THE BROOKLYN TRACE
An Eddie Daley Mystery

BILL JONES JR.

PANTHERA PRESS

Panthera Press™ and the Dread Lion™ logo are trademarks of the Panthera Press Company. Logo design by Maria Jones-Phillips.

Book cover design by Panthera Press. Front cover photography by Emanuel Hahn and Mubariz Mehdizadeh via Unsplash.com.

ISBN-13: 978-0985336639

Acknowledgments

I'd like to offer a special thanks to my early readers, including those who followed along with the serialized excerpts on my blog. Finally, a giant thank you to my wife, for whom I write all my stories.

Chapter 1

I'd been driving all day, sucking in western Oklahoma road dust, and I wasn't in the mood for any more damned mysteries. Nevertheless here I was, at the intersection of a brown field the size of Africa and some grit and gravel road to infinity. According to the signs I was on highway 56, or 385, or 412, or 64. The hell if I could tell which; they all pointed to the road I was on. None of them told me what this endless cross street was. The Camaro was down to her last quarter tank, and I was running even lower than that. So here I sat, looking up at thunderclouds gathering in the distant purple sky, wondering if I should turn around, and shaking the crap out of my useless GPS unit. All it could tell me is I was halfway between Cimarron and West Butthole counties, and this dinkhole of a pockmarked town I was searching for was nowhere in sight. I was just about to chuck the damned thing out over the convertible top and into the field when a cloud of rick-rackety, noisy dust came clombering down the clotted gravel road, right in my direction. I swear to God the thing appeared out of nowhere, like kids from a Stephen King cornfield. Just for safety I reached into the glove box, pulled out my best friend, and laid her under my seat. She was fully loaded and always in a bad mood.

To my relief the dust cloud turned out to be a rattly old Ford pickup, made sometime in the late sixties but nowhere near as well maintained as my own '67 Chevy. Still, from the way she purred I got the distinct impression that my old gal kind of had a crush on the beat-up truck. I did too, truth be told.

"You lost, mister?" asked the blondest blond farm boy I've ever seen. With my Irish roots I'm not exactly the color of mud, but this kid was pale enough to be a fire hazard around all that dried grass, what with the way the sun was bouncing off his skin like a convex mirror. He must've been around seventeen, with an aw-shucks air about him that just naturally made you smile. So I did.

"Well, I'm not lost, but this damned GPS unit sure as hell is."

The kid laughed. "Yeah, even satellites don't wanna fly over this place. Where you trying to get to?"

"I'm looking for a small town name of Ridgley. Got some business there." I looked at the gas gauge and, in a fit of delayed intelligence, turned off the ignition. "That is, if I don't run out of gas first."

"Oh, you're okay for gas. Old Man Showalter's got a station just yonder up the road." He indicated Highway 5,638,541,264 directly ahead of me. "He can point you to pretty much anywhere you wanna go, too. Old Bubba's lived around here since the War." The blonde showed a mouth full of crooked teeth and laughed. It made me laugh too. "Civil War, I reckon. He'll be movin' pretty slow, but he'll fix you up right pretty."

I nodded and thanked him, and he clattered off along his way. Turns out "yonder up the road" is precisely six-point-seven miles, in case you ever find yourself in the Bible Belt with a faulty GPS unit. You may want to write that down. After what seemed like hours, Bubba Showalter had filled my gas tank, checked the oil, crammed my belly with "chicken fried chicken"—which I estimated to be seventy percent grease—drawn me a map to Ridgley that would make those Google guys envious, and talked me into buying his old pump-action shotgun. Lord could that old man talk. I liked him a lot, but it was getting late and those storm clouds were looming in the exact direction Bubba's map was sending me.

I gave Bubba my thanks and thanked his wife for the chicken sandwiches in the greasy paper bag, then headed straight to Ridgley. Thank God she packed napkins or I might have lost control of the steering wheel and skidded off the road. Chicken grease is a damnable reason to die. The people in those parts were friendly, but I was already half a day behind schedule, and if every encounter turned into some southwestern version of Old Home Week it was going to be hell to secure my target and maintain some semblance of schedule. This trip was, after all, about money. So I cranked up the Camaro and let her loose on those Oklahoma back roads. That clattery old pickup never could have handled my girl.

She's loud, fast, and bitchy… exactly how I like 'em.

"You checking in?" The woman asking was young; I guessed mid-twenties, with long, dark brown hair that covered half her face and cascaded waterfall-straight to her mid-back. Despite her tanned skin she was awash in freckles; they started at her hairline and settled along her nose to both cheeks, with a few strays landing on her chin and along her shoulders like so much drifting snow. At the top of her cherry lips two freckles surrounded a light mole that demanded my attention. She caught my stare and smiled, barely, breaking the moment by sucking on an electronic cigarette. It looked as out of place on her lips as a robot at a rodeo.

"Yeah, no more than two nights," I answered. Two nights was all the schedule I had left. It was still light, at eight twenty-five, with the early May sun setting in an hour. That gave me time to get set and maybe grab myself something to eat.

"No sweat, you can pay by the day. We ain't exactly being overrun by tourists in these parts." She twiddled on her computer and booked the room, happily accepting the sixty-dollar per night in cash upfront. "There's a ten dollar cleaning deposit for the dog, plus an extra fifty if he does his business on the rug."

"What dog?"

"Um, the one about to die from the heat in your car out there."

"Oh shit!" I'd forgotten about the stupid mutt. It was another gift from Mrs. Bubba. Apparently, her German Shepherd had a litter of ten pups, and I got one of the thirty-five-hundred dollar beauties *gratis*. I figured that if I came up empty on my client's skipper I could sell the dog back home and pretty much cover the cost of the trip. That is if I could remember I now had a dog and didn't let it roast to death in the Oklahoma heat. I rushed out, grabbed the little bugger, and headed back to collect my key. I felt doubly bad because, instead of being mad, the little guy was licking my face like I was the best thing in the world.

The girl was shaking her head at me and squinting from the fake, minty smoke wafting around her head. "You always that attentive?" She'd already found a bowl of water for the puppy.

"Not always. Just got the thing. I guess I'm not used to being a daddy yet."

She offered me the key. "Good to know. What's the name?"

I was surprised by the question, since I'd already checked in. "Daley. Eddie."

She shook her head. Her hair floated around like there was a breeze that blew only on her. I envied that breeze. "Not you, the dog," she said.

"Don't know. He hasn't told me, and I didn't ask."

"Apache," she decided.

"I'm not sure about that. I don't want anyone to think I'm insulting their people by naming my dog after them. Ever heard of the Redskins?"

"You wanna name him Sioux instead? Might give him a complex. Ever heard of Johnny Cash?" She looked at the dog. "What do you think, Apache?" The pup barked, wagged his tail, and that was pretty much that. I was still apprehensive, but the girl was cute and her smile won the debate. I nodded my thanks, took the key—on the second attempt, since she pulled it away the first time—and turned to leave.

"Lemme guess. Skip tracer, bounty hunter, or rent-a-cop."

That last guess made me stiffen. "Something like that," I answered without turning back.

"Well, let me know before you check out if you found anything interesting while you're here." I'd taken a step out the door, but that stopped me in my tracks. I could practically hear the vapor cloud leaving her lips as she said it. Smokers may smell like crap, but they're sexy as hell, assuming you can get past the ashtray breath. I never could, but like I said, her fake cigs smelled like mint. A carcinogen with a candy aftertaste: the perfect consumer product.

"See you in the morning, baby," she said.

I stopped again. "Uh, yeah."

"I was talking to Apache."

"Oh, yeah. Say goodnight to the nice lady, Apache."

"The name's Mina. Thanks for asking."

I can't tell you how many times I do that. Not a good habit for a detective.

The next morning I got up early—well, early for me, especially considering I'd spent a few hours the night before working the local bars. I'd traced my skipper to this town from tax records my assistant, Debra, had "found," so I was almost sure he was here. Once in small towns like this, you'd be surprised how much you can learn from the local diner, barber, hairdresser, or, in this case, bartender. My target was named Frank Taylor, a wannabe badass apparently and absolutely a deadbeat dad. He was also a pretty heavy drinker with a penchant for not paying his bar tab. I got a lot of info just by investing forty bucks toward his bill. Given it was Mother's Day weekend, I felt it especially important to track the guy down and collect the almost twelve grand in back child support he owed. Fortunately, my client didn't much care what I did to get it, or at least she never brought up the subject of limitations. That always makes the job easier. Of course, I reasoned she didn't want him too hurt.

I walked Apache, grabbed us both something to eat from my stash, and set out to find my guy. I was still blinking in the sun when I noticed a pair of elegant feet and absurdly long legs stretched out on the hood of a dinged-up pickup, which I presumed must be the Official Vehicle of the state of Oklahoma. The legs were attached to a pair of denim shorts, which in turn met a flat, bronzed stomach and a bounty of chest freckles sprinkled between halves of a tied-up buoyant blue plaid shirt. I could just make out the hint of a scar above the jeans and below her floatation devices before she caught me staring.

"Hey cutie," she said, blowing a poor attempt at a fake cigarette smoke ring.

"Say hi to the lady, Apache." I took his paw and made him wave at her. I felt stupid the second I did it.

"Wasn't talking to him."

"Hey Mina." I let myself return her smile. If she was trying to rattle me, she was doing a good job.

"Aw, you remembered my name." She sat up and slid off the truck. "Got any smokes?"

"I don't smoke."

"Me neither." She reached over and scooped up Apache, who started licking the places I'd been imagining kissing. That dog was starting to win my heart. "About time you got up," she said.

"Were you waiting for me?"

"Nope. Waiting to clean the room. I'm the maid too, plus maintenance and pretty much everything else that happens when the sun's still up."

"You run this place?"

"Naw, I just own it. Mostly it runs me. My folks bought it, but my dad died and Mom moved back home, so me and my dumbass brother got stuck with the family fortune."

I looked around. The place looked deserted. "I don't see him around."

"Nope, and you won't either, not until night. He does the overnight shifts. That's when the drunks and hookers show up. I don't want anything to do with that business."

"Don't blame you," I said, reaching to take Apache. "Bouncing drunks isn't the sort of thing for …"

She waited for me to finish the sentence and offered a bristly, "Say it. A girl."

"Actually, I was going to say *lady*, but then I thought that might offend you."

"Why would that offend me? I am a lady." She puffed on her faux cigarette, extending her pinky to prove her gentility. "I made some coffee. If you have a fork, you can grab yourself a cup." She produced a mug, seemingly by magic, and took a sip. "Dark and bitter, like my ex," she said.

"Sounds exactly how I like it. But I got some pretty good leads last night, so I think I'm probably going to head out to my … meeting and then straight back home once I wrap things up downtown."

"Downtown," she repeated with a breathy laugh. "Is that what they are calling it now?"

"I dunno. It's not so bad around here. Kind of quiet, and the people are friendly. I like it."

Mina looked around as if she were surveying the place while turning in a slow circle. In the sun her hair glinted with auburn highlights that didn't show up indoors. She was made for the sun, with her skin showing just a trace of reddish brown beneath her blizzard of freckles. "I guess you're right," she finally said. She turned and fixed her gaze on me. "It's a shame you can't stay. I'd show you more of the sights."

"What sights are those?"

"You're looking at 'em. Want a tour?"

I choked a little, but managed to regain my composure before I made a fool of myself. She gave me a pretty intense look I couldn't read. Maybe she was insulted I didn't jump on her offer right away. I wanted to take that tour, believe me. In fact, I wanted to buy all her tour tickets and tour my tourist ass off. But I was on the clock and it was ticking. Even so I found myself posing a little, subtly letting my shoulders flex as I leaned against my car. Years of weight training and two tours in Afghanistan had left me in decent shape. I figured I looked just about as tough as a man could look while holding a ten-week-old puppy that was licking his face. "I don't suppose you give rain checks," I said.

Mina's eyes narrowed at first, but then she smiled, slipped on her sandals, and turned towards my now-vacant room. When she walked, her hips didn't so much sway as sing, and I knew the tune by heart. "Just give me a call if you want to take that tour. I left a card with my number on your car's windshield."

I reminded myself for a full minute that I was on a case and could not follow her into that room, then two more minutes. "I'll do that," I eventually said to the empty space where she'd been standing. I fought off the urge to pick up the prints her bare feet left, climbed in the Camaro, and Apache and I headed out to work.

Frank was right where the folks at the bar said he'd be: at a crumble-down garage with a sign proclaiming the name Ridgley Motors, even though the words *Harley's Texaco* were still visible as faded paint stenciled on the old brick. It was a small shop with just two bays and as many pumps. Inside was dark and empty except for a small cloud of cigarette smoke and a trio of mechanics playing cards on a rickety table. Outside there were five or six wrecks of cars, none of which I reasoned were worth more than parts. Apparently the staff at the shop agreed, since no one was working on any of them. I stood in the dead-car lot for a time, with the bright sun at my back, figuring that made me all but invisible to the smoke-eyed greasebunnies inside. The dim whine of drunken fifties country music leached from inside the garage, so I pulled myself erect and headed toward the small office before the music began to rot my brain. By the front door was a tall, wiry, beaver-toothed man I instantly recognized as my guy. He was standing outside, taking a break from doing nothing inside.

"Frank Taylor?"

"Who wants to know?"

I exhaled, suppressing the urge to smack him. I was holding Apache and scratching the back of his neck and didn't want to set a bad example. "Mr. Taylor, I represent the interests of your ex-wife in …" It was as far as I got before he took a swing at me. I managed to twist my torso in time, avoiding his fist, released Apache's neck, grabbed the back of Frank's head with my free hand, and introduced his face to the brick wall.

Apache started to growl, probably because the man interrupted his neck scratching. By now I really liked this pup. I set Apache down and he quickly set off chewing on now-gap-toothed Frank's pants cuff.

"Call your damned dog off'n me!" His voice was a high, lispy whine and he was dancing a country jig, trying to shake off Apache while holding his bleeding mouth with one hand. I jerked Apache's leash once; he released Frank and looked up at me, panting, with love in his eyes.

Two of Frank's co-workers strode out of the garage, each wearing gray coveralls covered in grease. Between the pair I estimated an extra eighty pounds of belly fat, like they'd eaten a pig each without bothering to slice it up first. They'd likely have heart attacks before they caused me much consternation. By the time they showed up I had Frank restrained, holding his hands behind his back. From what I knew of him I'd not expected resistance, so I didn't have time to pull out my handcuffs.

"You alraht out here, Frank?" asked the older of the two, all the while glaring at me.

I pulled out what's mostly a fake badge, meant to create an air of authority, and showed it to them. "My name's Ed Daley, and I represent Mr. Taylor's ex-wife and children. Mr. Taylor here has gotten in arrears in his child support. He and I are having a little negotiation session as to his repayment schedule."

The older man's face drew into a deep scowl. "Dammit, Frank, you tol' me you took care of that."

"I-I've been aiming to get a check in the mail, Daddy. Just got a little behind this month."

"Mr. Taylor hasn't made a payment in over twenty months," I corrected.

The two fat men frowned and shook their heads in a kind of pudgy man choreography. "You're on your own here, Frank," said his daddy. "You need to take care of them kids. Tammy can't do ever'thang on her own." He stopped and poked a fat finger in Frank's chest. "Them's my grandbabies. You best make things raht."

The men spun on their heels and returned to their card game. I noted that Frank's father made no effort to contribute to his grandbabies' care before he left.

Most apples rot right near the tree, my father always said.

I tried to get Frank in the car, mainly just to calm him down so we could talk. Instead, as I was loading him in, he shot out a leg and kicked Apache square in the side. The little fella gave out a hearty yelp, and I was in such shock a man would kick such a cute little dog that, for a moment, I just stood there gawking as he took off down the dusty road. I let him have his run, but only because my little buddy was crying up a storm. I felt bad for getting him hurt—no man left behind and all that.

After a couple of minutes I got Apache calmed and we jumped in the Camaro and chased old Frankie down. You should have heard that puppy bark. He wanted a piece of Frank bad. That ended up being a bit of good fortune, as Frank turned out to be deathly afraid of dogs. Afraid of spiders, sure, but puppies? For crying out loud.

In any case, Frank and I negotiated a while by an abandoned feed store, aided by Apache's intense interest in Frank's nether regions. Lucky for him, the puppy was way too short to reach anything important. We went back and forth for a time, before I was able to close out negotiations with a boot to the back of Frank's skinny ass. By two thirty we were at the local Ford dealer, trading in Frank's 2011 Mustang for cash. He could have gotten more selling it directly, but I was in a hurry. It didn't net the full twelve grand, but it was close enough to make my client happy.

"You sure you're okay selling this, Frank?" asked the business manager. "I thought you loved this car." He eyed me pretty hard, as well as Frank's lumpy and bruised face.

Frank looked at me, fought back a tear, and said, "I'm sure."

The manager sighed and handed Frank a check. I took it from him. "What the hell happened to you anyway?" he asked. He was glaring at me by now, especially since I was holding the money.

"Negotiations," I said. I reckon I only looked a little better than Frank.

"Negotiations? What the hell was you negotiatin'?"

"Mr. Taylor owes quite a bit of money," I said, taking Frank by the arm and pointing him towards the door.

"Why's his face like 'at?"

"He's a bad negotiator."

When we got outside I asked Frank if we were going to have trouble with local law enforcement. I had all the right paperwork, but it would have screwed up my schedule. Frank shook his head. "Naw. I never did feel right about making them car payments, knowing …"

He didn't finish the sentence. He didn't have to. Even a jackhole has a bout of conscience every once in a while, especially once they've had some sense knocked into them. Within an hour Frank had taken me to the bank, turned the check into cash, and even threw in a little package he took from the trunk of his former car. An hour after that my new partner and I were headed back towards Arizona with a load of cash and a belly full of pride from our first successful job together.

Apache and I made good time on the way back home. We managed the four-hour drive to Santa Fe in only three and a half and, after a nice dinner, we checked into a little motel just south of the city. Another early start; we were past the Turquoise Trail, through Albuquerque, across the state line, and into Flagstaff just after noon on Sunday, May 12 – Mother's Day.

After a thirteen-hundred-plus mile round-trip trek, Ms. Taylor's home was only two miles from my office. It felt good to see those peaks back where they should be. It's hard for folks who don't live near mountains to understand what it's like to look in the direction they should be and see only sky. It's disconcerting, and you never quite feel at home anywhere they aren't. Albuquerque and Boulder come close, but Flagstaff's prettier, like it's been frozen in time. Albuquerque's like a stain somebody spilled in the desert.

Still, adopted home or no, I couldn't shake the feeling something was missing. I think Apache felt it too, even though this was his first time in Flagstaff. I could tell, because he was pissing on the floor of the Camaro even more than normal. I was going to need to get it professionally cleaned. No self-respecting girl was going to be seen in a classic convertible that smelled of chicken grease and puppy piss.

Anyway, I put the leash on my pup, grabbed Frank's packages, and knocked on Ms. Taylor's door at precisely one p.m., a full hour before my client's deadline.

"Yes?" came the tentative reply as I rapped on the door. The woman who answered was in her mid thirties, a few years older than me. It was a small second-story walkup apartment in a complex that probably looked better on the brochure than it did in person. Still, she kept it neat and clean, from the little I could see through the crack of the door.

"Ms. Taylor, my name's Ed Daley, and I'm currently in the employ of Miss Tori Taylor ..."

"Is this some kind of joke?" she asked. "Come here, Tori." She turned and, two seconds later, a round-faced girl with pink cheeks, brown hair, and inquisitive brown eyes appeared. "As you can see, Tori is only nine years old."

"Hi, Mr. Daley!" Tori shouted, waving. "Did you get it?" She slid in front of her mom, showing every one of her braces-covered teeth. She looked like a pretty, non-beaver version of her father, which took a considerable dose of DNA from her mom to accomplish.

"I sure did," I answered, handing her the envelope of cash and the other package from her dad.

Tori took them and turned to her now even more worried mother. "It's okay, Mom. I hired him to help you find Daddy. Happy Mother's Day!"

Before Ms. Taylor became too concerned, I pulled out the trusty badge and quickly explained that her daughter had secured my services via an Internet inquiry. My job was to track down her father and collect "some of the money he owes Mommy" before she and the two kids were evicted from their apartment. Ms. Taylor worked but, between car notes, rent, food, day care, and a frequently sick five-year-old son, money problems had begun to dominate their lives. So the enterprising Tori looked me up on the interwebs and "hired" me to track down her absentee father and convince him to help her mom out, mostly via FaceTime.

Our agreed fee was eleven dollars and forty-five cents – all the money Tori had in her piggy bank. I didn't even know kids still had piggy banks. Of course, my normal fees—plus expenses—are considerably higher, but I'd lost my own mother to breast cancer three years back, and I figured this was the kind of Mother's Day gift even my tough old mom would have approved of. I would have just had a lawyer friend attach his bank account, but he had not much more cash than his daughter—thus, the in-person trip.

I tried not to make too big a deal of things, but Tammy—by then she'd insisted I call her that—wouldn't let me go without cooking lunch. It was pretty good, considering she was crying so much I was surprised she could even see to cook. She wanted to pay me more than the fee her daughter negotiated but, as far as I'm concerned, a deal is a deal.

Between you and me, old Frank was an idiot. Tammy turned out to be a real stunner. Not one of those skinny model types, but a real woman, the mom type who's rounded enough to be womanly but who still tries to take care of herself. If it weren't for other business I had to get to, I might have tried to stay past lunch. It may be unprofessional, but if James Bond could mix business with pleasure, then why couldn't I? I'd never exactly been the settling down type anyway.

But I had other places to be. Besides, the way her two kids were with Apache, I was afraid if I stayed much longer, I'd have to throw him into the deal as well.

I'd decided to keep him for myself, instead of cashing him in to cover expenses. Money isn't everything, right?

"Eddie, this is all too much," Tammy said for at least the fifth time. "How on earth did you convince Frank to pay after all this time?"

"It took a bit of negotiation, but he eventually came around."

"Oh no," she said, whispering and leaning close enough that I could smell her perfume. "You had to beat it out of him, didn't you?"

The woman did know her ex-husband. "It wasn't that bad," I answered truthfully. "He fought back at first, but honestly I think he wanted someone to make him do the right thing for once. Mostly he was fighting at the end to preserve his dignity." I stood to leave and received two more hugs from the girls and a small fist bump from her son. As I reached the door I remembered the last package. "Oh! Tori, you didn't open the gift."

"Here, Mom, you open it. It's your day."

Tammy gave me a confused look, and then tore open the package. It was an almost-new digital camera, courtesy of Frank. "What's this for?" Tammy asked, while smiling and pushing away Tori, who was trying to reclaim it.

"Frank figured that since he's almost caught up on the child support, that maybe you could use it to take some shots of the kids and send him copies. He said his dad complains he doesn't have any photos of his grandkids."

Tammy nodded. "I'll do that." She walked Apache and me to the door. Once there, she tiptoed and kissed me on the cheek, her lips grazing mine on the way. I considered introducing our tongues, but Apache started growling at me. He was just what I need, a furry little conscience. "Do you think he'll pay the other two thousand he owes, or should I write that off?" she asked.

"Oh, I don't think you'll be having any more trouble with Frank. It turns out he's part owner in his dad's garage. If he falls behind again, we'll have the place attached. His dad will probably kill him."

Tammy giggled, blinked her smiley eyes at me, and Apache and I got the heck out of there before I did something gloriously stupid.

"Where are you going now, Mr. Daley?" Tori called after me from the door.

"On vacation. There's this tour I've been meaning to take." The pup and I waved, jumped in the car, and headed home to change and sleep before hitting the road again. It was going to be a long Monday on the road back to Oklahoma, and Mina.

Chapter 2

Apache and I didn't make it out of town until Wednesday. After spending Sunday night dreaming about bucktoothed vampires, I got myself a Tetanus shot and an HIV test first thing Monday. I figured I was okay, but you never know. If there'd been a bucktoothed-vampire shot, I'd have taken that too. That ol' boy Frank was long on stupid and short on hygiene. After that I packed and was ready to head out when my assistant reminded me Apache probably needed a few hundred bucks worth of shots from the vet himself. Next thing you know the whole day was wasted, since the little guy was under the weather after his shots.

Since I had to sit around anyway I followed up a lead on a quick trace job at home and conducted two initial phone interviews on longer-term work I could take with me on the road. The advantage of the skiptrace work I do is that much of it involves doing Internet searches via all sorts of databases, most attached via the web. As a result, about sixty percent of my job involves sitting in front of a computer or on a phone, which I can do anywhere. The rest is old-fashioned legwork. I suppose that makes me something of a cross between private dick and geek, but that's fine with me. Geeks make good money. Most folks listed as skip tracers make around thirty grand a year; however, I do most of my work for large corporations and groups needing information for background checks. Basically, they pay me to find the people no one else can find or to root out skeletons buried in people's closets. I'm clearing six figures a year:

not enough to be rich, but sufficient to keep me comfortable.

I spent a full hour Tuesday night cleaning the urine smell out of the car's carpet. Then I bought one of those air-cushioned puppy car seats, and Apache and I were finally ready to go see if Mina's offer was still good. Nerves and insomnia got the best of me and we ended up heading east at around five in the morning. I probably looked like a douche riding in a badass '67 Camaro with a fluffy-butt puppy riding shotgun while strapped into what looked like a baby's car seat. For the first hour I rode slouched in my seat with the top down and sunglasses on, despite its being barely light outside. But then, barreling along I-40 and the Painted Desert somewhere around full dawn, I passed a car load of young women who were *Aww-ing* and waving at Apache and me like a bunch of cheerleaders. It made me wish I'd bought a puppy long ago. After that we pulled over, rolled the windows up and the top down, and we were on our way. Girls still smiled as we passed, and nobody had to know I only bought that damned seat so he'd stop pissing in my car.

We stopped for lunch in Albuquerque and shared a couple of burgers at Blake's Lotaburger. Apache showed his innate intelligence by loving the place even more than I do. It was here that I finally called ahead and made a motel room reservation. The call was taken by a clerk who sounded more asleep than awake, so I was worried that I'd get there and no one would be waiting. With a hungry, tired puppy, that would be a problem. I spent the remainder of the drive screaming up I-25 and wondering if I should call back for confirmation or just trust the process.

I needn't have worried. As soon I reached Mina's little hotel the heavy, sleepy clerk took my credit card and mumbled, "Room eleven-A in the back," without once looking up. I saw just enough of his soggy, pale complexion and reddened eyes to guess he was either pulling an extended shift or coked out of his mind. Just in case it was the latter I grabbed my gun from the car and took it with me. Druggies attract trouble, even out in the sticks. By now it was mid-afternoon, I'd been traveling for ten hours, and I was beat. I looked forward to taking a long nap, maybe a shower, and then resting up for whatever adventure lay ahead.

The Oklahoma sky had darkened into a green, tornadic tinge, and the cloying smell of damp earth rose and thickened the already humid air. I looked up and had my left eye drenched by one of the water-sodden dust balls that passed for raindrops. "Time to go,

Apache!" We took off running, with my pup turning to bark at me every few paces to get a move on. We made it to the door to room eleven-A just as the skies ripped open and the ocean above flooded into the dusty plain below. Rivulets of blue-white lightning slashed across the sky as if some unseen energy had been building, waiting to be unleashed upon my arrival. I stood there for a moment, partly shielded by the building's overhanging roof, fumbling for the key and shivering from the cold fingers of rainwater streaming down the back of my neck and into my shirt.

I finally managed to open the door and found a surprisingly large suite, well-appointed and masterfully decorated with framed canvases of western scenes dominated by turquoise and magenta hues. It was as different from the room I'd stayed in before as a five-star Hilton was from your local Dewdrop Inn. There was only a single item out of place; standing in the center of the main room was Mina, dressed in a smile and a thin, red robe that complimented her skin. For a moment I thought I'd been given the wrong room and walked in on her by mistake. Then I noticed her ruby lips and fingernails the precise color of her robe. Her attire was just short enough that I caught a hint of freckles teasing up her thighs.

"Welcome. I didn't think you were gonna show."

"Like hell you didn't," I answered, grinning.

"Most men would call a lady when she brazenly leaves her number."

"Most women wouldn't have hypnotized a guy so he had no choice but to return." It was false bravado. Mainly I hadn't called in advance because I feared she'd come to her senses and tell me not to come.

She walked over to me and, in one motion, snatched my shirt over my head. She stood, silent, just looking, mainly at my arms and shoulders. Mina placed one hand on my chest, running her fingers over the horizontal scar I'd had since my second tour in Afghanistan. From there she touched the semicircular scar that could have been nothing other than teeth marks, courtesy of Frank. She leaned in as if she were going to kiss my chest, then blinked, frowned, and slapped the holy freaking shit out of me. Outside a flash of late spring lightning shattered the glowering darkness and the room shook with its thunderous reverberation. My head was echoing the sound, my teeth rattling in harmonics with the storm. I thought the lightning flash was brain damage from her slap.

The adventures were starting almost immediately.

"That's for leaving me in your damn hotel room, waiting for you to come in and feeling like a fool." Mina stepped away from me, rubbing her hand. I hoped it hurt like a bitch. "Just so you know I'm not some desperate slut who screws every great-looking guy who stops by." I was barely listening except for the "great-looking" part. Mainly, I was trying to keep my eyes from watering.

"What the hell, Mina? I told you I had a meeting, and you said you were going to clean the room."

"When was the last time you saw someone clean a hotel room wearing sexy little shorts and sandals? Do you know how nasty hotel guests can be? I'm hardly going to touch dirty sheets with my actual skin." She glared at me. "I was looking cute for you, you jerk."

"I guess I wasn't thinking." At this point I gave in and began rubbing my throbbing face. She'd hit me so hard my teeth itched. "Besides, I asked you if you were waiting for me, and you said no. I took you at your word."

"News flash, Eddie, girls don't always tell the truth, especially when their dignity is at stake."

"So, what were you doing, exactly?"

"Offering myself to a complete stranger, for just about the first time in my life. Taking a chance. Rolling the romance dice. Trusting that life would stop being a bowl of shit. Silly me, having hope." She gave a bitter, breathy laugh. "It never occurred to me you'd turn me down." To my surprise she looked genuinely hurt. The girl was nuts, but sweet ... underneath, somewhere.

"I didn't turn you down. I finished my other business so I wouldn't have to leave right after ... you know. I may be a dumbass—almost certainly am a dumbass—but I know you don't follow a girl into a hotel room and then skip right out of town if you ever plan to see her again."

"Maybe I would've left with you," she said. Her eyes were unreadable, and there was something about her words that suggested I was with some lovely, powerful falcon, trapped in a very small cage. Perhaps she really liked me, or maybe I just seemed like a guy with a key to the cage's lock. Whatever the case, the cool veneer she wore when we first met was gone now, washed away in the tempest. She was lightning, and it was about to storm.

"I came back," was the only thing I could think to say.

It was enough. She placed a soft hand on my face, which was

still sore enough to make me wince. Her touch was gentle, however, and her eyes met mine as if needing something at that moment that only I had. I kissed her, our first kiss, and it lingered enough that when our lips parted her robe was gone, her skin was warm, and my hands began their tour. She undressed me there in the living room of her apartment, where she'd had her brother book my stay, and we never even made it to the bedroom for the first tour, knocking over furniture and scaring the hell out of the poor dog, who spent most of the time cowering in the corner. I didn't know whether our storm or the one outside was the cause, but I knew Mina and I generated more power.

The second tour was slower, with more sights to see as I learned every curve, fault, and corner of her, and we found each other's imperfections and made them whole. She sported a jagged scar from her right hip to mid-thigh, and marks on her side that might have been gunshot wounds. Neither of us said a word, but merely traced the maps of our flesh with touch, kiss, and fevered passion. There would be time for questions after. For now, there were storms and love and Mina's thunderous orgasms. Whispers are for kittens. Mina was a lioness, roaring her pleasure. Finally, when I thought I was spent, consumed by her, she left the bedroom and reentered with a tray full of food. We gorged ourselves, falling into wanton gluttony, unable to get our fill of each other. I'd been with more than a few women before Mina, more even than my share, but when we were done and her soft, fragrant hair was scattered over my chest like fallen auburn leaves, I knew that I'd been a virgin up to now. There'd been only one woman in my life, and she was mad, and I was too, now, for her.

The sun woke me the next morning. If God had given me a remote, there would have been an eclipse of biblical proportions. I'm not sure if there is such a thing as a sex hangover, but if there is, I had one. I cracked open one eye once I realized I was in bed alone and let my arm fall over the side of the bed. Each previous day that had been my signal to Apache that I was up and he'd rush over and start with the morning kisses. This morning, there was no Apache. No kisses.

I climbed out of bed and stumbled to the john. I looked terrible, except for the silly grin that crossed my face when I thought of the previous night. I showered, lingering under the stream, washing the soreness from my muscles. I returned to the bedroom, but still no Apache or Mina. Even worse, my bags were gone. Hoping she'd stowed my gear, given how meticulous her place was kept, I went to the closet. No luck. In fact, either she was the least clothes conscious woman I'd ever met or most of her stuff was gone too. By then a touch of panic was setting in; I rushed to the living room but there was no trace of her there … and my car keys were gone.

She'd bolted, I realized, and stolen my damn car and my dog too. What kind of person steals a man's puppy?

I flung open the door and rushed out into the sunshine, forgetting that I hadn't a stitch on. As I feared, my car was gone. I stood there exactly long enough for the door to click shut behind me as two old ladies walked by, staring. One was frowning as if I'd cooked her cat. I was so pissed I would've shaken my willy at her, but the other was giving me the eye and winking. I covered myself as best I could and backed up to the door, hoping against hope it would open. It did not. The two ladies continued on their stroll, one shaking her head and the other shaking her bosoms at me. She used her hands to do it.

This would be a good time to die, I remember thinking. Fortunately, right then, my Camaro came tearing into the parking lot, kicking up mud and dust like a demon. The old ladies squealed in fright and quick-lumbered to their room. The flirty one stood there for a moment, winking a blue-lined eye at me and puckering her wrinkled, stubbly, crustpocked lips. I would have been mortified, except I was too busy trying to decide whether to be angry that Mina took my car or grateful that she hadn't ditched me.

I chose both, mostly.

"I'm sorry, sir," she said, climbing out of the car with my damn traitorous dog, "but we have a no daytime nudity policy here at the Sleep Sooner Inn. I'll have to ask you to return to your room." The flirty old bat frowned at Mina, went inside, and slammed her door. "Eddie, what the hell are you doing?"

"I thought you left."

"Uh, with your car and your dog?"

Mina shot me a hard look and unlocked the door. It was at this point I realized I was caught in a girl trap. Those are like falling into a briar patch. It hurts going in, and the only way to extricate yourself is to stop squirming and wait until someone lets you out. If you try to weasel out of it on your own, you'll get torn to shreds.

"Well, I woke up and you were gone, so I went outside to find you—"

"Naked."

"I … I was still mostly asleep. I'd just showered." I knew how lame that sounded.

Mina gave me one of those half eye rolls women give you when they know you're full of shit but they don't want to argue. She took off her cowboy hat and tossed it on a table. Her hair was shades lighter, a straw brown that turned almost blond when it caught the sun.

"When … when did you have time to change your hair color?" It was a stupid question, but I was beginning to feel as if I'd somehow missed a day.

"You sleep too much, Eddie." She pointed to the chair in the bedroom, where she'd neatly stacked a change of clothes. I guess I missed those. "Get dressed. You're holding us up." She walked over to me and kissed me on the cheek. And just like that, she let me out of the briar patch. My theory, looking at this in retrospect, is that she let me off easy because of she knew great adventures require a cohesive unit. The last thing she wanted was a big fight. She turned and began packing snacks in a cooler and said nothing else about the public nudity or my basically accusing her of being a dognapping car thief.

"Um, where exactly is the rest of my stuff?" I asked. No longer worried about theft, now I was concerned I was deservedly being kicked out.

"It's in the car, with mine. By the way, I had your interior cleaned. It smelled like piss."

"Sorry, I thought I cleaned that."

"Yeah, you man-cleaned it. But I'm a woman, and we have actual noses." She bit into an apple, grabbed the cooler, and headed to the door. Apache was following her around like I'd been demoted from alpha to beta in some silent coup d'état. That dog was too smart for his own good. "Hurry up," she added from the door. "I want to hit the road."

"Road? Wait, where are we going?"

She closed the door and was gone. I told the closed door I liked her hair, but it didn't respond.

I met her outside. She was sitting demurely in the passenger seat of my car with both of her pretty feet sticking out the window. Not exactly safe, but this was Oklahoma; who was going to complain? Hell, in parts of Texas that was part of the driving test. She lifted her butt and handed me my gun. "You have a license to carry this thing?"

I nodded and told her I was a licensed private investigator, among other things. I was amazed that not only had she found it among my gear but that I'd forgotten I took it in her apartment in the first place. I checked to make sure it was on safety, removed the clip, and leaned over to put it in the glove box.

"Is that a lock box?" she asked.

"Yeah, I had it built in."

"Cool." She leaned forward and pulled a Glock from behind her. "Put mine in there too."

I sat staring for a minute, waiting for an explanation. She sat quietly not giving me one, eating her apple. After a pause she looked up and offered me a bite. I sighed, locked the weapons, and fired up the Camaro.

I avoided that apple but good. "Where to?" I asked.

She pointed to the parking lot's exit. "Make a left."

"Thanks. That's helpful." Twenty minutes later we were traveling east on US-412 heading toward Kansas.

"Why do all the highways in Oklahoma have three or four different numbers?" I asked.

"Because we're three or four times as cool as everybody else."

"That explains it."

"Actually, they're hoping to confuse the tornados so they end up in Texas. Make a left up there," she said, pointing to a sign reading *Kansas: KS-27 North*.

"You going to tell me what's in Kansas?"

"Wheat, barley, corn … stuff like that."

"Never mind."

"Couple cows."

I gave her a dirty look and we turned onto the highway, followed closely by a shitty Ford pickup with tinted windows. It was black and expensive, one of those special edition F-250s with a trailer hitch, but it was hauling nothing but ass. He ran up on my tail and hung around there long enough that I thought he wanted to mate. When I didn't take the bait and accelerate, he swung around next to me. It was a risky move for such a big truck at that speed, and especially given this stretch of highway was only a single lane in either direction. The only other vehicle on the road, however, was a piece of slow-moving farm equipment that I could barely make out in the flat distance ahead. The truck sped up and slowed down for about a quarter mile, just long enough for me to begin to relax. Serial killers make me jittery. A dumbass in an overpriced truck just annoys me. This, I figured, was nothing more than a farm boy wanting to test his hot new truck out against my beast of a Camaro. I smiled and said, "Okay, let's see what you got."

The pickup was ahead and to the left of me now, and I needed to accelerate or get trapped behind the tractor ahead. I'd barely tapped the accelerator when the truck's passenger-side window rolled down and a shot rang out, spidering the windshield.

"Shit," Mina said, slouching in her set. It wasn't a yell, more the type of reaction you have if you realize your fly is down in public. Apache abandoned his seat and landed on the floor in the back. He was growling. I ducked too just as another shot rang out, shattering the windshield. Whatever he was shooting it was high caliber to take out the safety glass like that. "Shit!" Mina repeated. "Why'd you lock up the guns?" She sounded pissed.

"Because you told me to!"

"Take the left there!"

I followed her direction, making a rubber-peeling left onto a stretch of road that took us back to the only houses for miles, not far from US-56 from whence we'd just come. Behind the truck shuddered to a stop and made a U-turn, digging grooves in the farmland that bordered the road.

"Get down!" Mina yelled, pushing my head to the steering wheel just as what had to be a rifle shot exploded the rear window, tearing the hell out of my ragtop in the process. I hit the gas, accelerated through the small town, and pulled the Camaro to a stop in the middle of someone's yard. I turned off the car, tossed Mina the keys, and she unlocked the lock box. If they wanted a gunfight, we would oblige them. To our surprise and relief, no truck came. We knelt there in the grass, shielded by the car for ten minutes before relaxing and climbing back in. If Mina was rattled, I couldn't tell.

"We better get out of here before whoever lives here comes back home," I said, accelerating and tearing up the rest of the lovely yard. "What the hell was that all about?" I asked. I was looking at her, not accusing, but trying to read her expression. The girl was born on planet Vulcan.

"Whoever they were, it was meant to be a warning," she said.

"How do you know?"

"We aren't dead."

"You going to tell me what we're being warned against? People don't just randomly roll up on you on the highway and shoot out your windows."

"How the hell should I know? I heard what you did to Frank. Maybe he and his friends wanted to send you a message. You make a lot of enemies in your line of work."

I didn't reply, but I couldn't imagine chicken-shit Frank having the guts to do an Oklahoma drive by. Besides, this was a deflection play. The best way to defer suspicion is to pretend to be suspicious of the other person. Her expression told me she knew more than she was telling, but that was the problem; she wasn't telling. I decided to bide my time. Besides, like I said before, I was already hooked on the girl.

"Turn right here," she said, now back in GPS mode. "We can take my truck. We had to stop at my brother's anyway. We'll just switch vehicles."

"You have a truck?" I'm not sure why that surprised me. Maybe until that point, I suspected I was nothing more than a ride out of town. She'd told me the beat-up truck I first saw her on was her brother's. Mina was full of surprises, as I was beginning to realize. We pulled up to the modest two-story home that housed her brother and his wife, and she had me pull straight into the garage. I argued that I needed to file a police report and then call my insurance agent to start the repairs.

Mina waved that off by telling me the local police was headed by Frank's cousin. This was a small place. "It'll be safe here until we come back," she said. "Besides, I don't want to spend my vacation talking to cops. If Frank's behind this, they'll just mess with us even more."

On that point, we were in agreement. Just because I work with cops doesn't mean I like them. Mina pulled the cover off the other vehicle in the garage—her truck—and grinned. It was a 1956 GMC pickup, dark green, with cream-colored interior. The truck was mint from the bullets of its aggressive front bumper to the covered short bed in the rear. In between the small cab had been extended to add a full leather-covered rear bench seat. Whoever did the custom work had dropped the old truck several inches, giving her a low, mean profile.

"This is badass," I said, running my hands along her lines. "It's yours?"

"All mine. My brothers did the bodywork and I did the mechanicals. Everything underneath it is brand new."

"You did this?" Mina didn't answer, but gave me a look that was more annoyance than pride. My reaction had nothing to do with her gender, however. "You and I are gonna get along great," I said. Her expression blossomed into a full-on grin. She opened the door and disappeared into the house.

By the time I'd finished transferring our gear and locking the guns in her lock box Mina had reappeared, holding a dark-haired little girl about a year old. "Here, hold Nona." She handed the girl to me and I took her, mostly because she'd caught me off-guard. We stood there, the kid and me, she in my hands and me with my arms fully extended, trying not to break her. The girl said nothing, simply hung there, staring at me, gnawing on one knuckle. She was cute, if you go for that sort of thing.

Mina glanced over, having secured the car seat. "She likes you."

"How can you tell?" The kid's expression hadn't changed.

"Look how she's looking at you."

All I saw was another Vulcan. She was clearly related to Mina. "Um … hi, Nona?"

Mina heard the question in my voice. She took the little girl, who continued to stare at me from over Mina's shoulder. That is until she saw Apache, who'd staked his claim to the pickup. Mina installed his seat next to Nona's, and he and the kid started a new staring contest. I guess it was love at first sight. Nona awarded him with a brilliant four-toothed smile. Apache's tail began to wag feverishly.

Mina climbed in behind the wheel and patted the passenger's seat. "Let's go. You're burning daylight."

I stood at the door, sighed, and looked at the two lovebirds in the back seat. "Please tell me you didn't break into this house and kidnap that baby," I said.

Mina cackled with laughter. "You are so funny. That's my daughter, Winona. I call her Nona for short." She held up her arm. "I thought you'd be able to tell by the freckles. You met mine last night."

"Winona?" I gave her a look that said her referring to the prior night's adventures in front of the kid made me uncomfortable.

She smiled it off. "Winona Good Crow. Her name's Lakota like her mommy's. Well, Winona's the Anglo version. It means firstborn daughter. Mine means eldest daughter." She turned to her daughter and grinned. "Isn't that cool?" Nona returned the grin.

"Cool." I repeated. My head was starting to hurt. "I didn't know Native Americans had freckles." To this day I still don't know why that was the part that surprised me.

"Don't be racist. Come on," she said, "Let's go. I'm excited!"

"Go," Nona said from the backseat.

"Go." I said, climbing in—me, the least excited person in the truck.

Chapter 3

We rode for the next several miles in silence, with all the romance leaking from the truck's cab like air from a deflating tire. It was partly due to my headache, but mostly due to the fact that I felt ambushed. Though I'd had no preconceived agenda when I came to visit Mina, after our intense night together I'd envisioned something different than a family outing with the kids. It never even occurred to me she had a kid. She was a hardbody, not a soccer mom. I guess I'd discovered what stereotypes were good for: nothing. That isn't meant to imply the previous night or even the chemistry during our meeting on the previous trip was about sex. There was something about this girl, something special that I was drawn to. But the sudden appearance of her child shook reality into my little romantic notions and, in the real world, I had not a clue what to do with a child. As I thought about all this I obviously let the silence leach too long into the air; as she turned toward me, her face furrowed with concern.

"You gonna tell me why you're suddenly so quiet?" she asked.

"No reason. I'm just nursing a headache."

"Headache." She glanced at me and then back to the road. "Does your headache by any chance wear diapers and give spitty kisses?"

"Your kid … *daughter* is not a headache. I wasn't saying that."

"Then what exactly were you saying?"

"It's … look, when you said we were hitting the road I just figured we'd be having a romantic weekend getaway somewhere." I was talking to the side of her head, which was disconcerting. She was hard enough to read when I was looking in her eyes.

"And you feel we're somehow diminished because I have a child?"

Ouch. "Well, if you're gonna twist my words—"

"What part of that isn't true, Eddie?"

"Look, I like you a lot. I hope Nona and I eventually like each other a lot. But kids scare the crap out of me. Hell, I'm still learning how to take care of a puppy."

She looked at me. The angry, red glint in her stare made me wish she would go back to being unreadable. "You sound like every other guy who doesn't want the responsibility of handling a kid. That's bull, Eddie."

"Yeah, I suppose it is. Except for one difference."

"Oh yeah, what's that?" Her words had formed a crystalline layer of frost.

"Last night I didn't promise you I'd be perfect. I only promised you I'd still be here in the morning. Well guess what? I'm still here." She fell into silence, but I could see the tension in her face slowly melting away. I turned around and looked at Nona, who merely gave me the Vulcan death stare. It made me laugh. To my surprise, she laughed too.

"Told you she liked you," Mina said.

We drove north on Kansas's Highway 27 for an hour before I finally broached the next subject. "You going to tell me where we're going now?"

"Oh, didn't I say? We're heading for South Dakota."

I quickly decided I didn't mind. I'd been a lot of places, many I wish I'd never been to. I had never, however, been to the Dakotas. "What's in South Dakota?"

"My mom. I miss her." She launched into a description of her family living barely north of the Nebraska border. Mina's mom was a Swedish-Lakota blend and her dad had been a full-blooded Oglala Lakota Sioux. For the entirety of her family's memories they'd lived in or near South Dakota. Mina, however, was a restless soul and, prompted by the lack of opportunity, had left at nineteen.

"What did you do when you left home?" I asked.

"Bounced around for a few months, then joined the Marines."

"You're an ex-Marine?" I asked.

"No such thing as an ex-Marine."

27

"Huh?"

"My LT used to say there are only two types of Marine: Marines and dead Marines. I'm not dead yet."

"Typical jarhead answer." I tried to hide my being impressed behind the barest of smiles. The Marines train all of their recruits to kill, even though only a fraction end up in the infantry. It explained Mina's previous calm under fire. It turned out she fixed helicopters—mostly stateside, but I got the impression there were other orders she'd been debriefed not to talk about. Whatever the assignment, it'd earned her a Purple Heart and a couple of sexy scars from an IED, an Improvised Explosive Device. I tried to charm the details out of her but all I got was "Don't ask questions you may not want to have answered, Eddie." I knew the look she gave me; I'd seen it enough. Someone had hurt her and she'd killed them.

I didn't want the details after that. I had enough horror stories of my own, most of which still haunted me at night. "So, how'd you end up a mechanic?"

"My brothers taught me the basics, the Corps taught me the rest. I actually wanted to be a chopper pilot, but I didn't have the education. In any case, I got enough time in the simulator that I could probably fly one if I ever needed to."

"So, how'd you get from there to the Sleep Sooner Inn?"

"I told you, it was my dad's. My sister left home, then I left, and then the whole family decided to try their luck somewhere else. I think mom was worried the boys would leave too. So they bought the motel. When I got out of the service I got a great job working for a contractor, doing basically the same work for a lot more money." A scowl crossed her face, like a cloud passing beneath the sun. "But then I met Derek. Got married, got pregnant, got indicted for tax evasion … you know, the usual story." She looked at me with a twisted smile that spoke volumes.

"Tax evasion. That's serious stuff."

"Yeah. The IRS seized pretty much everything we owned. I lost my clearance and my career. The only reason I didn't end up in federal prison was that my lawyer convinced them my ex never told me he wasn't filing returns. He stopped filing even before we married." She looked at me and seemed to be gauging my reaction. I'd heard worse. In my line of work, hers really was the usual story. "Anyway, I was broke and pregnant. I needed a job. So I went to work for my dad in Oklahoma. He'd gotten too sick to work and we couldn't afford to sell the place." She began to tear up. "Randy and I took over the Sleep Sooner and the rest moved back home. Six months later Dad died of lung cancer." She looked at me again. "A motel is never home, Eddie."

Mina fell silent awhile, and I allowed her the space. When she sniffled and smiled at me again, I began probing. "How old's the baby?"

"Seventeen months. She keeps me anchored."

The double entendre wasn't lost on me, but I wasn't about to bring it up in front of her daughter. Kids know more than grownups think. I figured I'd change the subject and jumped over the IED directly into a minefield. "Where's your ex now?"

"Out of the picture. It's only Nona and me ... but I have my sister-in-law to watch Nona while I'm at work. I do okay." She laughed. "Just poor as hell."

"Doesn't your ex help you out?"

"Are you kidding? I don't even think he knows her name. Her last name's not even his. Good Crow is my family name."

"Mina—is that why I'm here, to help you find your ex?"

"What the hell does that mean, Eddie?"

"I only mean it's kind of what I do for a living. Maybe he's the one who sent those guys after us. I just wondered if you were ... looking for a little help." I didn't mind helping, to be honest, I just don't like being used without consent. Women as pretty and smart as Mina usually have a reason for everything they do, in my experience.

Mina's face was anything but pretty at the moment, however. If she could have looked me to death, I'd be dead. "You're here because I thought you'd want to come. Silly me assumed last night meant you liked me." Her voice rose to a roar. "And if I need to find Derek, it won't be that hard. He's doing time in a federal penitentiary."

"I just meant—"

"Look if you don't fucking want to be with us, Nona and I can fucking let you out at the next fucking town, fucker." She repeatedly stabbed the air with her index finger and her nostrils were flaring like gills. It was fascinating, in a mad psychopath sort of way.

I turned and checked on the baby, given the flurry of expletives. She was asleep, gently rocking with the movement of the truck. Apache was asleep too, lying more in her car seat than his. Mina's outburst didn't make me angry; the last thing you need in my line of work is a quick temper. I figured she wouldn't have gotten that mad if all I'd been to her was a weekend of fun. That was when I realized I'd truly fallen for the woman. I was glad she'd gotten pissed.

I made sure my voice was calm and reassuring. "First of all, I didn't say I don't want to be here. Second, all that *fucking* was uncalled for."

"That's not what you said last night."

She didn't smile, so I smiled for both of us. She jammed on the brake, sending me lurching toward the dashboard, grinding the old pickup to a dusty, gravelly halt on the side of the road. There was little next to us except a wire fence strung along wooden posts and endless agricultural fields. We sat there idling for a second with Mina clutching the wheel with both hands. I was rubbing my forehead, which I'd banged against the sun visor.

"Serves you right, fucker."

"Are you putting me out?" I asked.

"No," she said, shutting off the truck. "You made me have to pee."

"How does that even make sense?"

"Because shut up, that's how."

Now she had me laughing, which only made her frown more. She got out, slammed the door, and turned away. A second later she turned back, glared at me, and then reached in and took her keys. Scowling at me the whole way, she crossed the front of the truck, bent the fence enough that the nearest post sagged to a sixty-degree angle, and lifted her long legs over the wires and into the pasture. With the lengthy set of skid marks she'd left on the road, someone would probably guess some drunk had veered off course and slammed into the pole. Nope, just Mina, needing a place to pee or hide the body. Still turning every ten feet to check on me, or plot how to kill me upon her return, she negotiated through the thigh-high crops to a point about fifty feet away. There, she unceremoniously pulled down her pants, squatted, and glared at me, with her head barely visible above a field of wheat, barley, or whatever the itchy hell was blowing around out there. It was hilarious, scary, and oddly sexy—enough so that I began to question my own sanity more than hers.

The baby was still asleep, but Apache was looking at me with this "What the fuck, dude?" look on his face. I just shrugged. I figured Nona's being asleep meant she must be used to outbursts from Mom by now.

Finished, Mina marched back to the truck, bent the fence once more, and popped her head in the passenger side window. "Kiss me," she said. I did. She kissed me dizzy, then pulled back and handed me her keys. "Scoot over, darlin'. You're driving." I took the keys and she climbed in next to me without another word. When the small block rumbled to a satisfying start, she mumbled, "Stupid temper tantrum ... *mumble, mumble* ... acting like a freaking little girl."

"You weren't that bad," I said. I didn't want her beating herself up. Heck, I thought it was kind of cute.

"I was talking about you. Say you're sorry."

I smiled. "I'm sorry." I paused. "We good?"

Mina stared at her lap. "I yelled at you and you smiled at me."

"I still liked you."

Her face lit up into a sunset of a smile, and we peeled the hell away from that damaged fence before some angry wheat jockey showed up with a shotgun.

Alone, Mina and I could have easily made it to South Dakota by nightfall, but with a toddler and a rambunctious puppy anxious to play with her we decided to make the trip a two-day affair. We stopped at a small diner in Cheyenne County, Kansas, in a town so small I didn't even catch the name. But there were plenty of wide-open spaces there, and Nona and Apache spent over an hour wearing each other out. After that we hopped back in the truck and headed north, darting briefly through Nebraska and into eastern Colorado. It was nearing dusk by then, and all of us were tired. Mina suggested finding a place to stay at the next town up, as that part of Colorado was pretty barren and not a place to be stranded if you're overtired.

The next town up turned out to be a place called Holyoke, so we decided that would be home for the night. I'm still not sure whether our phones were acting up or if there wasn't coverage but, whatever the reason, we ended up with no cell service and not a pay phone in sight. We were certain there were hotels, but couldn't search the web and couldn't call. After driving around for an hour on darkened streets, we found a rustic little bed and breakfast on the outskirts of town. Given the town itself was no more than a couple thousand people, we weren't surprised to find the parking lot deserted.

"It looks closed," I said as we pulled into the lot. There was a single sign lit by the amber light from a spotlight which read *Eastern Plains Bed and Breakfast*. It was the only place in sight. Though called a B&B it was a collection of small cottages, laid out roughly in a semicircle behind a two-story house. Given Mina's occupation, she fell in love with the place's "atmosphere" immediately. I was less convinced, as the atmosphere mostly looked moldy to me and there was still little evidence it was open.

"I think we should keep looking," I said. "I'm not liking this place."

"Nona needs to get some sleep or she will punish us all the way to Mom's house tomorrow," Mina answered. "Pretend you're a Marine and go knock on the door."

I was about to remind her that we Army types end up mopping up the messes the gyrenes make when all the lights came on. To be frank, it scared the bejeezus out of me. The door swung open and a chubby older woman came out, who I estimated to be in her late sixties. She wore a flower print dress covered with a white lace apron and reading glasses on a chain around her neck. She didn't say anything, but gestured for us to come in. Not much later we were in the house – which served as diner and hotel lobby – checking in.

Mrs. Kennedy, the owner, informed us there were currently no other guests, and we were welcome to choose any cabin in the place—except number ten, which was "undergoing repairs." I assumed repairs to mean exterminating giant Colorado cockroaches and picked number one, the furthest away. Mina, of course, asked which one was the biggest, and we ended up in number nine, right next door to the roach cottage.

As we were heading out, Mina picked up Nona and beamed. "See, baby girl? Isn't this exciting? You're staying in your very first hotel! Well, except the one you live in."

From the counter, the unsmiling Mrs. Kennedy said, "Oh dear, let's not have any excitement. Folks around here don't like too much fuss. Believe you me, peace and quiet is better."

Mina smiled, but the old bat creeped me out. The second the door slammed shut behind us all the lights in the main house went out, leaving only the dim parking lot lights and a series of low, amber lanterns leading us to cabin number nine. I jumped from the combination of the noise and darkness.

"I'm sure there must be a Motel 6 around here someplace," I suggested.

"Oh come on, jumpy." Mina and Nona happily walked ahead, whispering of "scaredy Army cats" and leaving Apache and me behind. My little buddy looked at me like I had to be out of my mind bringing him there. I couldn't wait for sunrise, especially when my little tough guy started whining.

Mina wanted to be romantic that night and, in truth, so did I. We didn't plan on being sexual mind you, just cuddly and cozy. The problem was twofold: first, the hotel gave me the willies. The room reminded me of my grandma's house and smelled like her attic. Second, every time I was able to put the setting out my head, I kept imagining Nona tucked in the bed next to us, secretly watching me kissing her mom and being scarred for life. Finally, with Mina reaching her peak of frustration, we heard a noise outside the room that sounded like heavy footsteps. Now, Mrs. Kennedy was a bit heavy, but even she wouldn't have made that much noise walking. She told us we were alone, and she was a widow, so unless she had a secret boyfriend someone was sneaking around outside.

"Go check," Mina said. "It could be those guys from the black truck."

"You said you didn't know who they were," I answered, whispering.

"I don't, and you're the man, so go."

"You're the Marine," I teased, "you go."

"I don't do recon," she responded, rolling over. "If someone's out there with a broken helo, give me a holler."

I don't think either of us believed we'd been followed all the way from the Oklahoma line but, in my line of work, you learn not to take chances. I threw on some clothes, took my gun, and slipped out quietly. It was pitch outside, with even the dim exterior lights extinguished. I walked to Mina's truck and back, but there were no other cars and no one in sight. If anyone was out there, they were gone. I opened our door but, just as I stepped inside, we heard a woman's scream, then another one. Mina and Apache were both up in a flash, with Mina's Glock appearing out of nowhere. I gestured for her to stay inside, just to make sure no one tried to grab the kid.

"Don't be a hero," she whispered before kissing me.

"I won't. I'll be a Marine."

She stifled a laugh and punched me.

Apache trotted out after, all vim and puppy breath, and I welcomed the company. Since cabin ten, the only one to our right, was shut for repairs, we checked the others first. We proceeded from eight to one, listening to the door and checking the knob. Each was locked and there was no sound. By this point I was beginning to think I'd imagined everything, except Mina and Apache had heard it too. We got back to our own cabin, where my buddy stiffened and began to growl. He was pointing toward cabin ten. I crept over, feeling both nervous and stupid.

Thump. Whump. Whump.

Apache growled louder, and this time I hushed him. Whoever screamed had to be inside this room. I tried the doorknob and, to my surprise, it twisted open. I lifted my gun and pushed the door open, letting it swing wide. The room was covered in blood: splatters on the wall, on the doorknob that would have led to the bathroom, and in a large pool on the vinyl floor of the kitchen area.

My heart started racing at this point, and I found myself automatically in combat mode. I nudged Apache behind me and braced my gun hand with my left. I took one silent step into the room when the bathroom door flung open and a large man with just a ring of short white hair charged from the room, carrying what looked like a bloody machete. That calm place in my mind that comes up in times of heavy stress momentarily wondered if this was the elderly Norman Bates. Fortunately, since the man was charging full bore and roaring like a maniac, the other parts of my brain emptied three rounds into his chest.

He slowed momentarily, looked down with an expression of dull surprise clouding his face, and resumed his charge. I backed up—not in fear, as there hadn't been enough time to get afraid, but to give myself sufficient room to try and blow his head off. Even if he were wearing a Kevlar vest, those bullets should have hurt enough to make him stop. I remember thinking he must be on heavy drugs. I kept moving backward, firing at his head, but no luck.

He swung his machete, barely missing my throat, and I stumbled backward, losing my gun in the process. Apache picked then to have a Rin Tin Tin moment and leapt for the guy's arm. It gave me enough time to retrieve my gun, and maybe saved my life, but now I couldn't shoot without risking my brave little puppy. By now Mina was out of our cabin, her gun in hand. The madman flung Apache off him and I backed up to where Mina was. Both of us were in firing position with my attacker slowly approaching, blood dripping from both arms. I couldn't tell if I'd hit him, Apache had gotten him, or if the blood came from someone else.

"Call the cops," I said to Mina.

"I tried. Room phone is dead and we've got no cell service."

The man took two more lumbering steps. We were frozen at this point, because no way we could back up and give him access to the room with the baby and, contrary to how things work in the movies, you can't just shoot people outside your home unless you can prove your life is in imminent danger. He'd tried earlier, but now he was just standing, watching us. Unless the man tried to kill one of us, it was a stalemate.

As if reading my mind, the attacker screamed and charged. Mina and I emptied our clips at him and he stopped, but didn't fall. I pushed her inside the cabin and yelled for her to lock the door. I heard it click just as I turned and felt the heavy blade kiss my back, leaving a horizontal sting of blood across my lats.

Satisfied that the girls were safe, I took off, hoping to lead the maniac away. I ran to the front, the madman roaring and swinging in close pursuit, and with Apache trailing him, but offering just enough of a distraction to buy me time. I rounded cabin one, reached the parking lot, and turned my head to see my enemy. It was a mistake. I went barreling over a concrete parking block, headfirst onto the dirt and gravel. I managed to roll over just in time to see the machete raised above me.

"Leave him alone!" It was Mrs. Kennedy, standing on the porch of her house, her face twisted in rage. "You've done enough here."

Just like that, the man stopped, looked at her, blanched, and rounded the far side of the first cabin. I jumped up after him but, when I turned the corner, all I saw was the dark field that bordered the complex.

"Mr. Daley, are you alright?" Mrs. Kennedy asked.

It remains the dumbest question I've ever been asked. "No pieces missing," I answered. "The girls are …" I was going to add "okay too," but she reentered the office before I finished my sentence.

"That lady is crazier than Captain Bath Salts back there," I told Apache. He wagged his tail in complete agreement. We returned to the cabin, but I stopped by number ten just in case. The door had locked shut and, though Mina and I had fired quite a few shells at and into the cabin, the placed looked spotless. I could see no blood. "We need Will Smith's weird-shit-o-meter, Apache," I said and joined Mina in our cabin.

My wit was completely lost on that dog.

The four of us spent the rest of the night in one bed, fully clothed, with Nona in the middle and Apache curled up at her feet under the covers.

The next morning we left the key in the room and took off, not even bothering to return to the office. It turns out there were a ton of hotels in the area, but we had missed them in the dark and ended up on the wrong side of the city. We found a quiet diner in town with seating at the counter, just like one of those old truck stops in the movies. And, true to form, the local police stumbled in, though I was disappointed to find he was a county cop and not a local sheriff. We'd decided not to talk to anyone about the episode from the previous night, not in small part because although we found nearly two-dozen spent shell casings outside of our cabin, there were no traces of blood anywhere. Either the guy was a spook or a magician, and I didn't believe in magic.

"Where'd you guys stay last night?" the waitress asked.

The cop looked over, obviously curious about the strangers with the cute puppy tied up outside. He was a wizened guy in his fifties who looked as if he'd spent most of his life in the sun, on a horse, chewing nails.

Mina gave me a look and said, "A little B&B called Eastern Plains."

The waitress and the cop exchanged a stare, and the waitress laughed. "I think you must mean the Golden Plains, don't you?"

Mina said no and showed them the matchbook she took as a souvenir. The waitress took it, went fish eyed, and handed it to the cop.

"Did you sleep in your truck?" the cop asked, eyeing the baby and giving us a hard look.

Mina and I shook our heads in unison. "Of course not," she said. "Mrs. Kennedy gave us a room for the night."

"Mrs. …. Now you folks wouldn't be pulling my leg, would you?" the cop asked. He sized me up and then focused his attention on Mina's shorts, long, muscular legs, and cowboy boots. "Where are you folks from?"

"Is there a problem, officer?" I asked. I thought his eyes visited her legs a bit too long. Besides, I may have mentioned that I don't like cops.

He returned my glare and Mina placed a calming hand on my knee. "Phyllis, hand me that clipping you keep on the wall over there," the cop said. The waitress went to the wall, removed a small plaque, and handed it to him. "Can you describe Mrs. Kennedy for me?" he asked.

Mina did, not removing her hand from my knee. She was as calm as a windless lake.

The cop handed us the plaque. It was a yellowed, framed newspaper clipping, dated June 26, 1988. "Did she look like this?" he asked.

We looked down and Mina gasped. The headline read: "Local Woman Murdered at Eastern Plains." The article stated that one Francis Bean Kennedy was found butchered in her home office at the bed and breakfast. Police believed she was the eighth victim of a suspected serial killer, but few definitive clues had been found. The accompanying photo was our Mrs. Kennedy.

"All they found was pieces of her wrapped neatly and left in her room. No blood, no fingerprints, no signs of struggle, nothing," the cop said. "By then, she was mostly retired and hardly ever had any guests. The only reason we found her was that her sister kept calling and couldn't get through. We never did find any evidence, in the house or in the cabins." He sipped his coffee and looked away. I could see pain in his eyes. Mrs. Kennedy haunted him even more than she'd apparently haunted us. "We didn't have access to the forensics we have today. All we had was list of recent guests, but nothing to indicate anyone was involved. The official report was she was killed elsewhere and her body returned to the B&B."

"But you never believed that," I said. The cop gave me a look. No words were needed.

"Did her sister claim the body?" I asked.

He shook his head. "Too god awful, I guess. We had it cremated, per the family's instructions, and shipped the ashes back east. As far as I know, nobody's been back there since."

The waitress nodded. "The hotel shut down right after the murder."

"Well, you might want to focus on one of her guests," I offered.

"Why? What do you know about this?" The cop's tone wasn't accusatory; it was hopeful.

I shook my head. "Not sure you'd believe us if we told you."

"Try me," he said, pulling his stool closer.

Mina relayed our story, describing the events and the attacker as best she could. Neither the cop nor the waitress said a word. She finished, then added, "But who knows, maybe the Colorado sun did something to us and we fell asleep in the truck and dreamed all this."

"Is that what you really think?" he asked.

"What I think is you might want to get a hold of some of those fancy forensics and take a peek at cabin ten again," I said. "After all, you said the place never reopened after the murders. Maybe the evidence is still there."

Neither Mina nor I were hungry after that, so we paid our tab and got the hell out of Colorado as fast as we could. My mind, however, was still back there with Mrs. Kennedy.

I was relentless. "Okay, I've got just one more question. If all we saw was ghosts, how come there's still a long cut on my back?"

"I don't know, Eddie. Maybe you have a vivid imagination. Or maybe the killer wasn't really a ghost."

"Yeah," I said after mulling that over a time, "Maybe he hangs around that place now, haunted by his crime, or he's looking for more travelers to kill. Except Mrs. Kennedy's ghost protects people, keeps him from killing again. Then he comes back, cleans up, and makes it look like nothing ever happened." I shut up and tried the shake the stupid out of my head. "What the hell am I talking about?"

"Can we please stop talking about this now?" Mina asked. She was sucking on one of those damned fake cigarettes for the first time since I arrived, blowing smoke rings out the window.

"You sure are calm about this," I said. "Aren't you even curious to know what went on back there?"

"I know what went on. Freaky stuff. I've seen enough of it to know I don't want to know more than I do now."

"Wait, you telling me that kind of thing has happened to you before?"

She waited quite a while before answering. "I sometimes have family members visit me when I'm sleeping." She looked at me. "After they die, sometimes they give me advice or warn me of something."

"Dead people visit you when you're asleep? I think they call that dreaming."

"See? That's why I didn't want to talk about it. I knew you wouldn't believe me. My dad visited me all the time right after he died. I think he wanted to make sure I was okay."

I had no response.

Mina exhaled more smoke rings out the window before putting the cigarette away. "Can we stop for some real cigarettes?" she asked.

"No, you quit smoking."

She sighed. "I did quit. I was testing you. You failed."

"How did I fail?"

"Because you suck, that's how."

I glanced over at her just as we passed a sign proclaiming we were fifteen miles from our destination. This meant I'd been talking about the damned spooks the entire trip. Maybe Mina was right. Maybe you just leave some things unexplained and go on with your life.

"Eddie, I think we should back off the sex a bit."

That was an unscheduled subject change. "You mean you want to have fewer orgasms? I don't know, I'd have to turn back years of skills building."

"Shut up!" she said, laughing. "You know what I mean. And I don't really need to hear about your many women."

"I never met a woman before I met you," I said.

She frowned. Obviously, charm wasn't the response she wanted.

"There haven't been that many, Mina." In my head, I added the word *lately*. She answered with a gentle touch to my cheek. That told me she wasn't trying to back completely out of the relationship. "What's going on?"

"I dunno. Maybe it's just because you're about to meet my mom, the cyclone. Or maybe it's … I don't know, this just doesn't feel like I thought it would."

"Meaning?"

"All of this—you and me—has been mostly on impulse for me. You blew into town, you were handsome and kind to puppies and old ladies. I just figured we'd have some fun and that would be it."

"And now you don't?"

"It just seems … I don't know, more serious than I expected."

She rearranged herself in her seat, her bracelets jingling like wind chimes. "Last night, with all of us in the bed ... it felt like, you know, a family."

"And that's why you want to slow things down between us."

She gave me a huge smile. "I knew you'd understand."

"Mina, I don't know what you're talking about." In truth, I thought I did. She seemed to be explaining why she didn't want to be a couple. What I didn't understand was why she was so darn happy about it.

Her jingling came to an abrupt stop as she folded her arms and sulked. "I swear to God, you are gonna drive me to start smoking again."

I decided it was a good time for me to shut up.

"Man, what is this place?" We were in a quick blink of a town that looked as if it'd been caught in a time vortex. It was small even by small town standards, with the only movement surrounding a couple of liquor stores that lined the street. A beer delivery truck, way too large for such a small population, rumbled ahead of us. Further up the street there was another, larger truck, and past that a group of protesters prostrate in the street. Police stood nearby watching, but not interfering. We drove around the group, Mina scowling silently.

"This seems like a lot of drama to be out in the middle of nowhere like this."

"This isn't *nowhere*, it's Whiteclay, Nebraska. You can tell because, if you look closely, you can see my people's shattered dreams spilt here in the street, drowned in the river of alcohol your people continue to supply."

"Um ..." My attempted subject change was interrupted by her pointing across my seat toward the opposite side of the street. Slumped among a dozen or so beer cans was a sleepy drunk in a John Deere hat.

"These fuckers are supposed to keep liquor at least ten miles from our tribal borders. Alcohol isn't allowed on the tribal lands, so they come here to be poisoned. You Americans ..."

"Aren't you American?" I stupidly asked.

"We were Americans for about ten thousand years before you were ..."

"Fucker," I finished for her. I got a grin in response.

"Stop making me like you. I'm trying to blame your Yankee ass for the ruination of my people."

"Where I come from, you can get shot for calling someone a Yankee. Besides, one of my grandmothers is a Trini."

"What's a Trini?"

"That means she's from Trinidad, in the West Indies."

Mina gave me a long, blank stare. "What difference does that make?" she finally asked.

"Grandma's part Afro-Caribbean and part Chinese."

Another long stare ensued.

"Mom is French and Polynesian."

"Quit changing the subject, Yankee." She looked at me and burst out laughing. "Wait, your grandma is Nicki Minaj?"

Her cackling sent me into a sulking silence for the last few miles of the trip. We continued up the road, quickly entering South Dakota. The town Mina's family lived in was little more than a series of one-story houses in the open plain. The property wasn't on the Pine Ridge Reservation proper, according to her, but it bordered the tribal land. We turned up a long driveway that consisted mostly of grass, which bifurcated two one-story houses, one blue and one beige. The blue house was the smaller of the two, a simple rectangular structure that couldn't have housed more than two bedrooms. The beige house was larger, an L-shaped rancher that would have looked at home back in Arizona.

"My grandpa built that house," Mina said, beaming, her eyes scanning the beige house's front door. She leaned over and blared the horn, scaring the dog and waking up the baby, who immediately began to cry. Seconds later, emerging not when the horn sounded but when the baby cried, came a lovely woman who looked to be no more than forty. She had Mina's high cheekbones and perfect skin, sans the freckles, with light brown hair that spilled past her shoulders. She was tall and shapely, dressed in jeans and a white blouse. "Mommy!" Mina was out the door and embracing her mother before I'd even cut the motor.

They stood there, hugging, crying, kissing, and embracing some more, while I let Apache out and struggled with the car seat. Fortunately, my ten-thumbedness seemed to amuse the baby, who rewarded me with a gurgling smile. I was, in truth, less being a gentleman than I was stalling, suddenly wondering why I was meeting the mother of a woman who'd just declared we should maybe be only friends.

"Here, give her to me before you break her." The voice was deep and rich, like Mina's would be if she'd had Marlene Dietrich lessons. It startled me just enough that I slammed my head on the ceiling of the truck.

"This is my mom, Katherine," Mina said, touching her back and acting for the world like a little girl. "Mom, this is Eddie."

"Hi, Eddie." The greeting was almost in passing as she took Nona from me. She flooded the baby with kisses, accompanied by the usual endearments. That was followed up with, "Lord, child, you stink!"

"She's been in the truck for hours, Mom." Mina took her daughter and started rifling through the cyclone the back of the cab had become, searching for the diaper bag.

"Yeah, Nona's an awesome traveler," I offered. "Never fussed at all."

Katherine looked me in the eyes, essentially for the first time. "Oh Mary, he's cute."

I looked around, wondering to whom she was talking.

"Is he a good kisser?" She gave me a wink and turned to grin at her daughter.

"Not funny, Mom," Mina said, carrying stinky-butt Nona and the diaper bag toward the house.

"Who's joking?" Katherine asked. She was still grinning at Mina. Before I could protest, Katherine grabbed my face in both hands and planted one right on my lips. It was soft, just-a-barely-brush your lips sort of kiss, but I was caught off-guard enough that I automatically kissed her back. In my defense, until meeting Mina, I'd rarely needed to practice resisting kisses from beautiful women. I heard Katherine offer a surprised, "Oh!" and then she kissed me for real. Next thing I knew, my eyes rolled shut and my knees were buckling. But then my um, *resolve* hardened and I pushed her away.

Those damned lips run in the family.

"Man, you are a good kisser!" Katherine stepped back, laughing and fanning herself. I managed to look over her shoulder to her daughter, who was standing on the porch, watching. There were no signs of amusement. Mina scowled lightning at us, spun, and entered the house, letting the screen door thunder behind her.

"Mina!" I called, fruitlessly.

Katherine looked at me open mouthed. "She told you her name was Mina?"

Now my mouth was open. "Mina's not her name?"

At this point, my head was spinning. I'd just spent two days with a woman who was secretly a mom and whose name I apparently didn't know. And then, when she introduced me to her mother, I got frenched in the front yard.

"Wow," Katherine said, her voice almost a whisper. "She must really like you." She turned, staring at the house as if she could see her daughter inside. Then she turned back towards me and placed one hand over her mouth, looking horrified. "Why'd you let me kiss you like that? I wouldn't have done that if I'd known. She ... she said you guys just met and it wasn't even serious yet." She looked at the house again and I realized she was trying to see in one of the windows. "She and her sister Kari used to always like the same guys. They fought over boys all through their teens even though I didn't let either one date...not that it worked. They drove her father and me crazy. I ..." Her voice became even quieter. "I thought it would be funny if ... oh good lord."

"Mrs. Good Crow ..."

"Katherine, or Wachiwi. I guess you're family now. After all, you've already had your tongue in my mouth."

That made me flinch. "If it's all the same to you, I'd be more comfortable with ma'am." I liked Mina's mom, despite the genetic insanity, but I was raised according to old southern traditions and you called your girl's mother "ma'am" or "Missus," but never by her name. Heck, Pops never once called his mother-in-law anything but Mrs. Purdy, and he adored her. Of course, he probably never tongue kissed her either.

"You don't feel comfortable...?" She stopped and looked intently at my face. "Ohmigod, you like her too!" She gave a little jump and clapped. "I knew it! She never brings guys here. 'It's too far to drive alone with the baby, Mom,' my butt. She wanted you to meet her mommy." My bewilderment must have been obvious, even as I busied myself unloading the bags, because she stopped me. "Mina's legal name is Mary Elizabeth Good Crow. We also have a Lakota name; in her case, Mina, in mine, Wachiwi. Mina always felt uncomfortable using her tribal name around anyone but family. Even her ex-husband called her Mary."

"She introduced herself to me as Mina."

"So she liked you right away." Katherine grinned and picked up the heaviest bag as if it were a feather. "I see more grandbabies in the future."

I've known her a week. I meant to say it out loud, but the words got stuck behind my burgeoning headache.

"Come on, slow poke. I want you to meet my sons." She stopped and leaned toward me. "They may harass you a bit, but don't worry, they're just being protective."

"It's okay, ma'am," I answered. "I have sisters myself."

"That ma'am stuff has to go. I'm only forty-five." That made her fourteen years older than me, which wasn't much. We reached the screen door, which she flipped open with her bare foot. "So when are you two leaving for New York?"

I stopped and the door slammed in front of me. After a five count, Katherine reappeared. "She didn't tell you about New York, did she?"

I wasn't about to reveal how fragmented Mina's version of truth had become, so I responded with, "Oh, she did, but I realized that in the excitement I hadn't even thought to ask."

"Oh good! Then you can at least stay a few days. We can get to know each other." She leaned toward me and whispered, "And try to forget that kissing thing, okay?"

Not a chance of that. Mina definitely got her looks from Mom. She reentered the house and I stood there awhile, taking in the great open plains. Whatever Mina had planned, I was beginning to suspect it was more than a simple vacation. But as I said before, I'd been to much worse places and I'd had far worse company to boot. Whatever little caper she was dreaming up, I fully intended to enjoy it. Despite her drama and the surprises, I was having a grand old time; mysteries are what I do best ... after kissing, apparently.

Chapter 4

I woke early the next day and had the coffee made and breakfast cooking when Mina woke up. One reason I was awake was that I had trouble sleeping without her soft skin or the perfume of her hair near me. Apache addressed my solitude by hopping on and taking up most of the bed. His hair smelled nothing like perfume. All night, I hung on the edge listening to birds chatter and longing for the soothing white noise of traffic. I welcomed the rising sun, since it at least got me away from puppy breath fogging up my neck. The other reason I was up early was that I figured I needed to do something to atone for kissing Mina's mother. I was uncertain what revenge Mina was cooking up in her Vulcan little head, given her unreadable expression and the fact that we hadn't had even a moment alone, but I knew it was coming. I don't think she cared I kissed her mom; she cared that I liked it.

Almost as soon as we'd arrived, Katherine had swept her daughter up and out of the house while I babysat Nona and Apache. I didn't mind, except for not knowing anything about kids. After all, she and her mom deserved some alone time. Plus, there was little else to do, as Mina's brothers still hadn't shown up. In any case, Nona and I eventually made out okay. Turns out Mina had been right; she seemed to like me a lot. At first, she spent most of the time staring at me and blinking back quiet tears. There's nothing sadder than a sad-faced baby girl. All it took to break the ice was for me to finally sit down on the floor where she was. Next thing you knew, I was the kid's second-favorite toy, next to my dog. When Mina and Katherine finally returned home, I was sprawled in the middle of the floor, sound asleep, and Nona was using my back as a chaise lounge as she watched some kid's video. I figured I'd get yelled at for falling asleep on duty, but instead, I got an enormous smile and a kiss.

Go figure. Women.

Anyway, the morning after, I heard Mina's stirrings around six a.m., and by six forty-five she walked out of her old bedroom wearing the same outfit she wore when she'd invited me to take her "tour." Even thickheaded me knew that was meant to say I was forgiven for the day before. I was glad I'd spent the previous hour cooking.

"Oh my god, I've never seen you awake this early," she said. I handed her a mug of black coffee and a fork. Mina giggled and kissed me. "Couldn't sleep?"

I shrugged. "I think I'm finally all caught up on my sleep. Besides, I wanted to talk to you alone… about New York."

"Mom told you about that?" Lines furrowed her brow. "She wasn't supposed to."

"Somebody should have."

"It wasn't her decision to make."

I waited for her to explain, but she merely sat at the kitchen table and sipped her coffee. "So?" I asked. I sat down next to her, but she didn't look up.

"I promise I'll explain what's going on, just not now, okay?"

"Okay, then tell me one thing, and I need the truth: New York isn't a vacation trip, is it?"

She looked at me and placed one hand on mine. "No. We're going to see my sister." There was something there, but I thought it was pain rather than deception. "I think she's in trouble," was all the explanation I could get from her.

"And you want me to help her."

She nodded.

"The mysterious Kari." How come your mom doesn't have any photos or videos with her in them?"

"My dad. Kari was his favorite because she's just like mom."

"You're like your dad?"

Mina nodded. "I'm good with my hands like him. Kari is too, but the rest of her personality is Mom's. She's really smart and super

46

nurturing. Daddy was supportive when I left, even when I decided to join the Corps. I guess he was used to the idea by then. But when Kari left, he was furious. Told her to *take all the damn photos* of her when she left."

"That seems odd. I would have pegged you all to always put family first."

She sipped her coffee and nodded. "Me too. But I think his heart was broken. Kari left a year before I did – just dropped out of school and announced she was going. Daddy expected her to be the first of us to go to college."

"So what happened with her?" I asked.

"She'd met some guy who convinced her she should be an artist in New York City. He was a slickster who saw her art in school and made her think she was ready." Mina swiped away a tear away with the back of her hand. "He was her art teacher. They just up and left."

"Jesus Christ." I hated the guy already. "Couldn't they arrest him or something?"

"She was seventeen. The age of consent here is sixteen. Maybe they would have fired him, but he'd quit already anyway."

"What's she doing now?" A hundred sordid stories began running through my mind. They were interrupted by her soft laughter.

"She's an artist in New York. Turns out he was legit, sort of. He was a perv, but he really did believe in her talent. He got her enrolled in some art school out there and even supported her while she was in school."

"Freaking child molester, in my book. Are they still together?"

Mina shook her head. "Kari realized that what he really wanted was control and she dumped him. Then she did what all girls with poor self-esteem do."

"Found another guy just like him."

She gave another laugh, and this time I recognized the hollow rattle it made. "You've seen this movie before," she said.

"Only a million times." She opened her mouth, then closed it. When she reopened it, I placed my fingers on her lips. I asked, "When do we leave?"

Huge smile. "Day after tomorrow, if you're up to it. Mom wants to spoil Nona into brathood, and she can't do it if I'm around."

"That's her job as grandma."

"Oh, you recognize she's a grandma now, do you?" she asked.

Girl trap. I walked right into it. "What do you mean?"

Her eyes narrowed, and I was positive I could hear the sound of a spring releasing. "I mean, your lips didn't think she was grandma material yesterday."

This time, I decided to hell with the trap. "What can I say? Your mom's pretty hot, Mina."

Mina laughed loudly. "Oh, Mom would love that."

"Mom would love what?" Katherine asked, carrying Nona into the kitchen, followed by Apache.

"Eddie thinks you're hot," Mina said, taking her wide-eyed daughter from her mom.

Katherine turned beet red and walked past us to the stove. Breakfast was done, just staying warm until everyone woke. "Oh, it looks great. Can we eat, or is it just for show?" She started fumbling through the cabinets for plates and utensils.

"Mom, tell Eddie how many men you've kissed in your life."

"Mina! Shut up for goodness sakes."

"Just tell him." She was grinning like a hungry shark.

Katherine gave me a sheepish look and answered, barely perceptibly, "Two."

I smiled at first, but then my brain kicked on. "Wait. I was … I was number two?"

A nod from Katherine and a Spockian smirk from Mina.

"Hey! We smell food! Where's my plate?" The voices came from two large men, one probably a couple of years younger than Mina, the other perhaps nineteen. Both wore their hair in long braids on either side of their heads. It wasn't hard to figure out they were her brothers; they looked quite a bit like Katherine.

"Dances!" shouted her youngest, chubby brother. Mina stood and embraced him, and he lifted her fully off the ground, twirling her in the center of the kitchen.

"Dances?" I asked.

They ceased spinning, and Mina smiled back at me. "Yeah, that's what he calls me." When I gave her a puzzled look, she added, "You remember that Kevin Costner movie, *Dances with Wolves*?" I nodded that I did. "Well, after my little encounter with the IED, I got shipped home to a military hospital. Anthony comes walking in, takes one look at me, and starts calling me Dances with Shrapnel. That's been my name ever since."

I chuckled. "Sensitive guy." Anthony took a bow. I stood,

shaking the older and more muscular brother's hand. "Eddie," I said, smiling.

"Mika," he said, smiling back.

"Eddie's my boyfriend," Mina said, watching Mika's face. "I caught him and Mom making out in the front yard yesterday."

"Oh Jesus," Katherine said, pinching the bridge of her nose, the words coming out in a breathy gush.

Mika's brow furrowed and his hand tightened against mine into a vice-like grip.

"Dude," Anthony said. "That's sick."

I should have seen that coming.

"Eddie wants to get the whole tribal experience," Mina said. "I think you guys should take him camping."

I wanted no such thing.

Mika's grip tightened, which I was surprised was even humanly possible. "Oh, he'll get an experience. I promise." Anthony nodded ominously as Mina sat and allowed herself a smile.

"Oh, Mina, do you really think that's a good idea?" Katherine asked. She was giving me the kind of looks you give a stage-four cancer victim. So not helping.

"Sounds fun," I choked out as I tried vainly to peel my right hand from Mika's grip. "Can't wait." It didn't sound like a bit of fun.

I spent an interesting overnight with the guys, in Custer State Park of all places. Looking back, I suppose the name should have given me a hint of what was in store. We had a fun day driving up, which included grabbing three horses from their cousin's horse farm, before ending up at the park. Mika and Anthony led me on a horseback tour of the park, highlighted by their leaving me there, stranded, about a four-hour walk in the dark back to where they had camped. It was a hilarious joke on the tenderfoot, right up to the time when I stumbled right into the path of an angry mountain lion. We had a brief encounter, but I was able to scare it off with a bit of bluster and a loud improvised rap. I guess big cats aren't into hip hop. After that I bonded pretty well with Mina's brothers, who were impressed I'd stared down a puma and won. It turns out Mina didn't send me there as punishment. She figured I'd have a blast.

The woman could read me very well. It turned out to be the most fun I'd had in years.

We let Anthony drive on the way back, since he was legally underage to drink and Mika and I had a few too many. Anthony had compensated by downing colas half the night. I figured between all the sugar and caffeine, he might not sleep until winter. It was a quick two hours back, but we stopped for breakfast and then hung around their cousin's place after we'd returned the horses. As a result it was nearly one o'clock in the afternoon when we approached Katherine's house. Clear as a bell I saw it and motioned for Anthony to stop.

"What's wrong?" Mika whispered from the back seat. He'd picked up my tension and was now on alert himself.

"That black F-250 in the driveway. That's the one that tailed us from Oklahoma and shot out my windows."

"You sure?" Anthony asked. "How'd they find you way up here?"

"I don't know. I don't even know who they are, but I mean to find out."

We were up the road from the house, shielded from view by a large tree in the front yard. Though the sun was in the back of the house by then, there was enough light that I could just make out that the cab of the truck was empty. That meant whoever was here was in the house. If I knew Mina, there was no way she'd invited them inside, not after our previous encounter. I told Anthony to wait until I positioned myself on the porch and then drive into the driveway, wait for my signal, and then tear the hell out of there and call the cops. He seemed skeptical, but Mika pushed him to the passenger seat and nodded his accord.

I ran a zigzag course to the rear of the truck, bending low just in case I was spotted from the house. No one seemed to notice, so I slid to my left and checked Mina's truck. She'd left the door unlocked. Smart girl. Being as quiet as possible I managed to open the passenger door, kneeling on the ground. She'd dropped her keys on the floor for me. These men must have taken her trying to escape. I grabbed the keys, pulled the lock box from under the seat, and got out my gun.

Then I peeked over the truck and, seeing no one, made a quick dash to the porch. Right on time Mika came roaring up the driveway, letting his truck's hemi do the talking. We made eye contact and then he shifted in reverse, tearing out of there in a cloud of dust and gravel.

From inside the house I heard, "They're taking off!" and a lanky man in a cheap brown suit came barreling out the front door. I was beside the door and clocked him in the head with my pistol. He was unconscious immediately, and I caught his sagging body before he could hit the ground. I kicked the door open, holding the man in front of me as a shield, and entered the living room. Standing to my left was a short, sweaty man holding Katherine from the rear, his hairy forearm draped across her chest and neck. He held what looked like a nine millimeter pistol aimed directly at me. Mina was seated barefoot on the sofa, her feet propped against the couch's frame. She held Nona in both arms, the child's face cradled against her chest. Her eyes were smiling at the sight of me. I met her gaze, smiled, and nodded.

Seeing I'd brought myself a shield, the other intruder turned the gun onto Katherine. My smile seemed to unsettle him as much as it reassured Mina. I decided to start with the obvious. "Who are you and what do you want?"

"I'm asking the questions," he claimed. His right hand was quivering. Mine wasn't.

I took a step towards him. "Don't make me ask you again," I said, being careful to leave any trace of emotion out of my voice.

"What are you, nuts? Stop or I'll kill this bitch."

At this point I knew his adrenaline was spiking, judging by his actions and the tension in his voice. It was time to take it down a notch. "Let her go, and nobody has to get hurt."

He gave what sounded like a forced laugh. "You ain't in no position to make demands. I'm telling you one last time to sit your ass on the couch with the Indian."

I stopped, speaking in even tones. "If you shoot Katherine— that's her name by the way," I said, nodding at my girlfriend's nervous mother. "If you shoot her, I'll kill you and put a bullet in your friend's head. If you try to shoot me, you'll miss and I won't." I dragged skinny another step. "Drop the gun, and maybe you don't die today."

He took a step backward, pulling Katherine with him. I noticed his eyes darting from Mina to me. He was in over his head here, which made him dangerous. Clearly, he hadn't thought about what happens if I showed up armed. He aimed his pistol at me, and I ducked behind my skinny shield. That was fortunate, as he squeezed off two quick shots, one sailing past my ear, the other slamming into his partner's face. I managed to hold on. Katherine screamed, but Mina didn't. Instead, she pulled the now-crying Nona closer to her.

"Shields work just as well dead," I said, blinking warm blood from my eyes.

I stood erect, raised my gun, and watched the next five seconds click off as if in slow motion. Mina yelled, "Mom!" and Katherine immediately pushed off against her captor, flinging herself to the floor. His eyes widened, he looked at me behind his dying partner, blinked, and swung his gun toward Mina. She pushed off against the sofa's frame with her feet, sending herself, Nona, and the couch backward. Mina hit the carpet, on her back, still holding onto her baby. The sweaty attacker fired his weapon a split-second later, the bullets sailing harmlessly over them.

I sent three bullets in his direction, one hitting his shoulder and two slamming into his side. I was on him in moments and kicked his gun away. After confirming the girls were okay, I stepped lightly on the man's side. He screamed in pain. Nona cried louder, and Mina took her from the room. I didn't see Apache anywhere.

"If you shot my dog, I swear to God I'm going to end you," I said. It was a dumb reaction, but honest.

"Apache's locked in the back," Katherine said. "He bit the skinny one on the leg. He got kicked, but he's okay."

Good dog.

I was still standing on the man's wound, applying just enough pressure that he understood I didn't care about his pain. "You're going to tell me who you are and why you're here, or I'm going to make you beg me to kill you." Corny, but again, honest. I stepped harder just to make my point.

He screamed again. Katherine turned away but didn't leave. "Okay, okay. Stop! Stop!" He was crying. I didn't care. "A guy hired us to tail you. Said this client of yours was poking around in things that were none of her business. He wanted me to scare you off."

I removed my foot. "Who is he?"

"I don't know. You know how it is. They contact a third party, the money's wired, nobody knows nobody else."

I knew he was telling the truth. These men were too unskilled for anyone to trust with vital information. "Why'd you try to kill us?"

"I wasn't trying to kill nobody. You had a gun aimed at my

face."

I switched subjects. That was going to lead me nowhere. "What information do you think I know?"

"Man, how the hell should I know? All I know is when you and the girl didn't go your separate ways, he told me to make sure you got the message."

"What message?"

"He said to tell her to let the dead rest in peace."

"What dead? Who're you talking about?" I asked.

His eyes fluttered as if he was about to fall asleep. I prodded him with the toe of my shoe. That woke him up pretty good. "I don't know, damn! I was told to give the message."

"And then maybe execute us?"

"Naw, naw! You got me all wrong. We was just maybe gonna rough you up a little."

"Right." I knew a load of crap when I smelled it. "How'd you even find us?"

"The guy gave us this address. Didn't take long to figure out where you were heading when we lost you back in OK." He rolled over onto his good side as the sound of approaching sirens wailed. "You didn't have to kill him," he said, looking at his friend.

"I didn't, you idiot. You killed him. I was bluffing." Katherine ran outside to meet the police. It was smart, as otherwise they might come in shooting. I stepped back and put my gun away before I became the target. I was ready to walk when another burst of delayed intelligence hit. None of this was making sense. I was working some cases remotely, but most were just background checks for a corporate client of mine. Other than that I only had a couple of deadbeat dad cases. I thought it could be one of them, since this perp claimed a woman client of mine had been the cause of concern to his boss. One of the dads was worth millions and did not want to share with his ex. Problem was, neither of them should have known we were in South Dakota. That left one possibility.

"This client of mine—did your guy tell you what she looked like?" I asked.

He moaned and his eyes fluttered. The loss of blood was causing him to lose consciousness. "The girl you brought here. She's your client, right?"

"Apparently," I answered.

I took a step and called Mina. That was when the room started spinning. She reentered and caught me before I could pass out in front of the cops. That would've been embarrassing. I bet Bogie never fainted on Bacall.

The cops wrapped up their investigation fairly quickly, as these things go. We were only up half the night. I thought I would be charged with assault or a weapons charge, but they verified I had the proper permits for the gun. It also helped that one of the bad guy's bullets had hit me in the upper arm, and I'd been too hopped up on adrenaline to notice the blood loss. In addition, the Good Crow women's statements convinced them that not only was it self defense, but I was something of a local hero. That was bullshit, of course. It could have gone the other way. Maybe if I hadn't been up all night I'd have had the sense to let the cops handle it. Mina and I gave them a promise that we would stick close to town, one neither of us had any intention of keeping.

We left the station by way of the ER at two in the morning. By then I'd been up for almost two days. Mina and I fell asleep in her room with our clothes on, and Katherine left us there. This time, even Mina slept through the day. I'm not convinced she was sleepy as much as she was just relieved I hadn't been killed. Still, I welcomed the company. I slept better with her nearby.

The night before we left Katherine invited what seemed like her entire family over for a celebration, or going-away party, or pre-wedding party, or a funeral, or God knows what. I tried to get Mina to explain, but her answer was, "You're the detective. You figure it out." Then she blew a gust of e-cigarette water vapor in my face. She was either annoyed or flirting. It was hard to tell with her.

After we all ate way too much food, an elder gave a blessing, partly in English and partly in the Lakota language. I tried to get Mina to translate, but she gave me a withering look that made me shut up. Then Katherine stood up and asked the group and those that went before her to bless her family, especially her two daughters' families, and me, "Who'd been brought into Mina's life for a reason." She stopped, choked back tears, and continued. I looked at Mina who was as teary-eyed as her mom. Even Mika and Anthony were looking somber. Something wasn't adding up. The mood was broken by music and dancing, as if we'd stumbled into a spur-of-the-moment powwow. Mika was one of the drummers, and Anthony sang in a beautiful tenor voice. Mina and Katherine danced with the other women, spinning and stepping with the grace of long-limbed birds. Then, as I was finally beginning to really enjoy the music, Katherine took to the center of the loose circle of people and extended her arms, silencing the crowd.

"All of you knew John," she said, referring to her late husband. "Except you, Eddie. You never had the privilege of meeting him. I'll never forget the day the two of us met. I was in the tenth grade and John was a couple of years ahead of me in school. He was handsome and popular and almost certainly didn't know I was alive. There were too many girls blocking his vision." The crowd nodded and laughed. "Everybody loved John, especially the girls." Katherine gave pointed though friendly stares to a couple of her female friends, each of whom covered her mouth and laughed.

"We were all on a school camping trip to Custer Park, where Eddie and the boys went a couple days ago. We had free time and, as usual, I was kind of off to myself, trying to forget the tall, handsome boy I'd had a crush on as long as I could remember. I climbed to the top of a hill and there, lying on her side, was a bison. I knew enough about animals to know she was giving birth. She'd already isolated herself from the herd, and she just kind of lay there in this little nest she'd made. I was watching so intently I never even noticed this boy had joined me. He sat next to me, accidentally brushing my back and scaring the daylights out of me. It was John.

"I liked to have fainted." By now, she had the crowd enraptured, including me. "Well, to make a long story short, we just sat there on that hill and watched the mother. In about an hour she'd given birth, and a little while after that, the young fella had been cleaned up good and was standing on his wobbly legs ready to join the herd. We stayed and watched until the two of them wandered off to feed. When they did I said a little prayer of thanks for the bison and John helped me up. We looked around and nobody, I mean nobody, was there.

"The whole entire class had moved on to the camp and forgot about us." She turned to one of her peers and pointed. "See Maria, we weren't making out. We were learning what happens if you do make out." The crowd laughed again, and Mina tittered and bowed her head.

"Anyway … anyway," Katherine continued, smiling and stilling the crowd, "it was getting dark, so we figured we better at least try to make it to camp. We started walking and it felt like we'd walked in circles all night. Native American instincts my butt. John had us so lost I thought we were in Canada. We came to this high hill and John tried to pretend he'd taken us there so he could see. I didn't mind because I was scared and John had been holding my hand the whole time to calm me down." She laughed and pointed to her daughter. "The moral of this story is, if the man you love has you by the hand, stay lost as long as possible."

"And never let him know you already knew the way," Mina responded.

Katherine grinned and gestured for Mina to hush. "Don't tell all my secrets," she said. The women in the audience laughed. "Well, we'd taken maybe two steps up the hill when this big cat jumped out of nowhere. I was terrified. I think John was too, but you'd never know it. He found a big stick and starting shouting and waving it in the air, making a big fuss. The puma came closer, and John just poked it with that stick. It snarled at him and tried to knock the stick away, but John held his ground. I guess the cat finally decided there were easier meals to have, so he turned and bolted back up the mountain, leaving me and John alone."

By this point, Katherine was in tears. So were Mina and Anthony, who were crying and smiling simultaneously. Even Mika was visibly moved. I was too, seeing a proud man like that unafraid to show his feelings in such a large group.

"Some of you know this story. I've told it often enough. But see, the part I never told anyone except my kids is that the whole time John was fighting that big cat, he never let go of my hand. Not once." She walked over to Mina and me, taking her daughter's hands. She continued speaking while looking at her daughter. "He held it when the cat wanted to rip him apart. He held it when I thanked him for saving my life. He held it when we kissed for the very first time right on that hill, and he even held it when the camp counselors finally found us and claimed we'd run off to make out. And years later, when he lay in a hospital bed, dying of cancer, in so much pain they even stopped giving him morphine, he was still holding my hand."

Katherine knelt down, let go of one of Mina's hands, and took mine. "Eddie, you are a good man, a brave man. I know you'll have a lot of choices in life. So, I'm only gonna give you one piece of advice. There will come a time when love is the most confusing thing you've ever faced. Common sense will tell you to do one thing, your morals will say do a different thing, and maybe your heart wants you to do another. But when you have to choose, the answer will be simple, even though love doesn't always make sense. Just trust your heart, and love who you love. Because the moral of this story is, when you find the girl you want to make your family with, you take her hand and don't you let anybody make you let go."

I met her gaze for a long while, watching her streaming tears and trying to make sense of her advice, especially because most of the people in her community were nodding in agreement.

"Okay," I finally said. It's not that I'm not the romantic sort, it's that I had the feeling this whole event was some kind of sales pitch.

"Forget all that," Mina whispered. "Just marry me. I'll make a great wife."

I turned and looked at her, expecting to see her laughing. Her expression was gentle but sincere. "I owe you an apology," she added. "I think I might be the client those men warned you about."

"I know. You want to tell me why I'm here now?"

"Why do you think you're here?"

"Because you want me to know how important family is to you. I'm guessing this is about your sister. Does she know who the dead guy is we're supposed to let rest in peace?"

Mina gave me a hard stare. "Congratulations, you're a great detective. You figured it out. You're also a pretty shitty boyfriend." She stood. "Oh, and if you'd been paying attention, you might have noticed I fucking already told you this was about my sister!" She punctuated her sentence with the same psycho-knife finger technique she'd used during her rant by the Kansas cornfield. I sat stupefied and, before I could respond, one of her aunts sidled over and pulled her away from me.

That was the last I saw of her for the evening. I should have taken my dog and gotten the hell out of there, and would have with any other girl I'd dated. However, I had an eleven a.m. flight to New York City with this crazy woman and I'd begun to get used to her surprises. More than that, whatever was going on with her sister, someone desperately wanted me to stay away. For a guy like me, that was enough of a reason to go. Plus, my girlfriend of one week had just proposed to me and yelled at me in the same conversation. I wasn't in a hurry to get married, but the ride to wherever our relationship was headed would be interesting.

Chapter 5

The morning of our flight to New York, well before sunrise, a perfumed, naked Mina woke me up by slipping into the small bed with me. I remember being in a dream wherein I was an antelope being chased by a herd of cougars, and the next thing I knew I was completely naked and this gorgeous woman was kissing my neck and telling me to wake up because I'd somehow made her horny. In between kisses and being submerged in her oceanic expanse of passion I probed, trying to discover what I'd done to trigger her arousal.

Her answer was, "You can be so dumb sometimes," followed by, "Hush. You're spoiling the mood."

Now, the way I see it, when a pretty girl wants to be in control and you are both nude, you yield. So I did. She was a tidal wave, this woman, lashing my shores until I feared that by the time she ebbed there would be nothing left of me but a driftwood shell. Afterward she rolled sweetly into my arms, smiled up at me, and fell into sleep. Even a hard case like me has to admit that was the best part.

By eight o'clock we were up, packed, and ready to go. I gave a last check of the room and ensured our guns were locked and stowed where Nona couldn't reach, then joined Mina on the porch. She was sitting and, to my surprise, smoking a cigarette.

"What the heck are you doing?" I asked, pulling it out of her mouth. I flicked it into the yard. "You don't smoke."

She gave me a cute pout I tried not to notice. "I used to smoke."

"You used to be single."

"Aw, you're trying to take care of me." She leaned against me and placed her head on my shoulder. Then she reached in her pocket and gave me the pack. "Just so you know, I'm going to get hugely fat now."

"No wonder you asked me to marry you."

She grinned and closed her eyes. "You didn't say no. Too late to back out now."

I thought it wise not to tell her that's not how marriage proposals work. I looked past her and noticed my dog in what looked like a yellow duffle bag. He gave me a look that could have only meant *Bail me out, dude.*

"Uh, why is my dog in a bag?"

Mina looked up at me with a smile, but otherwise didn't move. "That's a carrier, dopey. He can't just sit in a seat on the plane."

"Apache's going with us?"

"Of course."

I looked at him again. He looked ridiculous. "Couldn't he at least have a manly color? What is that, chartreuse?"

"He's not a man, he's a puppy. And yellow is one of the colors he can see the best."

"You're going to New York, boy," I conceded. I heard the thump-thumping of his tail inside the carrier. Mina shut her eyes but continued to smile. I said, "We aren't taking your daughter, but we're taking my dog to the city."

She pouted for the second time that morning. It was cuter than the first time. "Don't say that," she said. "I already miss my baby as it is. But I've been promising mom for months she could have a week." She opened her eyes and looked up. "Or two."

It was at this point I decided to change the subject. I could practically feel the briar patch all around me. "Where's Mika? We're gonna be late."

"I told him eight, so he'll be here at eight-fifteen. Relax, he's like a tape-delayed Swiss watch."

I checked my phone. "So we have five minutes. Cool, I still need to find your mom."

"She's been hiding from you."

"I know," I said, standing. "It's not gonna work."

I found Katherine where I expected her to be, in the backyard pretending to tend to her garden. Little Winona was with her, in a sundress, mostly sitting in the dirt and undoing whatever her grandma did. Katherine looked up at me and blanched.

"Oh, um, Eddie. I thought you two were gone."

"Nice try. Weren't you even going to say goodbye to us?"

She shook her head. "It makes me cry too hard. This is easier." She looked back to her patch of earth. "Thanks again for everything."

"Nuh uh," I said, squatting in front of her. "Come on. You know what I'm waiting for." I stood up.

Katherine sighed like she was being forced to enter slave labor. She laboriously took off her gloves, stood, and brushed the dirt off the front of her jeans. Then she walked up to me and tiptoed, her bare feet digging into the loamy soil. I kissed her, for real this time. It wasn't long, but it didn't need to be. When it was finished, I'm pretty sure she was the one swooning.

"Do you believe me now?" I asked.

She blew out a gush of breath and fanned herself. "Okay, okay. I believe you. I'll try." She pushed me away. "Now go, before you miss your plane and cause me all sorts of trouble."

"Bye, Katherine." I kissed her on the cheek, then kissed Nona and trotted to the front of the house. When I got there Mika had arrived exactly on time—fifteen minutes late—and was helping his sister load up the truck. They both turned in unison, with Mika giving me an intense look.

"Did you kiss her?" Mina asked.

I nodded.

"And?"

"And, she admitted maybe it was time to start looking for a boyfriend."

Mika gave his sister a fist pound. "Good," he said. "Mom's too young and pretty to spend the rest of her life alone. Dad would've hated that." He climbed into the truck and we followed. I'd just settled in the back with Apache when he added, without the semblance of a smile, "But he would have killed you for kissing her."

Mina nodded. "Me too, if you ever do it again."

This was going to be a fun trip.

Mina and I didn't talk during the flight east. She knew what I wanted to discuss and she was doing her best to avoid it. She, her mother, and her daughter had been placed in danger because someone thought I was working a case I knew nothing about. Mina, however, knew plenty. Cute little secrets and eccentricities are any woman's prerogative, but when it involves people pointing guns at me, it becomes my business. I didn't push it on the plane, as we were in coach and didn't have the privacy to discuss it anyway. I did let her know, in no uncertain terms, that we needed to talk. She spent most of the flight staring out of the window. As we entered the approach to JFK, Mina turned and looked at me. Her face was puffy as if she'd been crying. I hadn't noticed.

"I'm never going to marry you if you don't learn to trust me," she said.

I could have reminded her that I never asked her to marry me in the first place, but didn't. The way her eyes were scanning mine told me she was full of bluster. She was worried, a lot worried. Instead of being harsh, I said, "I know." I decided to leave it at that.

She looked at me a while and then nodded. We deplaned and took the long walk to baggage claim in silence. We were walking swiftly, since Apache's whimpers indicated he'd had just about as much of airlines as he could tolerate. Just before we exited security, Mina spoke. "I used the M-word again and you didn't freak out."

"I'm not generally the freak out type."

"That's good to know." Her smile began to blossom. "Oh! There's probably something I should have told you about my sister."

"Oh great, more surprises."

In lieu of responding, she grinned and took off at a full-on sprint. I'm not sure how she'd spotted her sister in the crowd, other than it must have been some secret sisterly radar normal people don't have. She'd bolted so unexpectedly it took me seconds of scanning to find her. Then I saw her waving and grinning at me, wearing a light blue top instead of the green one she was wearing seconds earlier. I took a couple of steps, wondering how she pulled off that piece of magic, when it hit me.

I stopped and almost dropped Apache's carrier onto a moving baggage claim carousel. There were two Minas. God, in his infinite, albeit flawed, wisdom, had given Mina an identical twin. I stood there, kicking myself for never putting it together before. Mary and Kari Good Crow were twins with old-fashioned rhyming names. No wonder Mina had always preferred her legal name as a kid.

Seeing I was frozen in place, Mina took her sister by the elbow and guided her to me. "This is my fiancé, Eddie."

"Hi, my fiancé Eddie," Kari said.

I blinked stupidly, first at Mina's announcement of my new title and then at hearing her voice coming out of this stranger wearing the Mina mask.

"He's cute!" she said, turning to Mina. "Is he a good kisser?"

Holy déjà fucking *vu.* This time I ran as fast as I could, while holding my bag full of barking dog, to our baggage claim carousel. From behind I could hear Mina's cackling laughter—in horrifying stereo.

Kari lived in a middle-class Brooklyn neighborhood, in a brownstone that had been converted into apartments and townhouses. The left-side door of the brownstone opened to a hallway that led to first, fourth, and fifth-floor apartments. Kari's two-level townhome had a separate entrance on the right. There was a basement level that Kari told me was only used for storage. Her unit was more than I'd expected for an artist, even a successful one.

Apache and I explored the neighborhood while Mina and her sister got reacquainted. The puppy had never been in a city larger than Flagstaff and, after days of carousing in the wide-open plains, Brooklyn was an entirely different planet. I was anxious to see how he'd react. Clearly he had no idea there were so many dogs in the world, and he tried to leave them scent messages every five feet or so. I had to buy him water to keep the little guy from getting dehydrated.

Having a puppy is as good a cover as a detective can have. In our slow walk around Kari's block we were stopped frequently by residents wanting to "pet the puppy." People are just naturally more relaxed when interacting with pets, and thus more approachable and less cautious with what they say. That's particularly true if you lead them to believe you already know the information you seek. I told the neighbors I was visiting a friend, "a sculptor who lived up the street." To my surprise, most either knew her directly or knew who she was. I probed under cover of friendliness and learned more about her in an hour than I'd learned from her entire family. Most of her neighbors began the conversations with expressions of remorse for the loss of Kari's husband and son. There were more tidbits of information that I quickly began to patch together into a story. It had holes, but holes can be filled. After learning as much as I could from strangers, Apache and I found a coffee shop with free Wi-Fi and we sat on the sidewalk as I delved into my host's life via the Internet.

Although hiding is easier than one might think, in order for people to hide they must first believe someone is looking for them. Kari did not. In the old Raymond Chandler days, a gumshoe made his mark by pounding the pavement, shaking hands, and asking questions. These days it's easier to pay a few bucks for access to the right Internet databases. You can find a world of information in a short time if you know where to look. I made my living by knowing where to look. No more than a couple hours after I set off, I knew what I needed to know and how to go approach the Good Crow sisters for the rest.

Apache and I played it cool for the rest of the evening, which was easy since we enjoyed both women's company immensely. He was busy taking a series of ear-scratch-fueled naps, and I was observing the sisters and taking mental notes on their dynamic. Though they looked alike, Mina and her sister were quite different. Kari was quiet and serious, more urban sophisticate than Mina's brazen country gal. While Mina was outgoing around long-time friends and family, her interactions with casual acquaintances were guarded. Kari, from what I garnered from neighbors, was friendly towards everyone. She managed to combine a quiet nature with extroversion, a combination I found intriguing.

They did, however, share a significant trait. Both women harbored insecurities that belied their capabilities, and which neither seemed to be aware of. There was one sister, Mina, who'd lived much of her life in small towns, but would jump impulsively from one major life change to another with neither plan nor parachute. She was bold enough to have become a decorated Marine by age twenty-three, but introverted enough that she had few friends outside of her family. She'd retreated to run her family's motel after her failed marriage, despite having a skill that fifteen minutes on the web told me was worth upwards of eighty grand per year.

The other sister had taken a single bold leap at seventeen, had been burned for it, and had taken few chances since. Kari was friendly and personable, but seemed to be the kind of person you smile at but don't really see. All the neighbors knew of her, but none gave me any deep insights. I figured that's because no one knew her very well. She was like a lovely canvas, painted by an artist you've never heard of, waiting to be discovered. Mina, despite her aloofness toward strangers, was always noticed. Always.

Kari had her mother's green thumb, with a robust "garden" that took up every inch of her balcony except for two reclining chairs and a small table. Her townhouse was filled with her sculptures, most western and Native American themed and most cast in metal. I recognized Kari as the creator of Mina's art back at the Sleep Sooner Inn. The townhouse itself was open and modern inside, in contrast to the classic brownstone exterior. Her furniture mostly consisted of pillows, throw rugs from her mother, a single, enormous sofa, and lots of clutter, from art supplies to half-finished projects. The mess made me feel at home. It sent Mina into a cleaning frenzy that wiped out what was left of her energy.

After dinner the girls were sprawled on the large sofa, sipping red wine and cuddling. Mina was lulling herself to sleep by petting my now spoiled dog. It was time to make my move. I stood, making sure they were looking up at me when I spoke.

"So, Kari Ellen Good Crow Sunay," I started. I made certain to pronounce her married name correctly, *Soo NAHY,* according to the sound files I'd found. That got her attention.

"Guilty," she said. Kari's choice of words told me she was ready for her inquisition. Mina looked over at me drowsily but said nothing.

"Married to one Mr. Fadil Sunay, late of Brooklyn, New York, and Washington, D.C. Originally from Turkey, emigrated to the U.S. in ninety-nine, right out of university in Turkey. He was assigned to the Turkish diplomatic corps at the United Nations." I looked at Kari for a response.

"Go on," she said, softly. "You're doing great." I detected no sarcasm in her voice.

"Met Miss Kari Good Crow, freelance artist and adjunct professor at the Columbia University School of the Arts, sometime in early two thousand nine?"

"It was September two thousand eight. And I'm really just considered an instructor, but go on."

"So noted."

"Boy, you're really being official," Mina said. She was starting to frown.

"Hush, sweetie, this is important," Kari said, not taking her eyes from me. She took Mina's feet and placed them across her lap. It seemed to soothe her immediately. I wish I'd learned that trick earlier. "Keep going, sweets," Kari said, this time speaking to me. "We have nothing to hide."

"Okay." Both her openness and affection were throwing me off my game, so I turned to my laptop, mostly keeping my eyes off the twinsation cuddled up on the sofa. "After what I assume must have been a whirlwind romance, the Sunays were married in June two thousand nine in a civil ceremony. My assistant, Debra, thinks she can get me a copy of the marriage license, if needed."

"Nope. I'm pretty sure I got married."

"Here's where it gets hairy, so stop me anytime."

"I'll never stop you, sweets," Kari said.

At this point I wished she didn't sound so much like my lover when she spoke. Her voice was different, however, just enough so that I could tell who was speaking with my back turned. I wondered if she was calling me *sweets* to try and confuse me. It was likely a game they'd played for most of their lives. It wasn't going to work with me.

"Things went well at first. According to neighbors, the couple seemed loving and happy and spent most of their non-work time together. Then, in early two thousand ten, Mr. Sunay was transferred to the U.S. Embassy in Washington, D.C. Around the same time, by my calculations, Mrs. Sunay became pregnant with her first child."

Kari sniffled a little and nodded.

"Do you have to sound so cold, Eddie?" Mina asked. I turned, expecting anger, but she looked sad instead.

"He's not being cold, sweetie. He's being professional so that it doesn't hurt as much." Kari looked at me. "It's okay. Keep going. I've been through this in my head a million times."

I gave Kari a weak smile of thanks. "Although this should have been the happiest time of her life, Mrs. Sunay didn't seem to be enjoying life very much. According to embassy press releases, Mr. Sunay had earned a promotion in Washington, and ..." I read part of the press release from my laptop. "*Mr. Sunay's loyal wife, renowned artist Kari Good Crow Sunay, remains in New York until they can arrange for living quarters in the Washington area.* Except I'm guessing that part never happened."

"No, it didn't. He claimed we couldn't afford to sell the brownstone in a down housing market, and it didn't make sense to

66

rent it out at a loss either. So the baby and I would stay here until we could all afford to move. He worked in D.C. weekdays and took the train up on weekends."

"How long did that last?"

"Until the baby was born. Then he started telling me he had diplomatic duties on the weekends, official dinners and the like. A few months after that he was taking business trips to Turkey and other places."

"What other places?" I asked.

"I don't know. He said he couldn't discuss them."

I closed the laptop then walked over to where they were seated. I took my place on the floor next to Apache. He immediately climbed into my lap to sleep. For this part I wanted Kari to see me as a friend, not a detective. I needed her honesty now that she understood I already knew most of the story.

"How long before he started hitting you, Kari?"

She began crying. Mina sat up and wrapped her arms around her, mouthing a silent *thank you* to me for sitting down next to them.

"It wasn't right away. He was sweet at first. But then we started arguing all the time. He was never here. I was a new mom with a job and no help. And on the rare occasions he was here, he claimed he was too tired to do anything. Then one night, I lost it and starting screaming at him."

"Is that when the neighbors called the police?"

Kari nodded. "Yeah. He punched me in the face and then started kicking me. I was screaming and crying. Fortunately, the idea that New Yorkers don't care about people is a myth."

"Do you think he would have ...?" I let the question trail off on purpose.

"Killed me? I don't think so. I think he just wanted me to know who was in charge. The cops came and I told them I wouldn't cooperate, so they didn't press charges."

"Why didn't you?" I asked.

"My son. Fadil told me the next time I called the cops he'd make sure I never saw Jeremy again."

I took Kari's trembling hand. She looked down at me and tried her best to stanch her tears. "Do you think that's what happened, Kari?" I asked.

She shook her head. "No. For a long time I did ... at least, I wished that were the case, that he was somewhere hiding out in D.C.

with my baby. But then I finally had to face facts." She pulled her hand away and covered her eyes. "My baby is dead. My husband is dead, both killed in a stupid traffic accident." She stopped, trying to suppress her tears and gather herself. She continued, "I was screaming at Fadil again, accusing him of having another family, and he just grabbed Jeremy and left. He didn't even take any of his things, just snatched my son, pushed me down, and walked out. I tried everyone I knew, every place I thought he'd go, and nothing. I went to the police on the second day. About a week later, the police knocked on my door and said they ..." She collapsed in tears and Mina held her closer.

Mina finished her sister's story. "The cops found Fadil's car on I-95 somewhere in Pennsylvania. They claimed he'd fallen asleep at the wheel, jumped a guardrail, and landed at the bottom of a creek bed. The car caught on fire and they couldn't even identify the bodies. The fire was so hot there was almost nothing left of the baby in the back seat."

Kari's weeping grew, and Mina pulled her head to her shoulder. "We tried to get an autopsy, but they shipped the bodies to be cremated without Kari's permission. Claimed it was an administrative error."

I mulled that over for a while, then spoke. "The papers say they were able to match some of Fadil's DNA. They found part of a finger, matched his print and even matched dental records."

"I know," Mina said. "They had time to do that, but not to do an autopsy? Come on."

"But you still don't believe it. You've never believed they were in that car."

Mina shook her head. Her expression was angry. "How did you know that? Did they have that on your Internet? Were you reading our old Facebook statuses or something?" She turned her face away from me and began crying herself.

I rose to my knees and wrapped my arms around both of them. Mina looked at me with a wounded expression. Kari kissed me on the cheek.

"I haven't looked at any of your private information, Mina," I said. "I know if you thought for a moment your nephew was dead, you'd never have talked about his death like that in front of your sister. Plus, I remember what you told me in the hotel. You said your family visits you in dreams when they pass on. But you only mentioned your dad, not your nephew."

"You didn't believe me."

"But you did. And anyway, I didn't disbelieve. I'm just ghost agnostic."

Mina blurted a short laugh. "So you'll help us?" she asked. She gave me a glower that meant, *Stop being funny. I don't want to laugh.*

"Mina, all you ever needed was to ask me. There was no need to be so secretive. And you didn't have to go through this elaborate road trip to get my help. I'd have helped you for free the day I met you."

Her expression flashed to hurt and then angry in seconds. She pulled herself away from Kari and pushed by me, standing in the middle of the room. "Think what you want of me, but I was never trying to con you into anything." She practically ran up the stairs to the bedroom.

"That went well," I said. I ran my hands over my face, trying to stem the oncoming headache.

"You know, she'll never marry you if you don't learn to start trusting her."

"Holy shit. Do you two share a brain?" I leaned my face on the sofa cushion to shut out the world for a moment. Kari began to rub the back of my head. I wanted to purr.

"Eddie, I'm the one who asked Mina to bring you. If you wanna be mad, be mad at me. She didn't even want to come here. I think she was afraid I'd get my hopes up. But she told me she was dating this *cool private dick.*" She gave me a sly look. "You don't look so private to me."

"Oh, Jesus."

"Anyway, when she told me about you, I asked her to see if you'd help us. I even got Mom to harass Mina into bringing you here."

"I thought you just said you were certain your son—"

"Is dead. Yeah, I said that. That's what the police said, the insurance company said, my counselor says. I'm supposed to say it too."

"Except you believe what Mina believes."

Kari's eyes began to mist, that tortuous state just before the first tear falls when you can tell she's still holding onto hope. "I don't know what I believe. I just need to know one way or the other. I can

... I can feel him, Eddie. I can feel Jeremy in here," she said, touching her chest. "Or maybe it's just wishful thinking."

I stopped fighting. "So Mina brought me here because you asked her to."

She nodded. "I'm sorry."

I closed my mouth and let silence clear the room that words had clogged like sour smoke. Kari broke the impasse, still looking at me with her watery eyes. They glistened like brown diamonds. "Eddie, Mina's in love with you. Why do you think she took you to South Dakota?"

I shrugged. "To meet your mom, I guess."

"Mom has hated every single guy we've ever introduced her to, and for good reason. Mina just wanted to show her she'd finally found a good one." She stroked my hair. "You really need to stop expecting the worst. She's a bundle of faults, but Mina's as loyal as your puppy."

I'd pushed Kari to relive the night her son died and she was busy counseling me and protecting her sister. I stopped feeling sorry for myself and climbed up on the sofa. Immediately Kari scooted to the opposite side and then stuck her feet in my lap. Even a dumb puppy like me can be trained. I began stroking her feet the way she had done with Mina's.

"I think Mom would marry you herself, if she could."

"Tell you a secret, the feeling's sorta mutual."

Kari snorted. "Let's not tell your fiancée."

"You know, we've only known each other a week. Not sure you could call us officially engaged, if you know what I mean."

Kari broke out in a wide smile. "Good to know." She looked down at my hands on her feet. "My hopes are officially up." She blinked, and this time the sparkle wasn't tears.

I really need to learn to keep my mouth shut and my hands to myself.

Morning came early for me. I left Mina sleeping while Apache snored on the floor next to her side, as always. I slipped on a pair of shorts and a tee shirt and headed down to make myself some coffee. Kari was there, dressed in a mid-thigh robe. The unmistakable smell of bacon and fresh coffee filled the air.

"Morning, sweets. Where's Mina?" she asked.

"I let her sleep in. We were up, um, talking pretty late."

Kari smiled and turned to the stove. "Yeah, I heard you, um, talking. You had Mina talking pretty loudly, as I recall. What was that, like three conversations?" She pressed down on her spatula and the bacon's sizzle and pop grew appropriately louder. I'd found another thing the twins shared: a devilish sense of humor. I was glad her back was turned or she'd have seen me grinning like an idiot.

"You must be a pretty good talker," she added.

"Alright, alright. Very funny. We'll try to be quieter from now on."

"Oh, don't mind me. I live vicariously through my sister anyway." She turned around, walked to the table, and handed me a plate full of food. "Don't wait for me, I already ate." She poured a cup of coffee from the coffee maker and handed it to me. "Let me guess. You're macho enough that you like it black."

I thanked her and took a sip. I wanted sugar but didn't want to be judged un-macho. "Just trying to be as macho as Mina," I said.

"You'll never make it, sweets. She was my brothers' big brother. Kept all of us in line."

"That I can believe." I started eating the omelet she'd made. It tasted so good I almost cried. "Oh my God, woman, you can cook."

She smiled but said nothing. Instead she just stood by, watching me eat. "It's good to have someone to cook for again," she said. "Henry doesn't like home cooking much. He's more the gourmand type. I think my South Dakota roots are too crass for his palate."

"Henry?"

"The guy I see on and off." She shrugged. "It's not really serious … at least, I'm not. I guess I'm not ready for serious yet. I've come to believe all men suck." She winked at me. "Well, I did a week ago, anyway."

That was close to flirting, but I liked it. "Your problem is you're dating a guy named Henry. Any man with even a spark of romance would have changed his name by now."

"Maybe that's why my sex life sucks."

I was again taken aback by the openness of this person with Mina's face. Actually, the more I looked the less identical she looked. Kari's face was slightly rounder than Mina's and not quite as long. They had the same features and freckles, and both even had moles over their mouth, but Mina had a dense cluster of freckles right by her left eye. Kari had a similar cluster by her mouth. As a result I found myself looking at Mina's eyes a lot; with Kari, I was looking at her lips. She caught me at it.

"I have something in my teeth, don't I?" she asked. She began to wipe them with a finger.

"No, I was just …" I trailed off as her robe slipped open, revealing the pajamas underneath. They were just an ordinary tank top and shorts, nothing overtly sexy or revealing, but it wasn't the clothes that caught my eye. On her thigh, mirroring Mina's scar exactly, was a tattoo. Without thinking I wiped my hands, turned to her, and opened her robe the rest of the way, running my fingertips over the skin art. The detail was intricate; the tattoo looked like a raised keloid in the process of healing. I'd seen Mina's scar enough to know this was a perfect match, except Kari's tattoo added stitching that started at the bottom of her shorts. Around this time I realized I was touching this almost-stranger's body like it was Mina's. I looked up at her and she was smiling at me.

"You like it?" she asked.

I paused because for a second, I thought she was asking me about her body. The answer would have been the same. "It's amazing." I loved Mina's scars, but these were almost better.

"When I saw her in the hospital she kind of came unglued. She was just bawling her eyes out and saying, 'I'm so sorry. We're not identical anymore.' So I traced her scars when they sedated her and got a tattoo artist I know to do the work." She lifted the bottom of her pajama top. "She did a fabulous job."

"I'm glad she didn't lose her leg," I added, joking.

"Yeah, I would've missed my leg," Kari replied. Her face was a blanket of seriousness that touched me deeply. I wouldn't even cut my hair to match my brother. On her abdomen, where Mina had taken both shrapnel and a bullet, Kari had duplicated the scars' outlines, but in the center, where Mina had only softly scarred flesh, Kari's "wound" opened to a pit from whence peeked out what could have only been a fairy staring up, hands raised as if surprised by the light.

"Inside all twins, there's magic," she said. "Mina's gonna get tattoos like mine while she's here."

I was so enraptured with the work, including the slightly raised skin beneath the tattoo's outline, that I didn't pay attention to the fact that I was now holding up my girlfriend's sister's pajama top and practically looking up into the bottoms of her breasts. Kari gave no indication it bothered her.

And of course that's when Mina walked in. "Isn't that cool?" she asked, seeming not at all distressed. "When she first showed me that, I thought I'd never stop crying. She was all, 'We're twins again, sweetie.'" Mina walked over to us, where I was still stupidly holding Kari's pajamas like a deer caught in headlights. She ignored me and kissed her sister. "I adore you," she said.

That gave me time to restart my brain. I let Kari go and grabbed the correct twin. "How're you feeling?" I asked.

She smiled, twisted out of my hands, and said, "Full of forgiveness."

"Yeah, he apologized the hell outta you last night," Kari added, heading to the stove.

Mina didn't flinch. She just sat opposite me, took my plate of food, and began eating. "Did you show him the Frankenstein stiches on your hip?" she asked. She looked happier than I'd ever seen her.

Her sister answered without turning her back. "No, I'm not wearing panties. He'd see all of my glory. Don't wanna scare him off." Kari was speaking softly and matter-of-factly about her sister's boyfriend viewing her male enslavement device. It frankly turned me on.

"Child, please," Mina said, talking around a full mouth, "he knows what you look like naked. You look just like me. Damn, these eggs are good!" Her eyes never left her plate.

"I'm not as muscular as you." Kari, knowing her sister, had left the stove with another plate of food and was headed straight for me. She set it in front of me, looked at Mina wolfing hers down, and shook her head. "See what I mean about people appreciating my cooking? Even Apache eats slower than her."

I started eating mine, being careful to look elegant in order to make Mina look worse. She didn't look up. "How come you never cook for me?" I asked her.

"Can't talk. Eating."

"Oh honey," Kari said, "trust me, neither of you wants Mina to cook for you."

Mina gave her sister a fist bump without looking up. "Damn right. But if you want a new small block dropped in that Camaro, I'm your girl."

I decided to play dangerously. "You know, put the two of you together and you'd make the perfect girlfriend."

The joke backfired. Mina stopped mid-bite, her mouth full of food, and gave me the finger. Kari plopped herself in my lap, looking sad. "Cooking and making babies is what Fadil thought I was good at, too," she said. It took me ten minutes of honest flattery to put that genie back in the bottle. By then my food was cold and Kari had gotten comfortable in my lap. Since I was starving, I ate around her.

"Don't you have a boyfriend whose lap you can sit in?" Mina asked.

"Yeah. Yours is better." She looked calmly at her sister with her arm around my neck.

A middle finger for Kari from Mina.

"How come you guys didn't live together when you left the Marines?" I'd learned that a sure way to distract my firebrand was to mention the gyrenes. It worked here too, saving my bacon.

"Oh God no," Kari said, smiling. "We roomed together seventeen years. That's long enough. Although I'm sure she could get helicopter work here no problem."

"Besides," Mina said, standing to put her dishes in the dishwasher, "Kari's too sloppy. Drives me crazy." She walked to us, jerked her sister out of my lap, and took the exact same position as Kari—in the way of my damned breakfast. "So what's the plan, Stan?" she asked.

Kari's eyes widened and she sat opposite us.

"Why do you only have two chairs for this big table?" I asked. I was getting annoyed despite the lovely, soft women fighting over my lap. This was about food.

"I used them to make life-sized statues," Kari answered. "Sitting Bull. He paid my mortgage for two months and people expect him to be sitting, for some reason. What is the plan, Eddie?" She was through with small talk.

"The bottom line is someone took a shot at me and almost shot Mina and Nona trying to keep me from investigating this case. That alone is enough to make me doubt the official story."

"Thank you," Kari said, breathlessly.

I held up my hands. "Let's not go too far too fast. For all we know, someone could have driven your husband off the road and doesn't want us investigating it. Or, maybe this is some insurance scam. I have a half-dozen other theories, too."

"I understand," Kari said.

"But you're going to help, right?" Mina asked.

"I'm all in." Kari ran over to join in hugging me, and I finally gave up on breakfast. After they'd calmed down enough to listen, I gave them my gut feel. "I can't help feeling that it was awfully convenient that Jeremy couldn't be identified. I get why there were no dental records, but there should have been something forensics could have worked with. That's especially suspicious since you think Fadil was cheating. In my experience, nines times out of ten, if the woman thinks her husband's a cheat, he is."

"You think he ran off with another woman?" Kari asked. The pain in her eyes could have cut me if I touched it.

"I don't know what to think," I answered.

"So what do we do first?" Mina asked.

I paused before answering. In the movies, the shamus answers *"You just stay out of the way and don't worry your pretty little head."* In the real world, detective work is time-consuming, tedious, and requires a lot of leg work. The more boots, pumps, and flip flops on the ground, the better.

I answered, "I'm going to try to find out where every single cent your husband ever made went and if anyone but you was a beneficiary of his death. I need you two to start making lists of everyone you know that knew him. Tell them you've found paperwork for an insurance claim, but you're having trouble reaching his family for some information you need."

"What will that do?" Kari asked.

"It'll shake the trees to see if anything falls out," I answered. "If this is at all about money, that'll get somebody interested."

"What about the two guys that came after us?" Mina asked.

"I have a good friend at the FBI, a guy I was in Afghanistan with. I'm going to call in some favors and see if we can find out who those two worked with." Mina nodded her accord. "Kari, the papers said they found one of your husband's fingers?"

"Yeah, it was caught in the door. The coroner speculated he tried to escape, but the door closed on him." She looked puzzled. "Why?"

"I'm not sure yet. I'm working on an idea. I'll let you know when I'm ready."

Mina stood, pulled me up, and kissed me, hard. "Thanks, baby. I love you." Before I could catch my breath, she said, "Come on, Kari, we need to find some detective clothes to wear." She practically sprinted out of the kitchen.

Kari, in contrast, walked slowly to me and sank into my arms, weeping. I held her and let her cry it out. I didn't need an explanation; I knew her reasoning. I was the first person outside of her family who believed that just maybe her son was alive somewhere. In truth, I wasn't at all convinced. But if he was, there wasn't a damned rock they could hide under to keep me from finding him.

Chapter 6

I spent most of the next two days bouncing between the computer and the telephone. Debra was glad to have a case to work on she actually cared about solving, and was proving to be a demon in research. Of course, she was pissed that I'd gone to New York without her, but I assured her I might need more pumps on the ground in the future. The info we'd turned up kept pointing towards my eventually taking a trip to D.C. She would be a big help keeping the investigation going if that came to pass.

Kari compiled a list of people who knew Fadil, and she and Mina spent fully six hours a day talking to them, asking questions about his job, his life and, importantly, about friends or enemies. Mina wore some of Kari's clothes and took delight in imitating her more-conservative sister. That part was my idea. Kari was far too close to the situation and emotional for the kind of delicate probing we'd need. By contrast I'd seen Mina's ability to get her way without disclosing any information of her own. She took the hard stuff, and Kari talked to mutual friends she trusted.

The first major surprise, at least to his wife, was that Fadil was no longer working for the Turkish government when he died. His "reassignment" turned out to be his resigning from the government and taking a job with a major federal contractor based in Northern Virginia. Whatever his other plans were, they apparently didn't involve moving back to Turkey. He'd gotten the new gig because he'd promised his new company he would become a U.S. citizen.

Kari made me a list of contacts at the U.N. and we managed to get one to speak to us by telephone: Fadil's former assistant, Miss Haleh Asker. She sounded young and pleasant over the phone, so of course I wanted to meet her in person. That's not as creepy as it sounds. I wanted to eyeball any attractive women that he spent a lot of time with. She agreed to meet me for lunch, as much as anything, I guessed, because she liked her former boss and wanted to help solve his death.

"Mr. Sunay was a nice man," Haleh said. "I enjoyed working for him."

I had her pegged to be around twenty-seven, pretty, with dark eyes. She wore a scarf, but a shock of her dark hair showed through in the front. She looked lost in her loose clothing, to the point where I wondered if colleagues listened at the restroom door for sounds of vomiting. She gestured when she spoke, waving a ponderous diamond that dwarfed her slender fingers.

"How long did you work for him?"

"Three years. He was such a devoted family man and a kind boss. He always recommended me whenever a better job opening arose."

"Did you leave to get married?" It was a purposefully dumb question. I wanted to be sure she wasn't engaged to Fadil.

"Oh no. He left to work as a … lobbyist I suppose is the best word, a director in fact. He even asked me if I'd go with him as his executive assistant."

"And you refused?"

Haleh gave a demure smile and averted her eyes. "He was quite insistent. He asked me several times, in fact. However, I was seeing someone who I thought perhaps would ask for my hand." She held the huge ring for me to see. "As you can see, I made the right choice."

I nodded and agreed she had. "I also made the right choice in not bringing my girlfriend to this interview," I said. "I have enough trouble already without your beautiful ring giving her ideas."

She cluck-clucked at me and gave me a little lecture on needing to settle down at my age. It broke enough ice that she dropped the formality and gave me the name of the man who recruited Fadil. She also told me it made quite the stink with his former employer, the Turkish government. In effect, he'd burned his bridges when he left. I thanked her for the time, paid for lunch, and was on the phone with

Debra before I reached the subway. By that evening she'd found a job posting with Fadil's recruiter, a Mr. Ken Satterhorn, from an internet cache I'm sure she shouldn't have had access to. The woman deserves a raise.

We couldn't find Fadil's new salary but, with the location and the job title, I was able to narrow it to a fairly good range. By the end of the third day I'd found his work location, his boss, their customers, and his pay scale plus or minus ten percent. Kari pulled out her old tax information and we did some comparisons. It turned out another thing the Good Crow girls shared was an unfortunate habit of trusting their spouses with complete control over income taxes. Kari had been told her husband made a hundred and thirty grand per year. I'd pegged his Director-level pay at around a hundred eighty. That meant fifty thousand bucks each year was going somewhere, and not to his very angry wife.

It took Mina's dragging her sister to a spa to keep the woman from spitting nails all evening. I also managed to convince her that what we knew was far from proof that Fadil had been seeing, much less keeping, another woman. In fact, no one I or Mina had talked to gave any indication of inappropriate relationships. Haleh had called him "a perfect gentleman, gallant and respectful." To her knowledge he never saw women alone in his office or outside of work, except for his wife and occasional family members. That didn't prove he was innocent, but if he were the type to throw money at women, Haleh, who had unrestricted access to him, would have known it.

"So what do you think it means?" Mina asked me, calling from Kari's cell.

"Either he wasn't seeing another woman or it started after he moved."

"Well, what, a hundred thousand bucks disappeared? Maybe eighty thousand after taxes? He had to spend it on somebody."

"Not necessarily. He could have been a gambler, drugs—"

"Kari said he was a fairly devoted Muslim. I don't see his being a druggie."

"Nor do I, to be honest," I said. "We're going to have to find out where the money went. I'm trying to see if I can get Kari authorization to search all his account records as next-of-kin, but if there was money in some foreign account we don't know about, we may never find it."

"She doesn't care about the money. I'm not sure she even cares anymore if he was cheating. She just wants to find her son."

I agreed we'd keep looking, but I told her it would take more than the week she'd originally allotted. I still hadn't mentioned the Washington trip because I didn't know whom I wanted to send. Besides, there were folks I wanted to talk to first. In the meantime, we had a sister who just discovered her husband's life was at least partially a lie. If we couldn't hold her together, finding out what happened to her son wouldn't fix anything.

Mina and Kari glided home after midnight on the wings of too little dinner and way too many drinks. I was watching Bogart, as usual. This time it was *To Have and Have Not*. Bogie inspired me when I had a case I couldn't solve. Bacall's presence was purely for joy. I'd only seen it ten times, so it hadn't gotten stale yet. The townhouse was dark and comfortable, the only light coming from the large TV. I was on my fourth Guinness, the result of not being able to put the pieces of the Fadil puzzle together or put the puzzle box away. A few tall, thick glasses of stout and Bogie were the perfect solution.

I didn't hear the girls come in, and they did their best to startle me. Without warning I felt soft hands around my eyes. "Guess who," she said, her voice deep and tinged with alcohol.

"Hi Kari. Feeling better?"

"How'd you know it was me?" She slumped on the big sofa in front of me, looking glassy eyed and disappointed.

"Yeah, and how come you knew it was me on Kari's phone?" Mina asked.

"I can always tell you apart. You forget, I met Mina first. By the time I met you, Kari, I already knew her voice and all her little quirks."

"I don't have quirks," Mina claimed. She sat behind me and put her feet against my back. "Rub my feet. Men have been dancing on them."

Kari leaned around me and laughed at her. "Dude. That's totally a quirk." They laughed hysterically. I didn't get the joke. Kari stopped laughing and looked serious. For a moment I thought the pain of our earlier discovery was coming back. Instead she leaned over and kissed me. This time, however, I wasn't as surprised as when Katherine did it, so I didn't kiss back.

"You shouldn't tell us apart. It's rude. We're iden … identypical, you know," she said.

"Atypical," Mina corrected.

"That's what I said. We're identical."

"Not completely. You have freckles in different places." I wasn't going to mention one had a fatter face.

"Cheater!" Kari said, jabbing a finger at me. "You're not allowed to count freckles." She looked positively livid; her eyes narrowed and the bridge of her nose was furrowed with wrinkles. Naturally, she leaned over and kissed me again. Mina was still seated behind me, dancing on my back, giggling. My lips remained faithful to the dancer behind me.

Kari leaned back and frowned again. "Nothing," she said.

"Why are you doing that?" I asked.

"I've been wondering if I'd like it." She'd made her voice absurdly low. Her sentence ended in laughter.

"What's funny?" Mina slurred.

"I'm trying to make out with your husband," Kari answered.

"Isn't he a good kisser?"

"I don't know yet. He won't help."

She kissed me a third time, and this time I gave her a little kiss back, mainly so she'd stop it.

"It's even better when you help," she said, again with the deep voice. She pinned her chin to her chest and lifted her eyes. It was The Look, Bacall's look. Quiet, serious Kari had been acting out the love scene from my favorite movie. I didn't know she'd even noticed it was on.

"You're a Bogart fan?" I asked, excited. Mina was Bogart apathetic.

"I like Bogart, but I love Bacall. You blew your line. I'm gonna need a new leading man." She stood up, pulled her sister's arm, and stood her up. They wobbled there together, looking as if they were fighting a private hurricane. "We're gonna change and then we'll be back."

It sounded like a threat to my buzzed mind.

"Hey! Were you making out with my boyfriend?" Mina asked, now frowning.

"That movie's over. We have to go fix ourselves up. We'll show this cheater who looks alike and who doesn't." They left to go upstairs, taking their bags. From the steps I could hear Kari still fussing. "Bogie would have kissed me back."

"That's not Bogie," Mina claimed, "that was Peter Lorre." They both cackled.

Insulted, I decided to switch from Guinness to the cheap vodka Kari stocked. In retrospect, it was a mistake. It was a mistake because beer and vodka don't mix so well, and because two drunk sisters take way longer to do anything than you'd think. I believe a part of me didn't want to be the only sober person in the house. The other part was just a guy in a house with two drunk, hot twins. If you've never been in that situation, trust me, drunk beats sober.

"Tell us apart now, Shylock!"

The voice startled me enough that I almost fell off the sofa. I don't know how long I'd been asleep or how much more I'd had to drink, but now I was seeing double.

"Sherlock, not Shylock," said her reflection.

"What's the difference?"

"Hush, you'll give it away."

"Which one's your wife?"

"I don't think I'm married yet," I answered.

"You keep that up, you never will be," one of them said.

I squinted, clearing my vision. They were dressed in identical green silk nightgowns that came to their knees. Each had spaghetti straps that showed off lovely, square shoulders. I'd never studied the shoulder freckles, so those were no help. Hair was a no-go. Mina's was long and Kari's shorter, but they were both tied in a bun. Whichever one was Kari no longer sported her natural, darker color. I looked to the eyes, but they'd put on identical make-up that hid the freckles on their faces. With the shadow in the dark room and their blush, I couldn't even tell which one had the longer face. Round face was Kari. They both looked oval. And perfect.

"So, which twin do you love?" the twin on the left asked.

I looked from one to the other and back. I tried to cheat and see through the fabric to the scars, but then remembered Mina had already gotten her tattoo done. I couldn't tell them apart.

"Well, who do you love?" she repeated.

"I love you both." That was easy. I wanted to lie back down.

The twin on the right said, "Aww," and tried to hug me.

"Shhh," said the twin on the left, pushing her back. Lefty looked at me. "Admit you can't tell."

"Yeah, surrender, Dorothy!"

They both cackled again. I didn't think it was funny at all. Before I could say so, the left twin sat next to me, followed by the other on my other side. "Pick one of us to kiss," the left twin said. "Whichever one you pick, that's the one you'll marry."

"No fucking way!" said the girl on the right.

"Hi Mina," I said, and kissed Miss Right. She was still frowning, but kissed me back. It was the most intense kiss I can remember, although I don't understand why. Maybe it was the idea that at that moment, and only that one, I felt as though I was with two Minas and I could have them both. Or maybe it was just the vindication of knowing I could always tell which girl I'd fallen in love with. In either case, the passionate serenity of the moment was brief.

"I wanna sleep with Eddie," Kari said.

Mina and I froze and turned to look at her.

"You can't. I want to marry him, Kari. Ever since I met him I've wanted to," Mina said. Her voice was gentle. Despite the jealousy her mother warned me about, she was as kind to her sister as she had been earlier when we discovered Fadil's lies.

"Oh, I know, sweetie. I would never actually have sex with him, even if he asked me. I just want to is all." She placed her face on my shoulder. "Thought you should know. I don't like secrets anymore." She was shaking her head "no" as she spoke, with her face still tucked against me.

"I already knew that, honey," Mina said. She reached over and stroked her sister's head.

I did not think that was a sufficient end to the conversation. I was drunk, but I wasn't that drunk. "Kari, I won't ever ask you to have sex with me." I hoped.

"Okay, that's good, because sometimes I lie to myself." Without warning, she fell backward on the sofa and passed out.

The three of us awoke the next morning still on the sofa, with me the middle of a tangle of bodies. There were three long legs on me and a breast in my face. In my hungover state I couldn't tell whose. Thankfully, neither girl was unclothed. I, however, was as naked as a newborn. The living room faced east, the only windows not blocked by other buildings, and the morning sun burned through my eyelids and drilled into my brain. I blinked awake and gently slid my face from under the breast.

"Ow," Kari said. "Watch the nipple." Pause. "Why are you naked?"

I covered myself and assured her I had no idea.

"He gets hot in his sleep. Takes his clothes off all the time," Mina answered. She looked a mess; her bun was undone and hair covered her face like a scarf. "I need coffee," she said, and slid onto the floor with a bump, startling Apache who was asleep next to us. She crawled hand over hand to the kitchen in search of the elixir of morning life.

I looked back to the couch, hoping to spot my clothes. Kari was sitting up, her hair mostly in her face. "You should model for me."

"What?" My brain was full of spiders and my eyes itched. I couldn't scratch because my hands were full of my remaining decency.

Kari leaned over and handed me my shorts. I waited for her to turn away, to no avail. "You're shy, aren't you?" she asked.

"Not usually."

To my relief, she looked away while I pulled them on. "So, what do you think?" she asked.

I assumed she was referring to the case. It was morning, and a hangover was no excuse to delay getting to work. "I'm feeling like crap, but I still want to meet my friend from the FBI. He is here in the New York bureau." I rubbed my eyes, trying to stop the itching and somehow switch them on. "I figure I'll have it together by noon and I'll meet him then."

"That's nice, but I meant about the modeling. You have a nice physique. You'd make a great cowboy."

"Um, Kari, I don't know."

Even as fuzzy-headed as I was, her prior-night's declaration rang in my memory as clear as a bell. "*I want to sleep with your boyfriend*" isn't something a guy forgets.

"I'm not sure we should spend so much time together," I said.

She held up her hand. "Don't worry, I meant what I said. I'd never let anything happen between us." She paused and brushed the hair from her face. "I'm sorry if I embarrassed you. I'm not sure why

I blurted that out. I guess I'm not feeling very attractive these days, between Fadil's secrets and my indifferent boyfriend." She looked at me and I could tell she needed something from me, but I didn't know what. I remained silent.

"I need to go lie down a bit," she said, standing and heading for the stairs.

Thirty minutes and two cups of coffee each later, Mina and I were standing in Kari's huge shower. Neither of us felt remotely flirty, much less romantic. In fact, the sole reason we took a shower together was that Mina was afraid she'd need someone to help hold her up. The one in our guest bedroom was too small for a duet. This one sported three showerheads and all the water we could use. We'd tiptoed past the unconscious Kari and I propped Mina up in the shower until the water began reviving her. She was standing under the shower head, her eyes shut and hair full of shampoo, too zonked to finish washing it. I was behind her letting the water wash my back when the bathroom door opened. In walked Kari, looking more asleep than awake. She was looking at her feet as she shuffled in. A few feet from the shower door she stopped and looked up as I covered myself yet again.

"Oh," she said. "Hi."

I had no response other than, "Hi."

To my great surprise, the first pleasant one in a while, she pulled off her clothes, revealing a lovely body that looked like a softer version of Mina's. My twin was a badass, truck-building hardbody. Kari was a city girl whose only exercise was walking. Had they done their test the previous night in the nude, I would have been able to pick Kari's form from Mina's with my eyes closed. In fact, that would have been a great deal of fun. Kari didn't seem the least bit modest or uncomfortable. In fact, she merely walked to the glass shower door, opened it, and invited herself in.

She looked up at me while I tried to determine what my response was supposed to be in this situation and said, "Can I borrow the soap?"

Mina handed me the bar of soap over her head without turning. I handed it to Kari. And yes, now I was smiling. I'd also released myself and my delight was readily apparent to the quiet, naked sister in front of me. With her eyes still mostly closed, she took the soap and glanced down. Kari blinked, her eyes widened, and she broke out in a huge smile.

"Sweets," she said, "you always know exactly what to say to me." At least now I knew what she'd needed from me earlier: proof she was still attractive. Smiling, and now singing, she turned away from me and reached back with the soap. "Do my back," she said.

Mina began squeezing herself by me, leaving the shower.

"Shit, you're mad," I said.

"No, I think I'm gonna throw up. I need to lie down." She squeezed by her sister and pushed open the shower.

"Wait, you're leaving me in the shower with your sister?"

"You both promised nothing would happen, right?"

"Right," Kari said.

"Then what do you want me to worry about? I'd rather you just see her naked than think about it all the time."

"Why would I think about it all the time?"

"Because you have a penis." She walked out of the bathroom, pulling a towel off the rack without looking as she passed.

"You do have a penis," Kari said, giggling. "It's not as cute as my glory."

I stood there for a few moments in shock. "You two have the strangest relationship."

"Mina can be very trusting with people she loves. It's a fault we share."

"That's not a fault. You just married assholes." I paused, listening to the sound of the shower and smelling the gentle perfume of Kari's soap. "So, what do I do now that she trusts me?"

"Be trustworthy." She turned her back to me again. "You going to do my back or what?"

"Why exactly did you invite yourself into our shower?" I asked.

"This is my bathroom, silly. You guys are the interlopers." She smiled over her shoulder at me and saw my confusion and discomfort. "Look, I'm an artist. My friends and I have all posed for each other, sketched each other, often in the nude. It doesn't bother me. If it does you, I won't do it again."

"That would be the saddest thing that ever happened to me," I said. I was looking at her bottom.

She giggled. "You are so good for my ego."

I started washing Kari's back, starting at her neck. When I finished she was squeaky clean and we were laughing and acting like idiots. At one point Kari decided she should wash my hair while jumping on my back for a piggyback ride. We ended up on our butts howling with laughter. Our energy, despite my initial excitement, wasn't overtly sexual. After a few minutes I was completely comfortable being nude with this girl, as if I had been all my life. Rather than sex, it was clear she simply wanted to enjoy a man's touch on her skin, one I was delighted to provide. It would not have surprised me if her desire to "sleep with" me meant precisely that.

If my girlfriend had wanted to ensure I never saw the twins as one person, that shower did the trick. Mina was sensuality personified. Even our slightest physicality was tinged with eroticism: the way she smiled an invitation when I looked at her, the flash of fire she brought, the way a touch became a caress based solely on her response. Kari, by contrast, was the pretty, goofy girl you go skinny dipping with but no one harasses because she's so sweet. I loved looking at her, and washing her body was enough to end my hangover, but I no more needed to possess her than I needed to own a Rembrandt. It was enough to be in that shower and see a part of her personality that I guessed no one knew except her sister.

Even so, a part of me wondered if it was wise for Mina to trust us so much.

Not *that* part, gutter brain. Okay, maybe that part.

The triple shower was a turning point in our relationships for a number of reasons, it would turn out. Initially, however, it left me even more determined to see this case through to the end. It was as if Kari's shower had washed away all my remaining skepticism. Somehow I could no longer fathom the idea that the fates would allow this woman to lose her child. I realized I was potentially setting us all up for heartache, but it was a chance I was willing to take. Mina insisted she hadn't left the two of us alone in the shower for just that reason—to seal my bond with her sister—but I had my doubts. Admittedly Mina can be very sweet, but she can also be devious. More than once I was glad she'd joined the armed services instead of a secret service like the CIA or NSA. She would have made them very dangerous.

I left with the girls in the midst of a brouhaha. Mina had been in bed nursing a hangover, so she was not in the most pleasant of moods. Of course, that was when Kari came sauntering into the bedroom full of vigor, courtesy of our romp in the shower.

"You shoulda stayed. I totally made your boyfriend wash my boobies. They feel all tingly now." She stopped, smiled, and looked at her sister. Mina gave her the Vulcan Death Stare, but otherwise didn't react. "Eddie has nice hands. I think I'ma try sculpture of his hands first, if I can convince him to pose for me. I want to do a full-size piece, probably with the both of you." Her monologue was followed by her plopping herself on the bed next to Mina and having her kissy lips met by Mina's stiff arm. Kari's pout was priceless. "Hey!"

"He washed your which?" Mina asked.

I took one look at the scowl that slowly eclipsed my girlfriend's face and got the hell out of there. I never washed any part of Kari but her back, but I doubted Mina was in the mood to hear that. The last thing I heard was Mina's voice yelling, "Sit your ass back down here. You and I are going to have a little talk about boundaries."

I chose to save the undeserved lecture which was certain to follow for later. I was glad they were having their fight, to be honest, because it allowed me to slip out without one of them insisting they join me. I needed information from my FBI contact and wasn't ready to share his answers with the girls quite yet. No matter how intimate our relationships, I was determined to treat them as clients when it came to the case. I was likely to turn up painful information and would need to guide them through it with care.

I met my contact, Special Agent Rodrigo Gaither, at a nondescript pizza joint in Manhattan. Gaither was a stocky guy, dark-complected, with black hair cut short enough to almost be a shaved head. We'd served together in Afghanistan and even traded saving each other's lives. As long as no one ever knew where I got my info, there was nothing Gaither wouldn't find out for me. After I got my slice, we sat in a corner, our conversation obscured by the bustling din of the place.

"So what's the story with those two clowns back in South Dakota?" I asked.

"What's the story with you eating a slice of pie with a knife and fork?" he answered. He was looking at me as if I were a giant roach.

"This is a new tie. I'm trying not to make a mess."

"Daley, fold that damn thing over and eat it like a man. I'm not sitting here with a guy eating pizza with a fork."

I sighed, picked up the oversized slice, and folded in it half. I looked like an idiot leaning forward over the plate so the grease wouldn't drip all over me. I had to throw my fifty-dollar tie over my shoulder like it was Snoopy's scarf. "Happy now?" I asked.

"Dude, what the hell happened to you out in Arizona? You used to be a badass."

"Yeah, well, you used to be scared of everything. People change."

Gaither shook his head, sprinkled his slice with red pepper and salt, and took a bite. "That's how a man does it. You should've joined the FBI when I got you that interview."

"Salting your food like that is how a man dies of heart disease."

"Dude."

"Black guys get hypertension when they're older," I said, responding to his raised eyebrows.

"I'm Puerto Rican. Were you my grandma the whole time we were in the Army? I never even suspected."

That made me laugh. "Just tell me what fine mess I've gotten myself into this time, Stanley."

"You and your old movies. You do remind me of my grandma." Gaither finished chewing and wiped his hands. He pulled out a tablet computer and began reading. "The dead guy's name was John Brohammer. Bunch of small-time arrests. In and out of jail since he was sixteen. Pretty much just routine works-for-hire stuff."

"So he was muscle."

Gaither nodded. "Pretty stupid muscle from all the reports. I don't think this guy ever committed a crime he didn't get caught for."

"Maybe his partner shot him on purpose."

He nodded again. "You're ahead of me. I'm thinking he was making sure Johnny boy didn't live to talk to you."

"So who was our main guy?"

"His name is Clydell Lee Coleman. Small-time stuff, same as Brohammer. But Coleman's connected."

"Wait, you think this is some kind of mob hit?"

"Mob hit? What are you, Tony Soprano? No, this doesn't look like any kind of organized crime at all. Coleman's a clown. He actually tried to tell the local cops it was you who shot Brohammer, even though the bullet matches his gun. No, it's the guy who hired him that's the pro."

I finished my slice and wiped my hands. I was still hungry. "Why would a pro hire two incompetents to cross state lines and commit a kidnapping?"

"See, that's why I want you in the Bureau. You haven't lost your instincts." Gaither turned the tablet so I could see. "I'm not showing you this stuff."

I nodded my understanding. An FBI clearance that allowed you to see personal info was pretty much equivalent to a Department of Defense Top Secret clearance. I doubted he was supposed to have it on his tablet.

Gaither pointed to a file with a photo of a thick-necked man who actually could have worked for the Sopranos. "This is Gus Sandersen, lives up in Queens. Calls himself a *Staff Augmentation Specialist.*"

"Nice."

"Yeah. Most of the staff he's augmenting is involved in drug running, minor enforcement, and the like. I suspect he also staffs the occasional hit, but he comes off clean. I can't prove a thing. Along with his contracted work he moonlights on the side, from what I can tell. That was my in. The big boys would be very unhappy if they found out one of their guys was getting his hands dirty with penny ante stuff."

"But he hired Coleman anyway."

Gaither nodded and pulled back the tablet. "Yeah, he pretty much admitted as much—off the record, of course."

"I didn't think the Bureau does off the record."

"We don't, but Sandersen doesn't know that." Gaither gave me a wicked smile. Old Gus was going to be in for a surprise at some point. "Anyway, we got Coleman to give up Sandersen by convincing him he was looking at capital murder for Brohammer. First degree in the commission of a kidnapping."

"Is that a valid charge?" I asked.

"I don't know. I'm not a DA. What do I know about charges?" Another wicked smile. Gaither was not your TV kind of FBI agent.

"So Coleman kills his partner to keep him quiet and pretends he thinks I did it. Then he ends up talking to keep from being executed for killing the guy."

Gaither nodded again. "I think he also figured if he killed him you wouldn't have a shield and you'd drop your gun. Most criminals are morons, man. It makes the work kind of fun. Anyway, Coleman led me to Sandersen and Sandersen finally gave up the name of the guy who hired him. Turns out the two idiots he hired weren't supposed to kidnap anyone. He's screwed coming and going."

"They shot up my Camaro."

"Your dad's old car? Damn. That ought to be a capital offense right there."

"I know, right?"

Gaither took his bag, put away the tablet, and handed me a slip of paper with a name and a description. "I didn't give this to you."

"Excellent," I said. "And I didn't buy you pizza for lunch either."

"Nope, never did. This guy who hired Sandersen, Henry Reilly, is strictly an amateur. If you find him, I'm going to need to talk to him myself. I'm not sure we can even prove a crime, since he can claim he hired Sandersen just to follow you and Sandersen did all the dirty work on his own."

"Wouldn't Sandersen testify to protect himself?"

"No. His real bosses would kill him if they found out. More likely Reilly would just turn up dead."

Henry Reilly. The name was ringing a bell, but I couldn't remember from where in the noise of the pizzeria. "How do you know he's an amateur?" I asked.

"Sandersen said the guy told him his full name. He had to cut him off. Told him *No last names. No credit cards.*"

"Jesus. So we almost got whacked by some jackass trying to pay for a hit on his Visa card."

"Yeah, so be careful. Amateurs can be more dangerous than pros. They make stupid mistakes, and they panic."

"Gotcha," I said, standing to shake his hand. "Did he say what this Henry wanted?"

"Didn't seem to know or care. He was paid to scare you off, make you decide whatever you're investigating wasn't worth the money they're paying you." He zipped up his bag and put on his shades. "What is the going rate for being a private dickhead these days?"

"Pro bono," I admitted. I was almost ashamed, especially given the look he gave me. "But on the other hand, I woke up naked with twins this morning and then took a shower with them."

"Dude," he said, slapping me on the shoulder. "You are

seriously overpaid." A smile crept across his face below the dark glasses. "I take back all the talk about you being a girl. You're still my hero, hoss." He turned and headed for the exit.

"Hey, if you want, I can try to get you an interview," I called after him.

He paused, then continued. Knowing him he wanted to give me the finger, but not in his official FBI-type suit. Gaither was a pro. Meanwhile I had to hope he never, ever met the girls. If they knew I'd been bragging about our shower, at least one of them would kill me.

I spent the remainder of the afternoon talking to Fadil's former co-workers from a list I'd received from Haleh Asker. I came up empty. Either they didn't know much or they weren't talking. After getting such a good lead from Gaither it was frustrating to dig a dry hole, especially since I'd been walking up and down Manhattan's east side for hours.

By four-thirty I was ready to call it quits. I'd been trying to reach Mina most of the day, but her phone kept going to voicemail. Finally, in a gloriously foul mood, I reached Kari while I waited for the train to Brooklyn. Grand Central was a zoo and I could barely hear Kari's soft voice on my outdated cell. What I did discern was that Mina was fine, but not with her sister.

"I'll tell you about it when you get here," she said. At that point the train arrived. Hearing her was out of the question.

By the time the forty minute trip to Bedford Stuyvesant was done I was too tired to really care what new adventure Mina was up to. Mostly I wanted to take off the damn tie and fall asleep in front of a beer. I reached Kari's place just as I was certain I couldn't take another step in my oxfords. Kari was out front with Apache. She was directing kids to run up and down the sidewalk in front of him, yet Apache sat still, watching not the children but Kari. As I approached my alert little buddy spotted me first and his ears perked up, but he didn't move. Instead he gave Kari an intense look along with a loud whimper. She turned, saw me, and smiled. With no more than a simple hand signal she gave Apache permission to go, and he bolted toward me at full speed. He was growing in leaps and bounds and, in his enthusiasm, almost knocked me over.

It's amazing how quickly you can recover when you're greeted by a happy puppy, a group of dog-loving kids, and a beautiful woman. Instead of the bath and beer I'd been picturing, I spent the next hour outside, playing with my pup and the kids. After that, however, Kari must have seen the exhaustion on my face. She thanked the group for helping her train Apache and dragged the two of us inside. Apache fell asleep in his normal position in minutes: on his back, feet in the air. I seriously considered joining him there in the middle of the floor.

"Why don't you go take a hot bath and relax?" Kari asked.

"You read my mind."

"Nope, your body language. You're drooping like a faded flower."

"I sure as hell don't smell like a flower."

"Use my bath, that way you can stretch out."

She got no argument from me. The master bath and bedroom were enormous in her townhouse, and the guest quarters much smaller. After being cramped in Manhattan all day, I welcomed the chance to relax. Fifteen minutes later I was up to my chest in almost obscenely hot water, stretched out, closer to asleep than awake.

"Here you go, sweets," Kari said. It scared the holy hell out of me. I jumped, splashing water out of the oval tub onto the floor and on Kari's jeans. She jumped back, managing not to drop what she was carrying as I scrambled to cover myself with a washcloth.

"What are you doing?" I asked.

"I brought you a Guinness and some snacks," she said. If she was aware it was improper to have invaded my bath, it wasn't obvious. Still, the beer looked awfully good. I took it and downed half the bottle at one go. Kari set a bowl of mixed nuts and a candle on the edge of the tub and smiled at me. "Feel better?" she asked.

"Kari, what are you doing?"

She pulled a lighter from her pocket and lit the candle. The scent of vanilla began to fill the room. "Aromatherapy. It'll help you relax."

"Kari, I don't think you should be in here."

"Oh shush. I've already seen your little dinglebopper."

"Not so little," I muttered.

She knelt on the floor behind me. Before I could object she pushed my torso forward and began scrubbing my back in circles with something that felt like a cross between a loofa and soft brush. Within seconds I'd determined that resistance was futile. Her twin was a Vulcan, but Kari was Borg, all the way. She continued to my lower back and then began rubbing my tight neck muscles. I objected vigorously, ten times, all in my head. My mouth mostly just made little moaning noises. When she reached around to scrub my chest I regained my sanity, courtesy of a surge of adrenaline.

"Look, we had fun this morning, but the washing each other stuff needs to stop."

She sighed, stood, and walked in front of me, shaking her head. "What am I going to do with you?" By way of answering her own question, she pulled her shirt over her head, exposing those perfect breasts for the second time in one day.

"Holy crap, Kari." I tried to sink under the water.

She was unconcerned about my recalcitrance. She removed her jeans and thong and climbed in the tub with me without saying a word. The woman sat opposite me, her arms draped along the sides of the tub, smiling at me. I tried to look everywhere but at her. Finally getting annoyed, she said, "I'm not leaving until you look at me, Eddie Daley."

I did. She looked good. Damned good. I told her so. "Kari, I'm dating Mina," I added as an afterthought.

To my surprise she frowned at me, picked up her loofa, threw it at me, and followed up by splashing water at me. "For the last time, I'm not trying to have sex with you!" She kept frowning, sitting there naked in my bath with her arms folded in front of her. She was adorable.

"Okay, okay, I'm sorry. I believe you." And I did, too. "But then why are you in the tub with me?"

Her frown faded. "I like being naked with you. I like how you look at me. What's wrong with that? You're fun."

Oh Jesus. Both of these women are crazy.

"Did you ever reach Mina?" she asked.

I was beginning to become used to the sudden subject changes both Good Crow women threw at me. Rather than being nonplussed I simply confessed that I had not. "Can you tell me what the hell is going on? When I left, you two were going at it. Now she's gone, and you're bathing with me."

Kari's face flashed discomfort. I gave her time to settle. "Mina's in Newark, at a friend's. I told her she needed to talk to you, but I think she was scared you'd be mad."

Without thinking I lay back and slipped my face under the

water. Maybe a part of me wanted to drown. Mostly, however, I was frustrated. But when I sat back up, I was almost in Kari's lap. She smiled and pulled me to her. I gave up and hugged her back. The Borg are irresistible.

"How'd you know I needed a hug?" she asked.

"For starters, you jumped in the tub with me. It's not hard to figure out you want attention."

She laughed her overloud, Kari kind of laugh and pulled back. "I suppose not."

"You really don't want sex?" I asked. I still don't know what answer I was hoping for.

She shook her head. "I just need to feel … I don't know, secure? Connected?" She gave me a pained look. "I promise you I know where to draw the line, okay?"

I wasn't convinced of that at all. However, I had a bigger issue to address. "Why is Mina in Newark?"

"Since she was in town she called some ex-Marine buddy she knew. Apparently, he told her to get her *butt to Newark ASAP* and he could arrange for a job interview fixing helicopters for a local company."

"And she jumped at the chance."

She nodded. "I told her to call you. I didn't even know she was considering moving here."

I was getting angry. "This sounds like some passive-aggressive bullshit to me. Maybe she's just mad because we're being so … intimate with each other." I suddenly wanted out of that tub in a jiffy.

"I don't think that's it. She's acting really weird, Eddie. Hot and cold, mad and happy. I don't get it."

I thought about the incident that morning; I wasn't going to let Kari off the hook that easily. "Why'd you tell her I washed your breasts? You knew that wasn't true. We were very appropriate. Well, appropriate considering we were roughhousing naked in the damned shower." I stood, climbed out of the tub, and wrapped a towel around myself.

"Eddie, Mina had to know I was kidding. We used to joke like that all the time growing up. Every time one of us liked a guy, the other would claim we'd just finished making out with him. I was trying to make her laugh."

"Then what was all the talk about boundaries?" I asked. This was sounding like hogwash.

Kari stalled and I gave her a look that let her know I was serious. She blew out the candle, climbed out of the tub, and found a towel. "I'm not sure, to be honest. Before she even told me what was really bugging her, she took the call from her friend. The next thing I knew, she was gone."

It was just what I needed: another mystery. "Well, you're her sister. What do you think is going on?"

Kari closed her eyes and exhaled. "Mina was the one who suggested I do a sculpture of you. I told her no, because I always start with the nude and add the clothing later. After our battles as teens I didn't want to start a war over your being naked around me. Posing takes a long time. It'll mean a lot of being together naked."

"You mean with me being naked."

She smiled. "Well, it's no fun if it's just you."

Unlike with Mina, I was beginning to see a method to Kari's madness. She kept us naked around each other in order to make my posing feel natural and not erotic. Which meant one thing. "Christ, you agreed to do the sculpture."

She gave me a sheepish smile. "She insisted. Said a sculpture of you would make an awesome ..." She stopped, looking uncomfortable.

"Say it."

"An awesome wedding gift."

I sat on the tiled structure that framed the tub. "Why is she in such a damned hurry? We've known each other for barely two weeks."

"I know, I keep telling her that. Look, I'll admit it, at first part of my flirting was so you'd flirt back and she'd see you're still not ready to settle down."

"You wanted to break us up?"

"Not at all, just get her to think. I was wrong about you anyway. You're totally ready." She sat next to me. She was shaking, whether from cold or anxiety I couldn't tell.

"None of that explains why she's not here. I could get just as comfortable with you while Mina's here."

"No, it doesn't." She was quiet for a long time, and I wrapped my arms around her to still her shivers. I could feel her shudders calm, and she leaned her head against me. The dampness of her hair cooled my cheek and, almost reflexively, I turned and kissed her head. This woman had been naked with me moments before and yet I felt closer to her this way, seated on the hard tub, saying nothing. Kari broke the silence. "Eddie, if we were going to hurt Mina, if we were going to be sexual, tonight's when it would happen." She looked at me and I was surprised to find her eyes were brimming with tears.

I stayed quiet, trying to determine if my girlfriend's sister was asking me to make love to her, and how to turn her down if she was. Then it hit me. "You think that's why she's in Newark, so we'll have sex."

Kari placed her chin on my shoulder. "I do. Why else would she leave?"

"Maybe she's really pissed at us about this morning. If it had been her and my brother, I'd have killed him."

Her voice deepened and softened and, for the first time, she sounded like her caretaker mother instead of Mina. "She's really confused, Eddie. Part of the time I think she's afraid you'll leave her. The rest of the time ..." She made a sound like air leaking from a tire. "I think she's hoping you'll sleep with me so she can break up with you."

"Holy shit." I was beginning to think I was in over my head. "I thought you said she trusts us."

Kari stood and turned away. "She knows I'd never do anything behind her back." I could hear the sound of her sniffles. She stood with fading sunlight illuminating her from the adjoining room.

"You think she's giving us her permission?" I was halfway to mad and halfway to worried about both of these women's sanity.

"I don't know Eddie. Maybe I'm wrong. Maybe this is some kind of weird test."

"Kari, is Mina ... you know, okay?"

"You mean, like, emotionally? I'm not sure. She was always the rock, you know? This is all-new territory."

Kari and I were quiet there for a long time, neither of us moving or speaking. Then I asked the big question. "If all of this is true, and maybe Mina is in need of some counseling, and if we're so trustworthy, then why did we end up in the bathtub together?"

She looked at me. "Because I'm really attracted to you, and you secretly wish you could have us both."

"I'm not like that," I said.

"So you don't want me?" Instead of answering, I pushed by her and headed into the bedroom.

She followed. "Eddie, I'm new at this. It's been a long time since I felt anything for anyone."

"I get that, but we shouldn't be playing with fire. It would crush Mina if she saw us here."

Kari shook her head. "I wish that were true."

"What does that mean?"

"I don't know. It's just … last night I was drunk, but not like Mina. I was just drunk enough to be brave, and I wanted her to know I was attracted to you so she'd be careful. She's practically pushed me on you ever since."

"Bull, Kari. She didn't push you in the tub or hold me down so you could climb in with me."

"No, but she did tell me to *Make sure Eddie isn't lonely tonight* before she left."

"You could have played Monopoly with me. Didn't necessarily require wet naked hugging."

"Naked Twister?"

I tried not to laugh. "I'm serious, Kari."

She shook her head. "No, you're right. I'm a terrible sister."

"No, angel," I said, "you're not. You're just hurt and lonely. I'm the one with no excuse."

"It won't happen again, I promise."

"I think I should sleep on the couch from now on," I said. "At least until I finish this case."

"Oh no! You aren't breaking up with her because of me, are you?"

"No, but I think we all need to be a little more platonic while we try to sort out what's going on with your sister. Whatever it is, I don't think it's healthy."

I turned to leave the bedroom. Kari called from behind me. "Eddie, is this a bad time to tell you about the dinner party tonight at Henry's?"

Henry's! I knew I remembered that name from somewhere. How could I forget the "boyfriend?" Perhaps because I was too busy *being* the boyfriend. I turned toward her, knowing that I had more news that would upset her.

Her expression changed, mirroring mine. However, she misinterpreted my meaning. "I thought you'd want to be able to talk to Fadil's and my friends all in one place." She stepped closer. "And see, I really had planned on making sure you weren't lonely without rocking your world all night." She gave me a smile that I was in no mood to return. Hers faded quickly. "What's wrong?"

"You need to sit down. I have something to tell you about Henry."

Chapter 7

Kari took the news of Henry's involvement in our case with surprising aplomb. There were no tears or angry rants. I laid out my version of the case: Henry had hired goons to scare us off because, for some reason, he didn't want Kari to find out what happened to Fadil. She listened, her face tightening with anger, letting me finish. "I don't know what he's trying to hide, but it's about time we found out," I said. She nodded, her eyes bright with rage. "What are you thinking, Kari?" I'd heard of cases where girlfriends shot their boyfriends for less.

"I'm wondering if my entire relationship with Henry has been fake. Maybe he only wanted to keep an eye on me." I was wondering the same thing. "You better go get dressed," she said. "We have to make a good impression tonight."

I stood to leave, stopping at the door. "If we want to be certain, we'll probably need to make everyone think we're involved," I said.

"Trust me. We will."

Kari came downstairs an hour later, dressed in a simple black dress that looked as if she'd been sewn into it. Her hair was loose, draping past bare shoulders. A light layer of makeup allowed hints of her freckles through. She stopped at the foot of the steps, her smoky eyes burning a hole in my suit.

"You look nice," she said, giving me a smile that made me shiver.

"Oh my damn," was all I could get out. The girl managed to look even better clothed than nude.

"Call the cab, sweets," she said. Sweets did as he was told.

Henry lived in a beautifully appointed Victorian row house in Harlem. The exterior was old brownstone, much like the one Kari lived in except instead of being broken into townhouses, this one was all Henry's. She told me that Henry was fully tenured at Columbia and had come from a moneyed family. It was obvious, looking at the care with which he'd decorated. The first level featured a living area with cherry-stained hardwood floors and wood trim. The only furniture in the austere living room was a surprisingly informal L-shaped sofa and low table, both of which sat opposite a large fireplace. A row of military straight pillows lined the sofa, none daring to slouch into parade rest. He had a few glum portraits that looked as if they'd have preferred to live in a museum.

The living room opened into a formal dining room that was lined floor to ceiling with flowery wallpaper. My grandmother would have approved. The door to the room was guarded by a grandfather clock that was older than any of the guests. I saluted it as we passed out of respect. Kari gave her first giggle of the night. We entered the dining room, squeezing past guests who were tottering about, holding plates of hors d'oeuvres. I knew I was in trouble from the music that filled the dining area, which was some obscure classical piece that sounded to my hip-hop-tainted ears to be cats singing to a harpsichord accompaniment.

Initially I believed the partygoers to be scattered about the home randomly, but a pattern eventually emerged. Kari led me through the dining room, introducing me to the others without mentioning our relationship or my role as investigator. Instead, she simply smiled warmly and held onto my hand. We received an array of curious looks, but no one asked any questions. Most of the women looked at Kari as if she might steal their food. Kari nodded to a tall, dark-haired man with penetrating eyes who returned the gesture. "That's Fadil's cousin, Talaz. He and Henry met at the memorial service. The rest are mostly Fadil's friends," she whispered. "Henry met Fadil in college, so they ran in pretty much the same circles."

"Yeah, I think it's the same circle my grandparents run in." Kari covered her laughter with a discrete hand over her mouth. I missed her loud horselaugh, but this wasn't the place.

Even though most of the guests were in their mid-twenties to mid-thirties, I felt as if we'd stumbled into a middle-aged dinner party after the opera. Not exactly my people, but we worked the room nonetheless. The tightly wound group stuffing their faces at Henry's expense offered little in the way of useful information, with the exception of one twittering bird named Chas whom Kari had never met. Chas was rather short, just south of five foot eight, with a tubular build, black eyes that seemed too small for his face, a hawkish nose, sagging jowls, and a mop of tight brown curls that sat on his head like a toupee. I imagined his curls were trying to disavow belonging to the little pelican.

"I am so awfully, terribly sorry to hear about your loss," he said to Kari, taking her hand from me and holding it between his two oversized mitts. "You are so very, wonderfully brave to have recovered so well."

To her credit, Kari gave no sense that his cloying words were upsetting her. I managed not to choke him. He was so totally, completely getting on my damned nerves.

"Recovery is a process," she said.

Chas, still enveloping her hand, asked, "Will you be moving to the Georgetown house, or are you staying here in the city?"

It took her a moment to catch his reference, but then a narrow bolt of anger flashed across her eyes. I wondered if Chas caught it. "No, Brooklyn's my home now," she said. "I'm not really familiar with the real estate market there, so no immediate plans."

"Oh, that's very smart. Georgetown is such a trendy part of D.C. You probably will want to let the market settle before you think about selling. It could bring you oodles of cash later." Chas released her hands as he spoke, his arms flapping.

We'd just discovered that Fadil kept a house in D.C. in addition to the Maryland condo we knew about, and Kari hadn't broken her smile. Bacall would have been proud. I figured it was time for my Bogart bit.

"Did Fadil own the Georgetown place?" I asked.

"Oh dear, you know, I'm not sure. I was just assuming."

He was just trying to be nosy is what he was doing. "Did you know Fadil from his new job?" I asked.

"At Hardaway Group? Oh, heavens no. I could never do the whole management consulting thing. I deal in art resales and estate liquidation." He leaned in conspiratorially, his fingers waggling like he was Edward Scissorhands. "Most of Henry's pieces I found for him, though I keep telling him they don't fit the bachelor lifestyle."

"No, but my grandmother would love the place," I said. Kari gave me a half-smile, half-glare and squeezed my hand hard.

Chas, meanwhile, laughed raucously and patted me on the chest. "It is rather matronly, isn't it?"

"He's flirting with you," Kari whispered in my ear.

"Where is our host anyway?" I asked, trying to ignore my sudden wave of discomfort.

"Oh, Henry's been in the kitchen the whole time. He's got some gourmet masterpiece planned. I'm sure it's divine."

I caught the eye roll that Kari threw out. This time I squeezed her hand. A tall woman with dark olive skin and curly brown hair walked up to Kari and flung her arms around her, all the while looking at me. She wore a white dress that set off her coloring like paint on a canvas. Kari gave a soft squeal and hugged her back. "Who's the male model?" the woman asked, still looking at me. She kissed Kari on the cheek and then kissed me, but not on the cheek.

Chas huffed and sauntered off toward the kitchen. "Thank you for that," I said once Chas was out of earshot.

"Oh, my pleasure, doll. Kari's way too sweet when it comes to protecting her territory, so I just acted in her interest."

Kari smiled and wiped lipstick off my lips. "Yeah, and you got some interest all over my boyfriend's mouth." We had agreed that was my role for tonight, but hearing it still made my heart beat a little faster.

"Boyfriend?" the leggy beauty asked. She leaned her face between the two of ours. "Does Henry know?"

"Eddie, this is Camara, my oldest and dearest friend. Camara is a brilliant photographer and teacher. Camara, this is Eddie Daley, war hero, investigator, and boyfriend."

Kari was really playing her role well, as evidenced by the way Camara's eyes lit up with her intro. I took her friend's slender hand and kissed it. I wasn't sure men still did that sort of thing, but Bogie would have done it for this dame.

When I freed her hand, Camara held it in the air, close to her chest, and stared at me. "I think I just released an egg," she said. She gripped her tummy. "It might be twins." Kari cackled in her real laugh, slapped a hand over her mouth, and pushed her friend.

"Shush, we're being grown-ups tonight," Kari said.

"Oh shoot," said Camara. "I was hoping we'd go get drunk after." She looked around. "Where's my girl?"

"Mina couldn't make it. She had a job interview," Kari said. Before she could answer more of Camara's questions, a small group of women from the living room came in and pulled her away. Kari went willingly, though she was looking back at me the whole way to ensure I was okay. I was fine, staring her six-foot-tall friend in the eyes.

As soon as Kari was out of earshot, Camara's demeanor changed. "I am so glad you're here," she said. "I've not seen Kari this happy since before the accident."

I took a sip from the glass of wine I'd been nursing, since I didn't know how to respond. It was just role-playing, but I couldn't exactly tell her that.

She must have read my expression. "Look, I don't mean to make you uncomfortable. I realize you can't have been dating long. A couple of weeks ago I thought she was still with Henry, for whatever that's worth."

"You don't think they were close?" I asked.

"Oh, you don't have anything to fear there." She moved close enough that no one else could hear. "Between you and me, I think the man is asexual ... you know, unless." She looked toward the door through which Chas had left.

"You mean him and Chas?"

"Wouldn't surprise me. I mean, you see Kari. Could you keep your hands off her for over a year?"

"It's been that long?"

She nodded. "If not longer. Kari claims they are intimate in spurts ..."

"But you don't believe her."

"No," she said. "If Henry spurts, it isn't in girls." I choked on my wine. She poked me in the chest with a long finger. "You better be good to her. She doesn't need any more hurt in her life."

I smiled. "I will. Cross my heart."

"Oh, I know you will, sweetheart. I know a man in love when I see one." I wanted to protest, but it would have blown my cover. Instead I changed the subject. "Camara, if you don't mind my asking, what is your ethnicity?"

"Me? All of the above." She started laughing. "My dad's

Russian and my mom's everything else. They used to call me Kahlua in college, since I'm kind of a black Russian. Come, there's a whole room full of Kari's real friends that are anxious to interrogate … I mean, meet you." She gave me a devilish smile and led me toward the living room. I almost got seasick watching her hips sway.

The atmosphere in the living room was decidedly different from the dining room. Rather than the stolid Young Conservatives Fundraiser vibe I picked up among the group in the dining room, the living room was full of mostly Kari's friends. They were young, artsy, and decidedly down to earth. A Stephen Marley reggae tune played from an mp3 player someone had hooked to a small set of speakers, and most of the crowd looked as if they would have been more comfortable smoking skunk on some tropical beach. Two of the women, plus Kari, had already ditched their shoes and were working the room barefoot. A couple of women sat cross-legged on the floor, one with close-cropped red hair and the other with short black hair that featured a shock of blue hair in the front. The blue-haired girl wore silver bracelets that dangled and clattered halfway up her left arm. These people were as different from the dining room group as Brooklyn was from South Dakota. The redhead was watching Kari and me like a hawk, with some kind of notepad on her lap.

"That's Lauria and Tanya," Camara told me. "They're married, the only married couple in the group."

"What are they doing?" I asked.

"Knowing Lauria? Working."

I didn't dare ask what kind of work she did.

By the time Henry made his grand appearance, the dynamics of the party were clear. There was Kari's circle and Henry's circle, and the two groups had almost nothing to do with each other. In fact, I got the impression that not a single one of her friends even liked Henry. They would have been far happier if the venue had been at our … *her* … Brooklyn townhouse. The sociology of New York dinner parties aside, which was as fascinating as it was foreign to me, the event begged a few questions.

First, if Kari and Henry were so different, and he was asexual as Camara asserted, why were they together? Kari had told me earlier that Henry had initially reached out as a friend when Fadil died, but later actively pursued her until she agreed to date. They went out together, enjoying the theater, lectures, art events, even weekend getaways and romantic dinners. What they did not enjoy was sex. She wasn't ready, she claimed, and Henry respected that. However, in my humble opinion, not only was Kari ready, her motor was idling in high gear. Any man even remotely interested in the woman would have noticed.

Secondly, why was it that practically everyone in Henry's cloistered circle seemed to know that Fadil was working for the management consulting firm, Hardaway Group? If Fadil was leading a double life, it was only a secret to his wife. It seemed that Henry's circle was also Fadil's circle. Kari was on the outside of both.

Third, and most important to Kari and her case, why was no one except her friends even remotely moved by her bringing a new boyfriend to her current boyfriend's dinner party? We'd been holding hands most of the night, trying to provoke reactions, and the only ones we'd received had been encouragements from Camara and her other friends.

Henry turned out to be a trim, well-dressed man in his late thirties. He was tall, around six-foot-two, with prematurely graying hair and laugh lines that made him look the professor he was. I got the feeling he was the type who fretted over a hair out of place or single speck of dust, since he and Chas brought in the three-course meal with Henry managing to look as if he'd been the *maître d'hôtel* and not the chef. I peeked in his kitchen as they brought in the food; it had already been cleaned. He was a better match for Mina than my messy artist date.

To his credit his concern only registered as a brief stare in my direction, though I could tell he was shocked to see Kari snuggled up to me in the buffet line. Thereafter he was the charming host, filling his guests with frankly the best food I'd ever eaten and wine that must have cost a small fortune. Once I tasted his cooking I no longer wondered why Chas was flitting around him so much. The pudgy little man was in love with Henry's cooking.

After dessert, with Kari ensconced in some well-needed laughter with her friends, I managed to pull Henry aside. "We need to talk," I said.

"Indeed, I suppose we do," he said. Henry led me past the milling guests and up the narrow staircase. We walked through a hallway to an enormous bedroom with parquet flooring, cherry columns, and a bay window that opened to the street. The furnishings here were formal and austere, much like the dining room downstairs. I could not imagine that anyone ever had a sexual notion in that room. Even my grandmother would have tried to brighten up the place. It did, however, give me leverage. I couldn't tell if Henry loved Kari, but he certainly loved his home.

He gestured for me to sit in what looked to be a nineteenth-century wooden chair. He sat on an enormous dressing table that could have doubled as a throne. He was taller than me now, which I assumed was his strategy.

"How can I help your investigation, Mr. Daley?" he asked.

"Ah, we're eliminating pretense. That'll save a lot of time." I didn't like looking up at the man so I stood, then sat on the writing desk that accompanied the chair. Henry's face hardened. He didn't like my twenty-first century ass on his nineteenth-century desk. That was good; I wanted him off kilter. "You can start by telling me why you hired those two thugs to kill us."

He shot bolt upright. "I did no such thing!" His brow was furrowed and the corners of his lips curled. It was a look of contempt, not fear, which meant my question pissed him off. He genuinely did not intend murder.

"Perhaps killing us wasn't your intent, but it was almost the result. One of the men you hired fired a pistol and almost killed a seventeen-month-old girl."

"Oh my lord," he said, and sank back into his seat. "I – I only meant for the twins to drop this foolish investigation before someone really gets hurt."

"A bit too late for that." I pulled a penknife out of my suit coat's pocket and began playing with it. "You still haven't told me why. Kari wants to know why, the FBI wants to know why and, most important to you, I want to know why."

Henry's eyes went from mine to my blade. "Is that knife supposed to scare me?"

"This little thing? Not at all. I was just admiring your desk and remembering one my grandmother had in her attic back home. My brother and I used to carve our initials in it with a knife just like this one." I unfolded the knife and touched the tip of the blade to his desk.

He was up in a flash, holding his hands in front of him. "No, no! Don't do that. That is an 1853 original. Clarence Darrow once owned that desk and it was already old when he bought it. It can't be replaced."

"Oh, I wouldn't dream of hurting such an important thing as a desk, Henry. It's not like it's, say, a woman, one who was already mourning the loss of her child. A desk is priceless."

He swept stray hairs from his brow and turned away. "I never meant to hurt Kari, ever. I was just doing what Fadil would have wanted."

"What, play with her emotions and then try to keep her in the dark about her husband's cheating? Why is that? Was he cheating with you?"

"You son of a bitch!" Henry shouted and rushed in my direction. I lifted a leg and shoved him back toward his seat with the bottom of my shoe. He landed heavily on the floor.

"Next time I'm not so patient. I asked you a question."

Henry stood and brushed himself off. It was all he could do to keep from baring his teeth at me. "Fadil and I were like brothers. I was trying to keep Kari out of trouble, trying to protect her."

"Against what?"

He didn't answer at first, so I pushed the tip of my knife barely into the desk's soft wood. He got much more cooperative. "I'd known Fadil since we were at university. He was prone to reckless behavior despite the wishes of his family, perhaps even because of it."

"His family?"

"Mainly his Uncle Emir. Fadil represented the family's legacy as far as his uncle was concerned, and the pressure he put on him was tremendous. Sometimes, Fadil couldn't live up to it. After he died in the crash, I became concerned that maybe it wasn't as much an accident as everyone thought."

"You think he was killed?" So did I, but I wanted to hear him say it.

"I suspect so, but I have no proof." His body posture sank. I was getting close.

"Who would want to kill Fadil?" I stood and approached him, putting the knife away. "Maybe a jealous husband? A spurned lover?"

"Fadil was a good family man. He was reckless, but he was no adulterer."

"So good that you needed to keep Kari from finding out the truth?"

"At first I thought maybe Kari hired someone to kill Fadil, but whoever did it hadn't planned on Jeremy's being in the car. So I hired people to watch her and I made sure I stayed close to her as well. But she was clean, heartbroken in fact. Later I came to the realization that Fadil had accumulated gambling debts. Whoever killed him wouldn't take too kindly to his widow's trying to dredge up information on him."

It made sense. All the pieces fit, and it would tie up the story nicely. There was just one problem: the way his eyes darted away from mine for a split-second before he told me about Fadil's gambling. It was an avoidance micro-gesture, a tell, and one that meant he'd just told me a bald-faced lie. I stood, grabbed him by his collar, and jerked him to his feet. "Here's what's going to happen now. You are going to tell me the truth, and if you lie to me one more time, I'm going to break every single thing in this bedroom, starting with you." To emphasize my point I twisted my torso and sent him flying toward the chair I'd been given, shattering it and sending Henry to the floor.

"That was irreplaceable," he said. He was teary eyed now.

"So is Kari."

I took a step toward him and he flinched. "Okay, stop, okay?"

"Why was Fadil hiding money? Why did he have a second home in D.C.?"

"He was seeing someone, a woman he met at work. I think he was planning to run away with her."

"Who killed Fadil, Henry?"

"I don't know, alright? Why don't you ask the people at his job about his life? All I was trying to do is keep his widow from being killed."

I looked at Henry cowering on the floor and wanted to pound the hell out of him. He was still lying, but I knew he'd given me all I was going to get out of him. Besides, Kari would be getting worried. I turned and left.

As I reached the door, he called after me. "You love her, right?" I turned and looked at him, but said nothing. "If you're really in love, drop this. Let it die. Whoever killed Fadil is still out there. Maybe I never loved Kari, but I don't want to see her hurt either."

"You just let me worry about Kari. You stick to your little dinner parties."

I left Henry there, in a pool of his own angry tears. I couldn't shake the feeling that what he felt for her wasn't protection, but contempt. What I didn't know was why. It certainly wasn't because he thought I was sleeping with her. Our pretense hadn't gotten so much as jealous frown out of him.

I did my best to straighten out my rumples and headed back downstairs. When I got there half the group was purposefully ignoring me and the other half watching with keen interest. The entire floor was a low din of unspoken harrumphs and attaboys that made me want to laugh. Camara was the first to approach, kissing me on the cheek and whispering, "There you go. You fight for her, baby." I didn't bother to correct her. Hell, I was beginning to think she was right.

We begged off Camara's invitation to go out for drinks. Kari was tired and anxious to hear what Henry had revealed, and I'd had my fill of drunken women for the week. Instead we found a gypsy cab for the half-hour ride back to Bed Stuy. I filled Kari in on my brief conversation with Henry, which ended in her tears on my shoulder.

"You know, I was almost sure we'd find out Fadil was cheating, but hearing it is still painful," she said. "I guess that means my marriage was officially a lie." She stopped and dabbed tears from beneath her eyes with a finger. Her perfect makeup was smeared, but she was no less beautiful. "I guess it's a relief too, in a way."

"How so?"

"Now I can stop mourning him and focus on finding my son."

I bristled at the idea she was mourning a sonofabitch who'd not only cheated on her, but beat her up once to boot. I thought about telling her not to get her hopes up, but sometimes hope is all you've got. By the time we'd crossed the East River into Astoria, she was fine. I noticed she was holding a rolled-up piece of paper in her lap that Lauria had given her as we were leaving.

"What's that?" I asked, wanting anything to talk about that wasn't Fadil or Henry.

She unrolled it. The paper was a beautifully rendered sketch of Kari and me standing amidst a group of people, smiling and holding hands. It looked like something you'd see in a wedding album. "That's amazing," I said.

"Lauria did that while we were talking. She's awesome. Does police sketches too, just for ready cash."

"You might want to hide that," I said. "Mina might not be too thrilled." I pointed to the primary detail of the sketch: our interlocked hands, which Lauria had enlarged and exaggerated in the foreground. She'd drawn in wedding rings. She even put herself in the sketch, sitting in the background, winking at us.

"Yeah, I suppose you're right," she said, sighing. She rolled it back up, her face almost a frown. "Would you be uncomfortable if I kept this?" she asked.

"Honestly, I'd be a kind of upset if you didn't." Before I could react she leaned over and kissed me. Her lips were softer than I'd imagined and her tongue quicker. For a moment, I wondered if we were still supposed to be in character.

I didn't get the chance to ask her, as the taxi suddenly veered into the left lane, tires screeching and horn blaring, while the driver screamed in Portuguese. The move slammed me against the window and Kari onto the floor. She screamed in fear and I only managed to shout "What the hell?" before a black sedan banged into the passenger side of the cab. I heard the sickening grinding of metal and the heavy sedan gave a final push, sending the taxi careening towards oncoming traffic. I could see the blinding headlights from a truck and heard the blaring of horns. Kari tried to get up, but I held her down. She'd be safer on the floor. The cabbie swerved hard left onto the sidewalk, then right across two lanes, managing to slalom the taxi around the truck and back safely into the eastbound lane.

"Hold on, hold on!" he shouted in a thick accent as we were struck again, this time from the rear. The taxi lurched forward and the driver slammed on the accelerator, throwing us against the seat.

We were weaving in and out of traffic for three city blocks with the sedan in close pursuit. As we neared a red light, the cabbie took a sharp right without slowing. The sedan attempted the same maneuver, swinging too wide, directly in the path of a neon green Smart Car. The little econobubble was crumpled into the side of a parked minivan and, while the sedan slowed, it didn't stop. The cabbie accelerated and the sedan, now damaged, made a U-turn in front of oncoming traffic and roared off in the opposite direction. As we rounded a corner I could just make out the sound of blaring horns and police vehicles behind us.

"What the heck was that all about?" Kari asked, now climbing shakily into her seat.

Fortunately for us the cab driver, from the little I could

understand of his Portug-english rant, assumed it had been a normal case of New York City road rage. He dropped us off a block from Kari's and I gave him a fifty dollar tip for "saving us from the maniac." We left him there, his hand thrust in the air, screaming into a cell phone about the damage to his cab.

When we were out of earshot, Kari asked, "That was meant for us, wasn't it?"

"I think so."

We hurried along for another half a block before she asked, "Do you think Henry was behind that?"

"I doubt it," I said. "He knows the FBI are onto him. But whoever it is, it means we must be on the right track."

We reached her door and she unlocked it. "That's not as comforting as you might think," she said and went inside.

"It's not comforting to me either," I said aloud.

Even the tingling in my lips didn't help my anxiety.

I spent a restless night tossing and turning with only occasional lapses of sleep. Even Apache finally abandoned the bed in the middle of the night for calmer seas. When I did manage to sleep my head was filled with dreams of car chases, fatal crashes, and even an imagined fistfight at a dinner party. In my dream it was not Henry and me but Mina and Mina, although one of the versions of her was doubling for Kari. I awoke in a hot sweat just as Mina was about to cut a long scar into her doppelganger's face with my knife.

Light had just begun to creep into the window and for a moment, in the blue morning haze, I was unsure of where I was. I checked the time: five forty five a.m. Mina would be up by now and, even if she weren't, I needed to talk to her. My emotions were a cluttered mess: part anger at her leaving without a word of goodbye, and a large part guilt at having kissed her sister in the back of a cab. True, Kari's innocent kiss of gratitude probably ranked lower than her having taken a bath with me, but the kiss was what rankled my conscience. I figured it was likely the fact we'd left Kari's friends with the impression that she'd finally found herself the "right" guy. I'd been called many things by women, but hadn't been called Mr. Right much.

I sat up in the bed, smoothed the hair from my face, and tried to figure out what it was I was going to say to Mina. I bounced between anger and contrition, settling on just trying to learn what was troubling the woman so much that even her twin was confused. I tapped her name on my phone and held my breath. After four rings, I heard, "He-hello?" in a shaky, breathy voice I'd rarely heard from Mina. She'd been sleeping.

"Mina? It's me," I said.

There was a pause of silence. Then, clear as a bell, I heard a man's voice from somewhere close by her. "Who's that, babe?" he said.

Next was the sound of hissing … no, Mina shushing whoever was speaking.

"Fuck," was all I managed to say.

As the call ended I could hear Mina saying, "Wait." I didn't. Instead, I turned off the phone, pulled on some jeans and a shirt, and headed out.

I got as far as the top of the stairs when Kari stumbled out of her bedroom, thick hair covering her face. She was wearing the little green nightie the twins wore when they'd dared me to tell them apart.

"Please take that off," I said, meaning only that I could no longer bear to see her as a reflection of her sister.

Kari looked at me, her brow creased with vertical lines. Without a word, she lifted the gown over her head and dropped it. She approached me, now dressed only in panties, her expression still deathly serious. "What's wrong, honey?"

"I-I didn't mean for you to …" I stopped and turned away.

"I knew what you meant," she said. "I want to know why."

I turned back and didn't bother to blink back the moisture clouding my vision. "Well, it looks like you're not the only one being cuckolded," I said. I regretted it the instant I said it. Kari didn't flinch; instead, she took a step closer and touched my face. I said, "I'm sorry. My little bullshit doesn't even compare to …"

She placed two fingers over my lips. "Go back to bed, baby." I shook my head no and turned. Kari ran around me and stood between me and the stairs. "Come on." She reached out, holding her hand for me to take. I took it and followed her to her room. She lifted off my shirt, unfastened my jeans, and pulled them down. I stood there like a mannequin. When she was done and we were both in our underwear, she climbed in the bed and held open the covers for me. I joined her there and she held me, not speaking, until I fell asleep in her arms.

I awoke again around eight-thirty. Kari was asleep, her arms still wrapped around me. The morning sun was in full force by then, and it lit her face and hair. The way she was backlit, with the highlights of her hair catching the sun, reminded me of the old religious paintings of saints. The sunlight was her halo; she was my angel. I wondered if we'd really been playacting the night before. Right then her eyes blinked open all at once, as if she'd gone from dreaming to full alertness in an instant. She smiled at me. It was all I needed, that smile.

I leaned toward her and kissed her. It was soft at first, like the first lolling wave on a tropical beach. But then the tide began to roar in and soon we were awash on the sand, watching helplessly as our resistance ebbed. The waves pulled us under and we drowned there in the beautiful lagoon of Kari's king-sized bed. I gasped, tore myself away, and came up for air.

"Oh god, I'm sorry, Kari." I wrapped my hands around my nose and tried to breathe in some sanity. I could find little.

"What's wrong?" Her voice was too small, a bit too sad.

"You aren't some rebound girl. You're the kind of woman a man wraps his life around."

I reopened my eyes and looked at her. Large, brilliant, brown eyes smiling at me. *Resistance was futile.*

Kari said, "Couldn't you have started being noble a little later?" She held up two fingers. "I was this close." Another smile, this time her lips.

Futile. Prepare to be assimilated.

I kissed her again and once more, and then a lingering, tropical replay that set our lagoon to churning once again. But she was softness, and softer, and softer still, and I pulled back again, this time joyously.

"You know," she said, "I've been known to orgasm just from kissing."

I stared at her for a long time. Then I stopped staring and started kissing. I've never been the type to back down from a direct challenge.

Chapter 8

We spent a lazy Saturday just hanging out—once we pried ourselves from the bed. That took some doing. It was comfortable next to Kari, and she'd drift off to a sleep so quiet I found myself getting drowsy just watching. Nearing ten-thirty Apache got us out of bed with his Dude-I'm-about-to-pee-my-pants-and-I'm-all-out-of-pants whine. That woke us up for good.

While I took my buddy for his belated morning walk, Kari packed us a picnic brunch and together we took about an hour's walk over to Prospect Park. Apache and I had been in the city for most of a week and he'd had little to no time to run around. Neither had I, for that matter. Once at the park, we ate and then fruitlessly tried to teach my stubborn dog to play Frisbee. He'd catch it fine, but then we'd have a major tug of war trying to get him to let it go. We eventually gave up and let him burn off energy by exploring the park.

We reached Lookout Hill, but I was none too keen about trying to get a German Shepherd to climb those ancient looking steps. Kari's stories of this guy or that one who'd been killed there over the years didn't do much to raise my interest. Instead we walked over to the lake and hung out there for what felt like a short while but what turned out be three hours. I was surprised to find a lake in the middle of the city; it was no Lake Elaine, since my mountains were missing, but it was relaxing.

By three in the afternoon we were hungry again. Instead of going home Kari took us through the park, exiting on Greenwood Avenue at another set of row houses. I was enjoying feeling like an urban sophisticate again, so I didn't bother to ask where we were going. Besides, with the upcoming trip I'd planned to the D.C. area, I welcomed the time not having to think or be in charge. Still, I was more than a little surprised when she rapped on a door and Camara answered. She was dressed in shorts and a halter top, but looked every bit as stylish as she had the night before. The address turned out to be not a home, but a shared artist studio space with a small room in the back where people could crash for the night.

Lauria and her wife Tanya were there, again sitting on the floor, working. Tanya was crafting some kind of handmade jewelry that I thought I could make a killing selling to tourists back home. Lauria was finishing a sketch of Camara, who was gloriously nude in the drawing. I was kind of sorry we hadn't arrived sooner.

Kari said, "We just wanted to come by to thank you again for the drawing." I gave her a suspicious look since she said it so loudly. She then leaned over and whispered something in Camara's ear, and the two of them turned toward me, grinning. I backed away. Kari had a Lucy Ricardo crazy-scheme look in her eyes and I was feeling very much like Ricky.

It was too late, however. Tanya stood and grabbed me from behind, effectively locking me into position. I could probably have gotten myself free, but she was shorter than me and had leverage.

Camara approached me, turned to Kari, and asked, "Can I?" Kari grinned back and nodded. Stopping only for a devilish grin, Camara ripped open my shirt in one motion, popping off around three buttons in the process.

"What the hell are you doing?" I asked, though I was laughing more than I was mad. Apache started barking at me, I assume telling me to shut the hell up before the pretty girl stops trying to strip me naked. While I was trying to shut him up and retrieve my shirt from Camara, Tanya grabbed me again, turned, and pulled me to the floor in one jiu-jitsu-like motion.

"Holy fuck," I yelped, since she made me fall on my funny bone.

"Quit whining, you big baby," was her empathetic response.

I gave her some token resistance, but nothing serious. She was just skilled enough that I couldn't break free without risking hurting her. I'd been trained for hand-to-hand combat, the kind that usually ended in some guy's death, not wrestling with cute lesbians.

Tanya said, "You aren't fighting very hard."

"What makes you think I'm trying to win? You're actually turning me on a little bit."

"Ew," she said and twisted her body. She managed to get me in an arm bar. When I tried to counter she released it, grabbed my right hand, and torqued it behind my back. I calmed again and she took the other one and locked it.

"You've done a little wrestling," I said.

"Three years varsity in high school."

"Did the other guys get a boner too?"

"Ew!" she said and tightened her grip. That made my elbow start to throb. While I cursed my elbow, tried to break her hold, stave off Apache's face licking, and tell the howling-with-laughter Kari I was going to kill her, Camara yanked off my jeans and my skivvies.

Tanya released her hold and looked at me. "Not bad, Eddie girl," she said.

"Very nice, in fact," Camara said, standing over me with my jeans in one hand and boxers in the other. She was scanning me like an old photocopier. "I've wanted to do that since I first laid eyes on you."

Kari started cackling louder. I didn't think it was possible.

"My turn next," I vowed, speaking to Camara. She winked.

So now I was sitting in the middle of the floor, stark naked, in a crowd of women, covering myself.

"You know," said the blue-haired Tanya, "you're kind of fun … for a guy." She had a twinkle in her eye that was more than a reflection from the jewelry that pierced her eyebrows. It contrasted her blank affect well.

"Okay, that was very funny and kind of sexy in an I'm-trapped-by-psychopaths kind of way, but I need my clothes back now," I said.

Camara said, "Aw, don't be mad. Since you're with Kari now, you're probably gonna get to see all of us naked at some point." She laughed. "More than you want to, actually." She lifted up her halter top and two velvety, round breasts came spilling out. "See? We're even now."

"Those are nice," I said, smiling and nodding. She cheesed at me and put them away, which had an effect like a cloud suddenly covering the midday sun. "Aw shucks," I said. "I was still using those." She grinned harder.

"Give me a break," said Tanya.

"Don't be jealous, T," I said. "I promise to look at yours next."

I was rewarded with my first ever smile from Tanya. "Don't make me hurt you."

Lauria, who'd resumed her sketching, looked at me, stared a bit, and smiled. "You're not upset at all, are you?"

I shrugged, being careful not to move my hands. "I've had worse things done by people I like a whole lot less."

"Oh, honey," she said, turning to Kari, "this one's a keeper."

"Now, will you pose for me?" Kari asked. She removed a sheet that was covering a small table, exposing sculpting supplies and clay. "I decided I needed to recruit some helpers since you were being uncooperative."

I looked over at Camara. "*Et tu, Brute?*"

Camara shrugged. "Hey, I just wanted to see you naked."

Kari walked over to me and winced. "You're not secretly angry at me are you?"

"Embarrassed, yes. Angry, no."

"Sweetheart," said Camara, "you have no reason to be embarrassed."

"Gag me," said Tanya. "Come on, pup, you don't need to see this." She took Apache and sat him next to her, covering his eyes. "Heterosexuality is so unnatural," she asserted.

I ended up posing for all of them, with the exception of Tanya, who sat working on her jewelry with her back turned to me. Camara was busy clicking away with a small camera, though I was dubious as to whether it was part of a genuine art project. To be honest, I didn't care. I was having fun, and my ego had never been healthier.

After a couple of hours, and a large pizza and beer as payment from the girls, we were finally finished and Kari was busy cleaning up. That was when I got my brainstorm. "Lauria, Kari tells me you do police sketch work."

"Yup, for ten years now," she said.

"If I were to describe someone for you, could you do me a sketch?"

"For another slice of your pizza, absolutely. Let me get my kit."

She got her stuff and we spent another forty five minutes with me describing a creepy looking guy with a ring of white hair and a large, square body. When we were done she'd rendered a perfect sketch of the psycho Mina and I had encountered in the bed and breakfast back in Colorado.

"This is perfect," I said.

Lauria gave me a two-fingered salute. "No problema. What's it for?"

"Just a guy I ran into once." I was going to stop there, but the whole room was watching me intently. I figured this was the right crowd to be open. "Mina and I ran into this guy back west. Something tells me he might be involved with a sweet old lady's murder. Maybe more than just her."

"A lady killer?" Lauria asked. "Well hell, I hope you catch the son of a bitch."

"Yeah, me too. I got a friend at the FBI who'll probably be able to help."

"Keeper," reiterated Lauria. Kari's smile was glorious.

We finally got back home at eight o'clock after too much pizza and a six-pack or two of beer. Tanya turned out to be a lot of fun, despite her pretense of tough aloofness. She may have scored a clean take-down during my undressing, but I beat her by a full two seconds in the Guinness-downing contest. She'd demanded rematches, which my buzzing head reminded me I won three to two.

"You'll probably sleep better tonight," Kari said, laughing at the stupid grin I couldn't get off my face.

"Is that an invitation?" I asked. I was feeling neither pain nor inhibition.

"We promised to be good, remember?"

"I was planning on being very good."

"Oh, you're just full of yourself tonight, aren't you?" she asked.

"You were kind of full of me yourself this morning."

She gasped. "I was not. I totally refused you entry, as I recall."

"I never asked for entry, is how I remember it. And as I recall, that didn't stop you from enjoying yourself … twice."

She hit me, but giggled. "That wasn't because of you. It was a dream I was reliving."

"Yeah, I've got your dream right here." I leaned over to kiss her, but she'd unlatched the door, and my added weight sent both of us careening into her living room. We crashed onto the floor, not drunk, but giddy. I looked up and was staring right into Mina's glaring face.

Her arms were folded and her jaw clenched. "Having fun?" she asked. Then she turned and stomped upstairs, the wooden stairs reverberating with each step.

"We're in trouble," Kari said.

"How can you tell?"

"She was barefoot."

"Ouch."

Apache, the world's most disloyal Shepherd, pushed by both of us and went bolting up the stairs after her.

"I'm selling that damned dog and buying a cat," I muttered.

Kari was pouting. I didn't even have to ask her why.

The tension in the house was unbearable for the next eighteen hours. As was typical with Mina, she and I didn't discuss her trip to New Jersey or what had transpired in her absence. Instead, she shut herself in the guest room. I slept on the couch. The next day she announced she had a flight to South Dakota. Kari was distraught. Mina, however, assured her she would return in a few days.

"I miss my little bean," was the only explanation she'd give us.

I let it go. In fact, I was still mad enough to not give a shit where she went. Kari told me the night Mina left that I was in the wrong. I guess twins' blood is thicker than kisses. I protested, of course, but her answer shut me up instantly.

"Trust doesn't end the first time you think someone's screwed up. That's when it starts."

I opened and closed my mouth several times before rolling my eyes and slumping in front of the TV.

"You mad at me?" she asked.

"A little," I confessed. I didn't need sociology lessons; I needed her to be on my side.

"Good," she said, plopping herself next to me on the sofa. "We'll watch some shoot-'em-up flick. That way you can be grumpy and enjoy yourself at the same time."

I sighed dramatically. "Is it always going to be like this with you?"

"You mean perfect? Yeah, we're buds."

I didn't give her the satisfaction of a smile. It took all of my effort, especially when she flipped on the Gene Autry movie.

Monday morning I took a flight to D.C.'s Reagan National Airport alone. I was happy to be back on the case. Chasing possible murder suspects was easier than trying to figure out some sort of twins-powered isosceles love triangle. I felt as if I were trapped in a Pythagorean nightmare. Kari and I hadn't cheated exactly, stopping at kissing, but I knew women well enough to know that's not why Mina was angry. It was clear that Kari and I had gotten very close while Mina was gone, that I'd spent the day enjoying her sister's company rather than sulking over the fact that she'd possibly slept with another guy wasn't lost on her. It wasn't lost on me either. I should have been hurt and furious. After lying in bed with Kari, however, all I felt was relief. I was off the hook.

Plus, as far as I was concerned, the only pair of our trio without a dysfunctional relationship was Kari and me. Mina and her sister were close, but there's nothing magical about being a twin that makes it okay to share your boyfriend. At the end of the day, they were sisters. Given they lived two thousand miles apart, it was clear they knew how to have appropriate boundaries with each other. Still, since the moment we'd arrived in New York, I felt as though I didn't know precisely whom I was dating. The first night, it was Mina: heady and passionate, as always. Since then I'd been in a sensual but not sexual relationship with Kari.

Triangles aren't as fun as you'd guess. In fact, I was feeling overwhelmed. A part of me wished I'd been with neither and had kept this job purely professional.

That was why I was grateful to be back at work. Solving mysteries is straightforward and simple. You follow the clues and see where they lead. Love? Totally illogical. Was I falling for Kari, or just using that relationship as a way to cool Mina's jets? I didn't want to think about it and wouldn't have to, at least until Mina returned in four days' time. In the meantime I was following the trail to Hardaway Group and Fadil's last boss, Ken Satterhorn.

I'd arranged to meet Mr. Satterhorn, or rather I had Debra arrange it as soon as I learned his name. He was reluctant at first, giving us the company line that he wasn't at liberty to discuss anything about employees. However, I'd coerced Gaither to intercede and he assured Satterhorn that he would be greatly helping a criminal investigation and nothing he said would be put on the record. I can't believe how often Gaither uses that "off the record" lie. The dude would arrest his grandma if he had the evidence.

Satterhorn, being a normal, patriotic government contractor—whose ego had been sufficiently stroked—agreed to meet me at a restaurant in Chinatown, within walking distance from his office. The food was excellent and the information just what I needed. In between stuffing his chipmunk cheeks with salmon, Satterhorn got straight to the matter at hand.

"I recruited Fadil because of his experience in diplomatic relations and his ties with the Turkish government. We'd been pursuing work on an airport renovation project and Fadil knew the right people to work with in Turkey, so we interviewed him and I brought him in as a director."

"How'd that work out?"

"Fine, at first. He seemed to know his way around the embassies and, although he was a little raw with the aspects of dealing with federal contracting, he was slowly making headway in clearing the needed hurdles. Plus, he turned out to have some invaluable contacts both in Turkey and the Middle East." He stopped talking and jammed more salmon salad in his face.

"High-powered contacts?"

"Higher powered than any of us had. I should have poked harder to find out how he'd gotten them but, to be honest, I didn't really want to know."

"You said things were fine *at first*. When did they stop being fine?"

He continued eating but resumed talking. I felt like I was interviewing a cow chewing its cud. "After the procurement timelines began to slip, Fadil began making excuses. This person was unavailable or that one was changing roles. Nothing much was happening."

"But you didn't buy his excuses," I suggested.

He leaned in. "Off the record, right?"

"Completely."

"He was keeping late nights. Started getting in the office late. Sometimes he came in looking as if he'd been up all night. Once I walked in his office and he was in a shouting match with a female employee. He hung up as soon as he saw me."

"Do you know who this woman was?"

He nodded. "Her name is Cynthia Roark, goes by Cindi." He spelled it for me. "I couldn't help but feel like something untoward was going on."

"Untoward like...?"

He made an obscene gesture with one index finger penetrating his other fist.

"Doesn't your company frown on that sort of thing?"

"Absolutely. Technically, Fadil was Cindi's supervisor. If I had proof, I'd have fired him."

I nodded and began scribbling in my notepad. Gaither was right; I needed a tablet computer—one with video software. When I'd finished writing I asked for her contact information, then asked him my final question: "What exactly was Ms. Roark's actual relationship with Fadil supposed to be?"

"We brought her on because she was experienced in offsets." I gave him a puzzled look and he explained. "Often when you're dealing with a large project for a foreign government you have to promise to do a sizeable chunk of work in their country, to offset some of the currency that's floating out of the country."

"Ah," I said, "jobs creation. We had that issue in Afghanistan."

He paused when I said Afghanistan and looked at me as if I'd grown in my seat somehow. "Exactly," he said, nodding. "Cindi was working with Fadil to try to arrange a big enough offset to make the whole program attractive to the Turkish government."

I was putting the pieces together in my head. "So did they travel together a lot?"

"Frequently," he said, "and alone."

"Thank you for your openness, Mr. Satterhorn."

"Ken. Glad I could be of service. If Fadil was ... well, I want to make sure whoever hurt him is brought to justice."

"We'll see to that. Oh, and one last item, if you don't mind."

"Shoot."

"Mr. Sunay's former assistant, Haleh Asker. Do you know her?"

"Haleh?" He stopped, trying to recall the name. "Ah, yes, I do remember her. I think I insulted her at first because I kept calling her Holly. I had no idea it was an Egyptian name."

I smiled. It was a professional smile. "Did Mr. Sunay ever mention wanting to bring her on board with him when he was hired?"

Satterhorn poked out his lips and shook his head. "No ... I'm pretty sure he didn't. I even asked him if there was anyone from his team he wanted to bring over with him, and he flat out told us no. As far as I knew, Haleh was basically just a secretary."

That was a very different story than she led me to believe. I noted I needed to have a little follow-on chat with Ms. Asker. Lies, especially seemingly unimportant lies, were always important during an investigation.

I thanked Satterhorn and the conversation switched over to the usual sort of chitchat that accompanies a business lunch. When we were done I paid the check and I was on my phone with Cindi Roark's office before I even got back to the rental car. She was tied up in meetings the rest of the day but offered to meet with me the next day after work, especially when I told her that her employer had concerns regarding her relationship with Fadil. I convinced her a good word from me would go a long way towards clearing her name. To my surprise she jumped at the chance.

I arranged the meeting at her home at seven p.m. That brief success was followed by my making my first major mistake in the case; I gave Kari a pretty accurate account of the day's events. She was technically my client and would normally be given a briefing. However, I'd responded to her as a friend. Were I being professional I would have realized she was far too emotionally involved to stay away and let me do my job.

We got in our first argument later that day, a screaming match really, in my hotel room via FaceTime. An hour in, when I continued to insist she needed to stay out of things, she called me an "insensitive ass" and disconnected. Thirty seconds later, my cell phone rang.

"I'm sorry for hanging up on you and calling you an ass," she said. "You're not, you're just insensitive."

It was a terrible apology, but more than Mina had ever given me, so I took it. "Kari, I know you have a ton of things you want to say. And you deserve to be able to confront her and get them off your chest. But one, we don't even know for sure this is the woman he'd actually been seeing."

"Yeah, right."

I ignored her. "And two, we're trying to find out who's responsible for your husband's death. I can't do that if you're busy trying having some kind of shouting match with her."

Kari was silent for a long time, which mistakenly let me believe I'd won the argument. Instead she said, speaking softly and deliberately, "You know, I thought you were supposed to be so adept at telling me apart from my sister. My name's Kari. You might remember making out with me in my bed." Then she hung up without another word.

I spent the rest of the evening flipping channels on the TV and trying to pull together a case file and a timeline. At the end, I realized I had more holes than data. So, I made one last call – this one to my assistant back in Arizona.

"Debra, "I said, "It's Daley."

"Mr. D, I've asked you a hundred times to call me Deb. Don't you like me at all?"

"I like you a little too much. That's why I call you Debra."

"Wow, what the heck did those twins do to you?"

"What's that supposed to mean?"

"You're being all honest and mellow and mushy. I think I like the old, bristly you better."

"Me too. Look, I don't have time for this. How's your schedule look the next week?"

"That's the Mr. D I love. I just have some late alimony payments to chase down for Mrs. Tolliver, why?"

"Because I need you to do some legwork. I'm going to need you to get me info on who legally owns some property here in D.C. I also need you to do a full background check on a guy name of Henry Reilly. Talk to his friends, colleagues, whoever you need to. I want to know everything about this guy you can find out. Same thing with Fadil's ex-assistant, Haleh Asker."

"Boss, that's gonna be challenging with a three-hour time difference."

"I know it is. That's why you're getting your butt on a plane to New York as soon as you can. It's about time you started doing some field work."

I pulled the phone away from my ear while she shrieked at the top of her lungs.

"If you're through trying to rupture my eardrums—"

"Sorry, Mr. D, I've just always wanted to see New York—"

"Yeah, I get that. Just remember: work first, party after, okay?"

"I'll be the consummate pro. Cross my heart."

"You always are … Deb."

"You so won't be sorry, Mr. D! I promise."

"I know I won't." Her enthusiasm was the highlight of my very dreary day.

We ended the call by agreeing on having her stay at a hotel near Kari's place. I was hoping she'd be able to crash on the daybed Kari kept in the backroom of the studio space she and her friends rented, but I thought I'd need to mend a few bridges before I started asking my peeved client for favors … especially once she got a load of Debra Jean Tuohy.

Did I mention the woman once caused a three-car pileup just by walking down the sidewalk? Did I also mention that was how I met her? Yeah, she looks that good. Cost me almost two grand to get the Camaro fixed. She was only nineteen then. Now, two years later, she can still stop traffic. She's a *good girl*, but fortunately she doesn't look like one.

If anyone could get Henry's cloistered group to spill the beans on him, Deb could.

I decided to sleep in the next day since I couldn't make much headway until I spoke with Cindi. Chas told us that Fadil had a space somewhere in Georgetown, but he didn't have the address. I hoped Cindi would provide that piece of the puzzle.

At ten o'clock I was still happily in dreamland when someone started pounding on the door. *"No limpiar!"* I called through the door, assuming it was the cleaning lady. A second later I climbed out of bed, feeling like a damned racist for assuming she spoke Spanish. Where I lived pretty much everyone spoke Spanish. Here in D.C. it was liable to be considered an insult. She knocked again and I pulled open the door, peeking around it in just my underwear.

"Good morning," Kari said and pushed by me.

"How the hell did you find me?" I'd been careful not to give her my hotel information.

"I called your admin—"

"Assistant," I corrected. Debra was very particular about her job title.

"Deb. And don't ask me how I found her. You're on the internet, dummy."

"Oh yeah, right."

"She was very cooperative once I told her you were my

126

boyfriend."

"Um, technically I'm your sister's boyfriend." I was still pissed from the night before.

"Whichever. Anyway, she told me where you're staying. She was so excited I could barely understand her, but I gathered you're bringing her to New York to help. I can't believe you were making her stay in a crappy hotel. I told her just to show up at the studio space and Lauria would find somewhere for her to sleep."

"Thank you," I said. That put a few hundred bucks back in my pocket.

Kari sat herself down on the bed. "I'd have sex with you, but I'm still mad."

The woman was just mean. She had no intention of having sex with me, but now I would be able to think of nothing else the entire day, and she knew it.

"Where are you taking me for breakfast?" she asked.

"I thought we were mad at each other."

"We are. That doesn't mean we can't still be friends." She waggled a finger for me to approach. When I did she leaned forward, her lips pursed and eyes closed. I leaned in for the kiss. "Psyche!" she said, and pushed me on the floor. She stood and walked to do the door. "Get dressed. I'll be waiting in the lobby."

And here I thought she was nothing like her sister.

We arrived at Cindi Roark's condo in a little town called Rockville, Maryland around fifteen minutes early. For a suburb it was a noisy enough setting, overlooking a "town square" that mostly consisted of people sitting around watching their kids play in fountains. I immediately wished Kari hadn't come after seeing the look she got watching all those moms with their kids. After a bit I took pity on her and had her wait for me at the rear entrance of the building, away from the noise and the children.

I left her chomping at the bit there and rang Cindi's bell alone, five minutes late. I wanted just enough time to throw her off and have her wonder if I'd be a no-show. When she opened the door I knew why a man would risk throwing his marriage away over a work colleague. Cindi Roark, was, in a word, alluring, which is an uptown, Henry Reillyesque word that means smoking hot. She was slender, around twenty-five, with shoulder-length, curly black hair and the kind of smoldering brown eyes that could make a man lose his marriage. I could tell she'd been home from work awhile, since she was dressed in a simple spaghetti-strap black top and shorts, with slender legs I tried not to see and pretty feet that I didn't even bother to try ignoring.

"Mr. Daley?" she asked, speaking through the partly open door. I said yes and showed her my badge. She opened the door and let me in. We exchanged niceties and she gave me a glass of tea she probably sweetened by dipping in one of her fingers. It was too sweet for me and I let it sit sweating on the coffee table.

"Ms. Roark, I'm investigating Mr. Sunay's death, and I'm not at all convinced it was an accident. So, as you can imagine, I want to gather as much information as I can." I paused and tried to gauge her reaction. There wasn't much of one. "You don't seem surprised at the idea of his being murdered."

She gave a half-hearted shrug. "The police and insurance investigators went through here over and over months ago. They all agreed it was an accident."

"What do you think?"

"What I think doesn't matter. It's just I figured you wouldn't be here if you thought all that happened was a traffic accident."

"Fair enough. So, how about I get right to the point?"

"I wish you would. I've had a very long day and I'd like to get in a run before it gets too dark."

"I'm sure we won't be long," I said. I pulled out a notepad on which was written absolutely nothing, but I figured it would make her feel like I knew more than I did. "As I indicated on the phone, I met with Mr. Satterhorn yesterday and he had some concerns regarding your relationship with Mr. Sunay."

Cindi's eyes flashed and her thin lips pulled taut. She was getting mad, which meant this interview was already heading in the wrong direction. I needed nervous. "Fadil was my boss and my friend. Maybe it was unusual or even inappropriate to be best friends with someone you work with. I don't know, but that's all there was."

"Just friends," I repeated.

"I was not fucking Fadil. Period. Ever." Her nostrils were flaring. She meant her use of the f-word to throw me. It did, but not enough.

"Whom was he having sex with then?"

"Hopefully his wife. Ask her." She stood. "If there's nothing else, I need to get going."

"You seem awfully angry considering I'm here trying to find out who might have killed someone you claim to have been your best friend."

She calmed and sat back down. "I'm sorry. I don't like being accused of things I didn't do."

"Actually, I wasn't the one accusing you. Your boss, Satterhorn, was. I'd hoped you'd want to help me help you."

"People think just because you're pretty that means any success you have is based on sleeping your way to the top. It's crap."

"To be fair, you are fairly young for a job that sends you traveling all over the world. Plus, I understand you and Mr. Sunay were alone on those trips a lot."

She pursed her lips, rolled her eyes up toward the upper lids, and slowly shook her head. Again anger, not nervousness. "First, I have a B.S. from Georgetown and an MBA from Wharton. Second, my travel *all over the world* was mostly to Turkey and back. And third, the reason Fadil picked me is because my grandparents are Turkish and I speak the language fluently." She said something to me in Turkish that I didn't understand, but I got her drift anyway.

"You just told me to go fuck myself, didn't you?"

She frowned harder for a moment, then snickered. "You speak Turkish?" she asked.

"No, I've just had a lot of women tell me to go fuck myself. I recognize the tone."

"I'm sorry," she said, after laughing. "I know you're doing your job. It just pisses me off that no one can imagine Fadil and I weren't doing anything wrong. Why is that so hard to believe?"

"Because, frankly, you're gorgeous. Not many men could stay focused if they were one on one with you."

She allowed herself the briefest of smiles. "And that's my fault?"

"Not your fault, it's theirs. But it is your reality and that makes it your problem. Men are pigs—well, most of us anyway. That's why they figure Fadil must have been one too."

"So, my career is over at Hardaway because I'm pretty?"

"I don't think so. Honestly, I think Satterhorn believes Fadil was entirely to blame if something was going on between the two of you."

"He never touched me. Not once."

I looked her hard in the eyes. "I believe you, and I'll make sure to tell Satterhorn. But I think you do know who Fadil was sleeping with."

Cindi turned away and shook her head. "I'm sorry. I can't help you. If he was seeing some woman on the side, he never told me about it." She stood again and this time gestured for me to head to the door.

I nodded. "Ms. Roark, if I may, do you mind if I use your bathroom before I go? I have a long trip back to D.C."

She said, "Of course," and showed me the way. Once there I sent a quick text message, flushed the toilet, and washed my hands.

We walked to the door, and I thanked her again for her time and the overly sweet tea. She nodded, but said nothing and pulled open the door. Kari was there, holding a photo of herself, Jeremy, and Fadil. Cindi gasped.

"This is the family I thought I had, Miss Roark. The little boy with the long hair is Jeremy. Fadil and I used to argue all the time over his hair. My people believe virile young men should have long hair. Fadil thought it made him look gay." She took a step into the condo and Cindi matched her, stepping backward. "Do you think he looks gay?"

Cindi shook her head quickly. Her eyes were streaming tears. "No, no I don't."

Kari began to cry too. "I don't … I don't have a son anymore. And I'll spend the rest of my life trying to learn how to deal with that." Another step forward, another matching step back. Kari shook her head, her straight hair billowing around her. "What I don't want to spend my life doing is wondering … wondering if I ever really had a marriage." Kari's face twisted with sadness. Like Cindi, she wasn't angry, but in pain. "Did I have a marriage, Miss Roark? Did I?"

Cindi turned and sat heavily on her sofa. She said nothing at first, but covered her face with both hands, her head propped up by both elbows against her knees. Then, after thirty seconds when Kari sat beside her, she said a single, soft word. "No." It came out as a whisper. She looked through her tears at Kari, who only stared ahead. "Kari, I tried to make Fadil tell you. I told him a hundred times he needed to release you. He just wouldn't hear it."

To my amazement Kari turned, wrapped both arms around Cindi, and together they cried. I had to leave, suddenly needing to watch children play in the fountains and mothers scold them for getting their clothes wet. I needed to see dads who knew how to play with their kids and who still loved their wives even though the sparks had died down and the fire was now just embers. I needed to be in a place where husbands didn't cheat and didn't lie. I needed to be someplace where gay men didn't feel they had to marry straight women and break their hearts just to meet society's expectations. Most of all I needed to not see Kari's face when Cindi Roark told her that Fadil was a homosexual.

I'd managed to compose myself by the time Kari came out thirty minutes later, her entire face puffy from crying. I was grateful for her large sunglasses so that I couldn't see the pain written in her eyes.

"Thank you for ... for giving us space up there. I think we needed that." She took my arm, but didn't look at me. "You're pretty savvy when it comes to women."

I started to let that go, but decided she'd been lied to enough. "No, actually, I was being chicken shit. I just didn't want to watch you cry."

"I know that. But you still did what I needed you to do."

We walked to the underground garage in silence. When we were alone in the car, I asked the hard question. "What did she tell you?"

"What we both probably suspected, that my husband was gay. He'd been having an affair with a man he knew from New York. His lover moved here, and apparently Fadil followed him."

"Damn. I'm sorry." After another pause: "Did she give you his name?"

She shook her head. "She said Fadil would never tell her his name, just that it was someone he knew from school."

"And you believe her?"

"I do," she said. "She gave me this." She handed me a slip of paper with an address and a key all by itself.

"Is this what I think it is?"

"Cindi thinks so. She says she was cleaning out his office after the accident and came across the key taped to a piece of paper that said Georgetown House. He'd called her from someplace in the District a number of times and she did a reverse phone lookup and found the address." Kari took off her sunglasses and looked at me. "The listing was under the name Good Crow."

"You gotta be kidding me."

"No. It's like he was daring me to find out his big secret."

"Or hoping you would," I added. "Maybe he wanted you to do what he never had the guts to do."

"Cindi told me one more thing. It might be the reason he was so determined to keep this a secret."

"Really?"

"Yeah. She said Fadil was terrified that his family would find out, especially his Uncle Emir."

"Have you ever met this uncle?"

"Sure. He's always there at family events, kind of the unofficial head of the Sunay family. I always thought he was a nice man."

"What did Fadil think of him?"

She shrugged. "He seemed to respect him a lot. Emir is very old fashioned and religious. I can't see his ever accepting Fadil's being gay."

"Well, from what you've told me they weren't wealthy enough for this to be about being written out of the will."

"No. Odds are Fadil figured Uncle Emir would banish him from the family. So I guess he found a fake family to make his uncle happy." She wiped away a final tear and stared out the windshield. "So, what's our next step?"

"Ever been to Georgetown?"

"No, but I heard it's really trendy. I might have some real estate interest there." She gave me a weak smile.

"You're taking this pretty well."

"Nope. Only compared to being told your son is dead. I'm torn up inside." Kari took my hand and I held hers tight. "Am I really so much of a loser that men aren't attracted to me? I mean, my husband was gay and Henry was pretending to like me. It turns out I haven't had a genuine relationship in at least five years. Maybe I've never had one. Maybe no man out there will ever want to make love to me, have kids by me, spend their lives with me."

I spoke before I could turn my mouth off. "I want all those things with you."

Kari said nothing so I released her hand, turned on the ignition, and started out of the parking garage. When I got to the exit, as twilight began to claim the day, she spoke. "You belong to Mina, Eddie."

"I belong to me, and it's about time I stop letting people decide for me whom I should and shouldn't be with. That goes for you,

Mina, and your mom."

"Okay," she said. "But remember what I told you about cutting my leg off for Mina. I meant that. I won't hurt her."

I was getting pissed. "Kari, I don't know how this will work out. I may never get married to anyone. But if we go through all of this and I do ask you, you damn sight better say yes."

After a long silence, she said, "Okay," and took my hand.

I can't drive for shit with my left hand, but I didn't let hers go again.

The Georgetown section of Washington, D.C. was an interesting place, with an old-world flavor mixed into urban sprawl. We drove down Wisconsin Avenue and made the mistake of turning onto M Street where life seemed to be a slow-moving parade of late shoppers, tourists, and teens cruising aimlessly. We circled the back streets until we found the address we were looking for. It was a plain looking townhouse carved out of siding-covered row houses. Our unit was an end unit, lined with yellow siding that was cleaved together with one with green siding. Double windows and doors showed the demarcation of one unit to the next.

"Don't get much privacy, do you?" I asked. "The one unit is like two inches from the next."

"It's not so bad," she said, glumly. "I kind of like it. Looks colonial."

Indeed, the modern unit did look like a late-twentieth century version of a Williamsburg colonial, stuck in the city amid pricier and more genuine versions. The street was crammed bumper-to-bumper with visitors' cars, so we drove in circles for another fifteen minutes looking for a space. Parking was at a premium, as evidenced by the blue sedan that seemed to mirror our tracks in the hopes we'd overlook a space they could jump on. Finally we found a vacant space on a darkened street that was pockmarked with private driveways warning visitors not to even try parking there.

"This must get old," I said once we'd finally parked.

"Yeah, I guess you have to buy one of the more expensive places to warrant your own driveway."

The blue sedan rolled past us and the guy in the passenger seat shot us a dirty look as they crept by.

"Sorry, dude. You snooze, you lose," Kari said.

We slow-clombered to the townhouse, which turned out to be only a block and a half from where we parked. The streets were quiet, with only the occasional sound of distant sirens and the clip-clopping of Kari's heels against the cobblestone walk breaking the silence. The night air was thick with the remnants of an overhanging blanket of haze, making the short walk an uncomfortable one. I began to long for my clean dry mountain air. It was approaching nine-thirty now, and life along the side streets was winding down as visitors began flooding back toward the suburbs and locals began hunkering down for the short summer night. We double-checked the address of the end unit; it looked deserted. Just in case, I walked around to the back, which consisted of almost no yard and a line of dense shrubs. There was a rear door, but the grass behind was uncut with no trail or visible evidence that anyone had been out there in recent weeks. I walked back to the front, to Kari.

"Ready to do this?" I asked.

She took in a deep breath and nodded. I strode to the door and rang the bell. No response. I tried again, then did my police knock that was certain to awaken the neighbors and certainly anyone in the house.

I turned to Kari. "No one home." I couldn't tell from her expression if she felt relief or disappointment. I imagined she was no more certain of her feelings than I was. She gave me a look somewhere between fear and resignation, and opened the door. We went in but left the lights out in case the neighbors had been watching. There was no way of telling if the resident had been gone for an hour or a year. We walked around, getting a feel for the place, which was homey but nondescript. After a time we began to feel more comfortable and flipped on a light.

"Look at that," Kari said, pointing to the dining room. On the wall was the same gaudy, flowery wallpaper we saw at Henry's place.

"Looks like my grandma's been here, too," I said, walking towards the cloying décor. All the vinyl flowers almost set off my allergies.

"More like Chas has been here." She joined me in the dining room.

She gave me a look and I got it. "If Chas is the common denominator …"

"Then no way Henry didn't know about Fadil and his

boyfriend." The final word of her sentence slipped out with no animosity, yet I could tell it stung her tongue on the way out.

"What do you think the odds are that Henry's known all along what's been going on?" I asked.

"A hundred percent. He's very loyal to Fadil, known him since they were in their teens at Columbia."

"How far would he be willing to go to help Fadil keep a secret like this?"

Her eyes widened. "I doubt there's anything he wouldn't do." I nodded my agreement. "Do ... do you think he's the one who ran us off the road the other night?"

"I didn't when you asked me then, but I do now," I said.

She opened her mouth to speak, but was interrupted when the front window popped as if someone had thrown a rock, followed by the glass front of a display case near her shattering. I dove, knocking her to the ground. Three more pops through the window and one through the siding and the wall, and furniture and bric-a-brac around the house began to shatter. Kari's eyes were wide as I lay over her.

"We need to get out of here," I said, trying to sound as calm as possible.

We crawled on our hands and knees back into the living room and towards the kitchen, which led to the back yard. At the room's exit I stood, flicking off the light switch. No sooner did I stand then the front window exploded in a burst of automatic weapons fire. A bullet ripped through my left shoulder cleanly, burning as it passed through.

"Eddie!" Kari reached up and pulled me down. I hit the floor harder than I should have due to the awkwardness of having an arm hanging numb.

I need my damned guns was the only thing going through my mind.

"Come on, baby!"

As the firing paused we hurried through the kitchen and out the rear door. No more than three paces past the high grass we were through the twelve-foot-high thicket of brush behind the house and out onto the backyard of pricey homes along a parallel street. I held my shoulder and tried not to pass out as Kari guided us through the backyards and onto the street. She stopped there, her eyes darting around nervously. She wasn't as cool under fire as her Marines-trained twin, but she was damned cool enough.

"You should call the cops," I said. "Maybe the sirens will chase those guys off and we can get back to the car."

"You need a doctor, honey."

I shook my head. "It was a high-powered bullet and it's already passed clean through. I just need stitches. You can do that for me."

"Eddie, I'm no doctor. What if you get an infection? You could get blood poisoning or something."

"I won't get sepsis if we're careful. I have a kit in the hotel room with thread, antibiotics, and gauze." I released my arm and touched her face. It left a bloody hand print on her cheek. "I promise it'll be fine."

"Why do you travel with an I-just-got-shot kit?" I tried to shrug, but it hurt too much. She shut her eyes and inhaled deeply. "You are so stubborn. Okay, we'll do it your way, but if you die on the way to the hotel I'm gonna kill you."

"I won't die. The bullet didn't even hit any major blood vessels. I promise. If it had I'd be calling an ambulance myself."

"Okay, but you better be telling me the truth." She called 9-1-1 and left a tip about hearing gunfire. The dispatcher told her they were already en route and to stay inside and away from windows until the cops showed up.

"Now they tell us," she said after hanging up.

We made it to the car and the hotel, and Kari did an admirable job of stitching me back up. I guess those years doing intricate work with her sculpting tools gave her steady hands. "You would've made a great surgeon," I said after she'd applied a bandage.

"No, I'd get too emotionally involved," she said. "Mina's the one who'd have been a great doctor." She made a face that was at least halfway to a wince. "I called her when you passed out in the car and told her what happened." She hesitated. "She wanted to fly back tonight. I told her to wait until we knew if it was safe back home."

I shook my head. "She can't bring Nona here. We don't want the baby caught up in this."

"Mina knows. She won't do that." She looked at me. "Eddie, that girl adores you. You should have heard her on the phone. She was frantic and yelling at me to ignore your stubborn butt and take you to the hospital." She lay back on the bed, staring at the ceiling.

I lay next to her, careful not to move my arm. "I adore her too."

"Then what are we doing, Eddie? Why are we acting like this?"

"Because you're the one I'm in love with." It was the first time I'd ever said that when I was sure I meant it.

"Fuck," she said, the first time I remember her cursing. It wasn't nearly as cute as when Mina said it.

After a time, as we were both drifting toward sleep, too emotionally drained to even undress, she asked, "Were they trying to kill us, or…?"

"Fadil's lover? I don't know for sure. But I'm starting to think Fadil wasn't the only one who wanted his affair to remain a secret."

"You think that's why he was killed, because he was gay? I mean, come on, we're in the 21st century."

"More likely because somebody wanted to make sure no one ever found out he was."

We let that ruminate awhile before drifting off to sleep. As sleep took us, I still refused to let the woman's hand go. Her mother's words echoing were through my head: *don't you let anybody make you let go.*

I bet this *anybody* never met Mina.

Chapter 9

We made it back to Brooklyn in one piece and together we paid a visit to Rodrigo Gaither. I had to come clean with him on the events in D.C., since I couldn't exactly hide them with my arm being in a sling. Kari was in rare form, thinking it hilarious she was meeting with a "guy named Rod" and "a big private dick." I was getting annoyed until I figured out she was purposefully being silly in order to charm him. She'd read his sense of humor well. By the time she was finished he would have mobilized half the FBI had she asked. Instead she got him to promise he'd secure someone from the NYPD to keep an eye on her house if we needed it. We shared the information we'd gathered and the few theories we came up with to tie them together. The single thing we agreed on is that none of us believed that Fadil's death had been an accident. Gaither took it upon himself to do a background search on Fadil's Uncle Emir and other members of the family. I had second visits to Henry and Haleh on my agenda, after giving myself a few days for my shoulder to get stronger.

Gaither reported that the D.C. cops had found little from the Georgetown shooting. Forensics found multiple spent shell casings, but little else. No one came forward as eye witnesses. They were treating it as being possibly drug related, meaning the investigators were being reassigned to cases they could actually solve. It was okay by me. Gaither was as close to a cop as I wanted to deal with anyway. Before we left I gave him the sketch that Lauria had produced of the madman from the Eastern Plains B&B back in Colorado. "What's this guy's connection to the Sunay case?" he asked.

"None. Kari's sister and I ran into him in Colorado. We think he may be connected to at least one murder in the area." I omitted the part wherein Mina and I saw his victim's ghost. I still wasn't letting myself admit that, even in my own head.

"At least one?" he asked.

"Yeah. I think he may be a serial killer. If he is, I'm convinced there's still some good DNA evidence back at the bed and breakfast where we spotted him."

"Well, serial killers like to haunt their crime scenes. Some even get sexual pleasure reliving the crime."

"Haunt is a good word," I said. "Do you think you can do anything with this sketch?"

"If he's in our database, yeah. This sketch is pretty realistic, almost like a photo."

"Yep, the artist is pretty good."

"I'll take it and see if I can get someone to run it through the facial recognition stuff we're testing. I'll let you know if I find anything."

I thanked him, gave him a few particulars, and then he escorted Kari and me back toward the exit. Before we left, he pulled me aside. "What's the real story with you and these sisters?" he asked.

"I met one, we started dating, she brought me to meet her sister …" I stopped, ashamed to go on.

"No. Don't tell me. Kari is the sister."

"Yeah."

"Dude. You fell in love with the wrong twin."

"I know." I felt a headache coming on. "It's that obvious?"

"Fuck yeah. You two may as well have tee shirts made."

"Mina's gonna kill me."

"The Marine, Mina?"

"Yeah."

He opened the door and I headed out after Kari. "Nice knowing you, son," he said, grinning.

Dude was totally jealous.

Two days later Deb had arrived and was working out of the Prospect Park studio and making headway, by her accounts. I'd been trying to nail down Henry for another chat without much success. I managed to arrange to meet Fadil's uncle, but scheduled it for after I was due to hear back from Gaither. While I waited Kari had me pretty much restricted to house arrest, claiming I wouldn't heal properly without rest. That was never the military's point of view, as I recalled.

We were in the kitchen. I was preparing my southwestern chili recipe while Kari made some artery-clogging devil food called frybread, which was exactly what it sounds like. Of course she reminded me the dish had been created out of necessity when the American invaders herded Natives onto lands that couldn't support their healthier diet. It figured that somehow it would turn out to be my fault. We worked pretty well together in her small kitchen, managing to twist and turn without banging into each other and avoiding Apache, who seemed to be trying to tackle us so he could get to the food. I think we were doing more laughing than cooking. We'd invited Lauria, Tanya, and Camara as thanks for putting Deb up in their space, and of course Deb, who'd managed to fit into their little group as if she'd known them for years. I was mostly looking forward to seeing what she'd come up with. Hopefully it would be good enough info to justify the news I had to give her.

Kari, being a good host, but not a good organizer, had allowed me to plan the menu and was focused on ensuring I didn't "manhandle" all the cooking. I, being a child of Texas and a resident of the Southwest, was insulted she would besmirch my good culinary name and was forcing her—rather, giving her the opportunity—to taste my chili. Having had her taste buds ruined by Henry's hoity-toity yuppie food, she was laughing vociferously and fighting off my free hand with the anointed tasting spoon full of God's Own Chili when Apache shocked us with a loud bark. We turned, prepared for the worst, but instead were met by Mina, who was standing in the kitchen's doorway, her arms folded, glaring at us.

"Mina! Hey!" Kari said, releasing me and starting toward her, her arms wide. Apache had practically broken his neck to reach his one true love already.

When Kari approached, Mina shook her head and took a step backward, avoiding her twin. "No," she said, still shaking her head.

"No."

"What's ... what's wrong, sweetie?" Kari asked.

Mina's face twisted into a snarl of hurt and anger. She jabbed a finger at both of us. "You two, that's what's wrong."

Kari's voice was quiet. "What do you mean? We're just making dinner for the girls. I didn't know you were coming today, but I'm glad you're here."

Mina shouted, "I'm not talking about your damned dinner! I mean the two of you! You got married when I wasn't looking!"

Kari turned and looked at me, flashing a quick look I can only describe as horror. She turned back to her sister. "Don't be stupid, Mina. We're just cooking."

"I'm not stupid." Mina began crying and shaking her head again. "That wasn't cooking I was watching. That was some kind of husband-wife kitchen ballet."

"How long have you been standing there?" Kari asked. Her voice was a whisper.

"Long enough." Mina walked up to me. I was still stupidly holding the spoon of chili in my one free hand. She bent, tasted the spoonful, and said, "That's pretty good." Then, she punched me in the face. Not a romantic movie heroine slap, not a TV fake punch, but a full-on, I'm-a-badass-Marine punch in the jaw. It hurt like hell. For a second, a terrible second, my instincts kicked in and I balled my fist and drew back. It hurt that much. But I caught myself and pulled my hand down.

Unfortunately, it wasn't before Kari jumped between me and her sister and said, "Don't you dare hit her." She practically hissed at me.

Mina turned away, her eyes still teary, and said, "Don't worry, he would never hit me. He's Mr. Nice Guy, remember?"

She turned, exited the kitchen, picked up her bag, and walked out the front door, shaking her punching hand.

Kari called after her, but didn't follow.

I glared at Apache. "Some watch dog you are. Good looking out." He barked at me, turned, and ran to the front door after Mina.

"What do we do now?" Kari asked.

I pulled off my cooking apron and headed for the door.

Kari grabbed my arm. "No, you're better off letting her cool off on her own. It's not like she can get back home right away."

I didn't respond, but tore my arm away from Kari and headed

after her sister. Apache was trying to dig his way through the front door. Kari pulled him away and I took off. Two minutes later I caught up with Mina on the street. She took another swing at me and I ducked under it. She took a third and I caught her arm, twisted it until she was off-balance, released it, grabbed one leg with my free arm, and pulled her over my good shoulder. She was still holding onto her bag, so I brought her back to the brownstone, slung over my shoulder and cursing a blue streak.

"What the fuck do you think you're doing?" she screamed at me when I dumped her on Kari's sofa.

"What I should have done the first time you ran away."

"What, assault me? You wanna fight it out, one arm?"

"No, telling you I love you and to stop acting like a scared little crazy woman." I was expecting another storm of anger, but that seemed to take the wind out of her sails. "Kari and I never had sex, Mina. Not once."

She sniffled but remained silent.

Kari sat next to her. "He's telling the truth. We were tempted … I-I kissed him, but we never let it go further than that."

"You kissed him?" Kari looked at her lap. Mina looked at me. "Did she tell you that's as good as sex to her? To both of us?"

"I'm sorry, Mina," I said. "I never meant to hurt you." Then, being a defensive ass as is my nature, I added, "It wouldn't have happened if I hadn't caught you with some guy."

"Eddie!" Kari said. I shut up.

Mina wiped her eyes. "No, it's okay, he's right. But he wasn't just some guy. He's a guy I dated while I was in the Corps. He was in my platoon. Dan heard I was in New York and he got me an interview with this helicopter tour service that operates out of Newark. He wanted me to sleep with him." She snuffled and wiped her eyes. "I figured out that was the real reason for the interview." She looked up at me with her puffy eyes. "I thought he was being a friend, but he was just being a guy."

"Then why was he with you when I called?"

"His place is a pigsty. I spent the whole night cleaning, you know, to say thank you since I wasn't gonna screw him. Fell asleep on his bed with all my clothes on." She started crying. "I woke up when you called me. He'd climbed in bed next to me. Nothing happened, Eddie. I'd have killed him if he tried." She looked at me. "Thanks for the trust."

I felt like crap. It was exactly as Kari had said. I still wasn't ready to surrender, however. "I don't get it, Mina. Why did you just leave without talking to me? Why have you been pretty much running away from me since we got here?"

Mina stood, walked over to her sister, and pulled her up. They embraced there, upset with each other, in the middle of the floor. They were both in tears and locked in the tightest clinch I'd ever seen. "This is my best friend, Eddie. She's my other half, the better half in fact. When I met you, I knew right away I wanted you to be mine. But then I saw you with my family…my mom."

"I thought your family and I got along great."

"You did, baby, you did. But that's the problem." Her voice became a harsh choke. She stopped talking and starting crying again.

Kari began speaking, as if Mina had somehow transferred her thoughts to Kari's brain. I'd seen them do it before, but it still freaked me out. "You're just like Daddy, Eddie. I'm a lot like my mom. Mina saw you with Mom and how she responded to you and she started thinking you'd be able to…" She looked in Mina's eyes and began brushing the hair from her face. "She thought…she thought maybe you'd be able to fix me." Kari looked at me. "And you did."

Mina gave her sister a sweet little kiss on the lips.

"Fix you how? You seemed fine when I met you, the same as now."

Kari released her sister's embrace and sat on the sofa with her knees drawn up to her chest. She said nothing, just sat there, rocking slowly back and forth. Mina watched her for a time. She looked at me, seeing the confusion written all over my face. "Stay here," she said. She turned and began heading toward the townhouse's front door.

"Wait, Mina," I said. "Don't go."

She stopped and turned back. "I'll be right back, I promise. You need to see something."

Kari's eyes widened and she jumped off the sofa, running to her sister. "No, Mina! You promised. No!" Her entreaties were almost painful to watch.

Mina was as gentle as I'd ever seen her. She held her sister by both cheeks and placed her forehead to Kari's. "Trust me, baby. He loves you. It'll be alright."

Kari sulked, looking as if she would cry. Then she turned and sat on the sofa, both feet up with her back to us. She said not another word.

"Stay here," Mina said again. She left, heading toward the street. I peeked out the window after her and, instead of exiting, she turned down the steps to the basement level. She opened the door and entered, closing it behind her. Mina was gone at least ten minutes, so I sat on the sofa next to Kari. She wouldn't look at me or respond. When Mina returned she was carrying an armload of paintings and a box of small sculptures.

"What are those?" I asked.

"Kari's work from the last eighteen months, since the accident."

I walked over to them and looked. They were amazing pieces, all, but clearly the work of a tortured soul. I knew Kari painted, but she told me she only used paintings as ideas for future sculptures. These painful works had no business suffocating in a dark, dank basement. Most were rendered in shades of gray, with occasional splotches of blood red that she splattered like an elfin Jackson Pollack had danced across the canvasses. There were multiple scenes of carnage: traffic accidents, mutilations, murders. Children died in most of them, in horrible ways. And, in the background, there stood Kari watching, always with her face strewn with tears. In the worst of them Fadil stood in the foreground, holding Jeremy's severed head in one hand and Kari's crying head in the other. I turned away. Mina wouldn't let me stop, however. She handed me the box. In it were four statues, all of Kari, all nude, all committing suicide. She'd been killing herself almost up until the time I met her.

"Now, here's one she probably didn't want you to see, the one she painted three days after you showed up. I wasn't supposed to know about this one, but I woke up early one morning and saw her painting it."

I heard Kari's soft crying on the sofa. Mina handed me the painting; it was small, no more than the size of notebook paper. It was a masterful portrait of Kari and Mina. They were standing, arms around each other's shoulders, smiling. In front of them sat Nona and a long-haired boy who looked just like Kari—Jeremy. In the background stood not a crying Kari, but me. I had wings, as if I were an angel. In the margin of the canvas, Kari had signed and dated the work, with the title *Hope Returns* in bold red letters.

"You're her guardian angel," Mina said.

I turned to Kari. My heart hurt. "Is this why you've acted so close to me, because you think I can find Jeremy?"

Kari turned to me, her face rippled with pain.

"Don't be an ass, Eddie," Mina said. "You're her angel because she loves you, not the other way around." She placed a hand on my chest. "There was a big hole here, and you're the guy who fixed it. I knew this would happen…didn't want it to happen, but knew it had to." She backed away as I reached for her. "So now we can all be broken together." She picked up her bag and headed upstairs.

"So now I guess you think I'm a crazy woman, right?" Kari asked.

"No. Who the hell knows what's normal? It's not normal to have to bury your child."

"I didn't get to bury him. They cremated him, remember?" She walked over to get her phone. "I'm going to tell the girls we'll have to make it another night."

"No, don't," I said. It wasn't just because I needed to connect with Deb, although that was reason enough. "Whatever happens from this point on, let's try to face it as a team. No more lies, no more secrets, no more pretense. Okay?"

Kari nodded. "Okay by me, but how are you going to convince Mina?"

"By telling her the truth. I can't do this without her."

Kari started crying once again. This time, I went to her and held her. "What's wrong?"

"I can't ever marry you, Eddie. She acts tough, but Mina's the soft one. I was terrified for her when she joined the Marines, but somehow she made it, and when I fell apart she was my strength. If we got married and broke her heart, she'd never let herself trust anyone again."

"Do you want to marry me?" It was an unfair question, but I didn't take it back.

"It's too soon to say so, but yes. More than anything."

"Then let's focus on one thing at a time, like making your last painting come true."

Kari looked up at me with a trace of hope returning to her eyes. "I'll try," she said.

For now, that would have to do.

Our dinner party was doomed to be far more dinner than party, given Mina and Kari's sullen moods. For my part I spent most of the time playing with my dog and avoiding the girls' harsh stares. For the first hour Deb had been a no-show, and I was beginning to worry. After the food was served and she still hadn't shown, I grabbed my phone and headed toward the door. I wasn't sure where in Greater New York I'd thought I'd find her, but I got didn't have to. I opened the front door and there she was, standing with Gaither, whom I hadn't invited.

Deb, as I mentioned, is a beauty and just his type, though I couldn't for the life of me figure out how they'd met. I'd mentioned his name in passing during my calls to her, but that was it.

"Hey Mr. D. You know Rod," she said, breezing by and looking at me as if I were Wile E. Coyote and she was the Roadrunner. I didn't mind, since that pretty much defined our working relationship anyway.

"Oh, I know him all right," I said. Gaither gave me a look as he passed that made me want to punch him in his grin.

"I called and invited him. I thought you'd rather have one briefing than have to travel all the way to Manhattan for a second one with him." Always efficient, that Deb.

Deb is five foot eight and looks like she just stepped out of a Dallas Cowboys Cheerleaders practice instead of Sunday school, which is where you'd more likely find her during football season. She was dressed as per normal for her: tan figure-hugging jeans that met her just at the roundness of her hips; a white, strapless, above-the-navel top that showed off her tanned skin and her Marilyn-Monrovian hourglass figure; bleached blond hair that fell below her shoulders and featured a streak of black locks that looked as if they'd been placed for contrast; a very visible jewel-encrusted drop-charm belly piercing that dangled to her belt line; and a crucifix that planted Jesus's feet just above the rocky crevice of her magical breasts. Plus she was barefoot and holding her flip flops, which were the only shoes I'd ever seen her wear.

She strode into Kari's living room, all twenty-one-and-a-half years of her, and immediately took over the room. She didn't actually do anything to make that happen – when Deb Tuohy entered a room, it just seemed to happen by itself.

"Why's everybody so glum?" she asked. She walked up to Mina, reading the room's hierarchy perfectly, and gave her a hug. Mina's hands hung at her sides. "You must be Mina. I'm Deb, Mr.

D's assistant." She kissed her on the cheek. I heard her whisper, "Don't worry, he's always a perfect gentleman with me. He's said such great things about you."

Mina glanced at me. She hugged Deb back, kissed her on the cheek, and immediately brightened.

Kari was next and, although I have no idea what Deb whispered to her, the introduction was followed by Kari's walking over to me and taking my hand. Mina looked at us, turned away, and started chatting to Gaither. After that the mood in the place improved enough that I could rightly call what we had a dinner party instead of the wake it felt doomed to be. It was enough to convince me I'd made the right decision regarding Deb.

I pulled her and Gaither aside and had her tell me what she'd learned.

"Okay, from what I've figured out this Henry Reilly is a piece of work. He has a circle of friends, none of whom seem to actually like him very much. It felt like they couldn't wait to talk to me about him."

"I wonder why," Gaither said.

"Were you dressed like that?" I asked.

"Yes." She gave me a smile.

"Oh, then you know why," Gaither said.

Deb smiled harder. "I don't know what you mean. I'm a good Christian girl."

"I bet you are," he said.

I looked at him. "If you're through flirting with my partner, I'd like to get her report."

"Sorry, Mr. D. Well, Henry ... wait, what? Partner?"

"Deb, could you please focus? We don't have all night to talk about your promotion." I was messing with her but, since getting her flustered was a rare happening, I meant to enjoy it.

"But ..."

"No buts. You've been keeping us afloat for the last year. It's time I did the right thing."

"Jeez," Gaither said, "sounds like you're marrying her."

"I am, in a way." I aimed a finger at Deb's nose. "But you have to finish your degree before we make the partnership official."

"I will!" Deb did a little jump that bounced Gaither's eyes almost out of their sockets.

"Deb's majoring in Criminal Justice," I told him as a means to get his focus off my partner's boobs.

"Um, er...oh, hey, that's great," he said. "You know, I can probably get you an internship."

"I bet you can," I said. "Find your own partner." I turned to Deb. "Let's hear what you got."

"Well, Henry apparently met your subject, Fadil, back in college. The two were roommates. Folks suspected they were lovers, but no one knew for sure. Fadil always had a girlfriend and Henry was a bookworm no one ever saw with a girl or a guy."

"Maybe a spurned lover," Gaither said.

"Maybe. Anyway, they used to hang out all the time until graduation. Then everything changed."

"What happened?" I asked.

"Apparently Fadil's family happened. Henry's friends think his uncle put pressure on Fadil to drop his friendship with Henry. They thought he was too...I guess, feminine."

"How'd Henry take that?" Gaither asked.

"Pretty hard. He kind of closed up in his shell. Got a teaching gig at Columbia and has lived within walking distance ever since. Other than official functions no one ever saw him around. Until a few years ago."

"When Fadil came back in the picture," I said.

"Exactly. Suddenly they were friends again. Henry's people thought maybe they had become lovers again, but then Henry showed up a university function with Chas as his date. Everyone was shocked—not that he was gay, but that he was finally out. Since then Henry has actually been socializing. Not well though, since most of his friends think he's kind of a boring ..." She dropped her voice to a whisper. "Ass. That's the word they used. They especially hate what he did to Kari. They could tell she didn't know he was gay."

"Kari takes people at their word," I said.

"That's never a good idea," Gaither countered.

"Did anyone say anything about whom Fadil was seeing?" I asked.

"No one knew for sure, but they were sure Henry knew. They said he went on a vacation to the Greek Islands with Chas and they were supposed to meet Fadil there. People suspected he brought his boyfriend, but Henry would get furious whenever anyone suggested Fadil was gay. Even though they were all certain he was."

"Pretty loyal friend," I suggested.

"Or just scared of the uncle," Gaither said. I gave him an inquisitive look. He continued with his report. "Emir Sunay, emigrated from Turkey in 1977 to attend school at NYU. Graduated in 1981 and finished NYU's School of Law in 1984. Specializes in international law with some pretty high-yield clients from Turkey and Saudi Arabia. We think he represents their interests with mostly real estate deals here in the New York area."

"So he does have money," I said.

"He's got enough. Apparently sometime after finishing school he got religion, and now prides himself on living a modest life style. But I've got him pegged at somewhere around fifteen million."

"More like fifty million," Deb said.

"How do you know that?" he asked.

"You don't want to know," she said. Gaither's eyes flashed a look of pure love.

"Anyway," Gaither said, still looking at Deb, "it looks like Emir has begun to step away from running the firm in favor of his two sons …"

"Uday and Qusay," I said. Only Gaither and me got the joke.

"I think one's named Talaz," Deb said, looking sincere. That made us laugh harder.

Gaither continued. "Emir's semi-retired and living out in central New Jersey. I've emailed you the address." The rest of his report was fairly routine, with one major exception. Uncle Emir's strict version of Islam forbade his nephew from having an adulterous relationship with anyone, much less with a man. Homosexuality was right out. That, we decided, was the overarching reason for Fadil's secrecy. "Fadil stood to lose a possible inheritance if he was found out."

"More than that," I countered. "If Emir's clients are as important as you say, there's no way they would allow a lawyer to represent their interests who had a major scandal attached to his name."

"Right," said Gaither. "That makes sense. So what do we have?"

"Two suspects," I said. "Uncle Emir, to protect the family name, for one."

"I got that one, but who's the other?"

"Henry," chimed in Deb. "He had to have been in love with Fadil since college. And he sacrificed his happiness in order to keep his friend's secret. Finally he meets somebody, starts getting out of his shell, and works up the nerve to go public with his sexuality. Even plans a lovely Greek vacation to show off his new man."

I chimed in at that point. "And along comes Fadil, who is supposed to spend the vacation lamenting what he'd given up."

"But instead he shows up with his new boyfriend," Deb finished.

"Had to make Henry wonder: why was he willing to be so public with the new guy and not with him?"

Gaither was nodding. "That makes sense too. Do you want me to talk to Emir? I can send a couple of guys out there."

"No," I said. "I don't want either of these guys thinking the cops are onto them. Let everyone keep thinking we buy Fadil's death as an accident. Besides, it's been a while since I was on the road. I'm starting to get itchy sitting still."

"Now how're you gonna keep up your film noir image if you keep living the Americana lifestyle?" Gaither asked.

"I'm my own genre," I answered.

"Right. Eddie Daley, Back Roads Private Eye."

The party pretty much adjourned after that, except for Gaither's razzing me about being surrounded by women just as everyone was preparing to leave. Until then I thought I'd get out of there with my dignity intact.

"In my experience there are two kinds of men who are as comfortable with women as Eddie here: no-good players and gay dudes."

"Seriously?" asked Tanya. I thought my little girl blue would pop him in the mouth.

"No, I'm just saying. I'm just wondering which type my boy here is."

Mina began waving her hand. "Ooh! I know this one," she said.

Kari, smiling, pulled it back down. "Hush, you."

Lauria and Tanya were both still frowning.

Camara came to my rescue. "We know too," she said. She walked up to me and kissed me, right on the lips. Tongue dancing. Gave me a little squeeze on the butt. "The good kind," she said.

She was followed by Lauria, who kissed me while still frowning at Gaither. Very soft lips. Trailing was Tanya, whom I knew not to try to kiss. She took a step past me, stopped, grabbed my hair, and bent me down backwards. Then she kissed me. Kari and Mina were holding each other and howling with laughter.

"That's how a woman does it," Tanya said when she'd stood me back up.

"I wanna be a lesbian," I gasped. My lips were tingling.

"Yeah you do," she said and followed her wife outside.

Then Deb gave me a smile, winked at Mina and Kari, and kissed me.

"Oh my damn," I managed to breathe out when she'd finished. "Good girls aren't supposed to kiss like that."

"I guess I should stop calling you Mr. D now, huh?" she said. I thought Gaither would melt. She turned to him. "I thought you were a nice man, but you're a little homophobic jerk." She took a step toward the door, then turned back. "For the record, Eddie's a sweetheart." She blew the twins a kiss each and followed her friends back toward their studio townhouse.

Gaither shook his head and walked over to me. "I effed that up pretty good," he said.

"Nah, Deb likes you. She's just teaching you not to be a jerk. I'll talk to her about you."

He nodded. "Thanks. I owe you one."

"I'll probably be calling to collect. Either Henry or Emir have tried to kill me twice. I'm not expecting a bundle of roses when I go talk to them."

My friend gave a discrete glance at the twins who were busy cleaning up and handed me a gun. "It's clean, untraceable. Don't use it unless you absolutely have to." I took it and dropped it in my pocket. "Eddie, be careful. That woman you spoke with, Cynthia Roark? She turned up dead last night. Maryland cops are treating it as a likely homicide."

"How?"

"Home invasion, maybe. A friend found her in bed with a pillow next to her face. Local cops think she was smothered with it."

"Jesus. We went to see her and led whoever this was right to her."

"It's not your fault. I'm sure they already knew about her. Probably they were trying to shut her up, but you got to her before they could." I nodded my understanding, but it didn't make me feel any better. "Do yourself a favor. Don't tell Kari about this." He looked over at her. "I'm guessing she'd never get over the guilt."

"Like I will."

"You're a pro, dude. It's part of the job." He patted my sore shoulder hard enough to make me squeak in pain and walked out.

"That was for letting my future wife kiss you," he said, calling from the stoop.

"Tanya is already married," I said and shut the door in his face.

Never let the FBI have the last word. You'll live to regret it.

Chapter 10

Mina and I visited Henry first thing the next morning. Given my new insight to Kari's delicate emotional state, I decided I'd rather have her at the studio working than dredging up bad memories with me. I wanted Mina around for two reasons: one, my shoulder was healing nicely and I no longer wore the sling, but I still needed someone around who could watch my back. Gaither was out, since he couldn't act in an official capacity without probable cause. That left Mina, who was a strong second choice. To be honest, she'd have been my first choice anyway. The second reason I wanted her around is that I hadn't spent much time with her. I needed to understand how I really felt about her; I missed the crazy little fireball.

It seemed that other than Camara and the Good Crows themselves, I was about the only person who could easily tell Mina and Kari apart. I was betting that applied to Henry as well. We were outside his townhouse at seven in the morning when Mina went to work.

"Watch this," she said. To my astonishment she shut her eyes, breathed deeply a few times, and then reopened them. The tears came immediately. She punched the cell phone and I heard, "Henry! Ohmigod! You have to let me in. He … he's gone crazy. I told him you and I broke up, but he won't believe me." She genuinely sounded upset. There was a pause while she listened, winking at me. Then, "Yes. Yes, I can talk him out of bothering you, but you have to give me something to prove you and I don't love each other anymore. Yes. Yes. I'm right downstairs." She hung up and wiped her eyes. "It's a gift," she said.

"Have you ever done that with me?"

"No," she answered, in a sullen tone. "You always make me cry for real."

Shit.

The door flung open and Henry poked his head out. Mina punched him square in the face, knocking him unconscious. "That's for playing with my sister's head, you lying sonofabitch!" She reached in her pocket and pulled out a pistol.

"Jesus, Mina, put that away." I looked around, pushed her gun hand back in her pocket, and stepped inside. She helped me pull Henry inside and we prepped him for questioning.

"How the hell did you get that thing on the airline anyway?" I asked.

"Didn't take an airline." She was fiddling around in Henry's refrigerator. "Ah, here we go." She pulled out a pitcher of ice water and walked over to where I was sitting, opposite Henry, whom we'd sat in another chair.

"Then how did you get here?" I asked.

"Flying lessons."

"All the way from South Dakota?"

She shrugged. "It's not like I won't get him the thing back. Helicopters take a lot of maintenance. I promised him a full overhaul for the flight here."

"The FAA will take your license."

"Don't have one yet."

"I'm sure that's not legal," I muttered.

"You're such a baby." She dumped the full pitcher of water over Henry's head, managing to douse me as well.

"Holy shitty fuck!" Henry gasped. He almost fell off the chair.

"Seriously?" Mina asked.

"What the hell is wrong with you, Kari?" He leaned in and his face blanched. "Oh God, Mary."

"Yeah, it's Mary, you asshole." She took another swing, but this time I managed to catch her arm and pull her away.

"Henry, I have a few questions for you and I'd advise you to give me honest answers this time or I swear to God I will step outside and let her finish with you."

Mina stopped struggling and looked at me. "You mean it? You

will? Honest?" She had the most beatific, completely insane smile I've ever seen. It was all I could do to keep a straight face.

"Ke-keep her away from me. I told Kari her sister needed help."

Mina swung at him again. This time I didn't hold her back, and she connected with the side of his face, knocking him and the chair to the ground. I leaned over him and lifted him up by the hair. He didn't like it. "Okay, I'm gonna make this simple for you. Somebody tried to kill Kari and me twice. I don't like it when people try to kill me, so I usually kill them first. Therefore you are going to do everything you can to convince me it wasn't you, starting by telling me the truth." Henry was making pained faces and holding onto my hand with both of his. I released his hair. "And if you tell me just one more lie, just one, I will shoot you."

Henry, to his credit, had gotten a wave of courage likely fueled by anger. "You're bluffing. There's no way you're coming in here and committing murder. You get the hell out of here right now, and maybe I won't call the cops when you leave."

"I didn't say you would die, Henry. I only said I would shoot you." I looked at him, allowing my eyes to scan him. I made a point of not showing him a weapon. "Which parts do you use the least? Maybe I'll start with those."

"Cock," said Mina, pointing. "His cock. He never uses that." I turned and gave her a hard look. "What? You asked."

"It was a rhetorical question, Mina. I think we all understood what I was insinuating."

"Well, I think you should be clearer."

Henry got a little too brave, stood, and charged me. I turned my torso, grabbed the back of his neck as he flashed by, and torqued him, slamming his face into the wall. It left a Henry's-face-sized dent in the wallpaper. Henry slumped to the floor.

"He's gonna get a concussion if he doesn't stop doing that," Mina said. I saw no irony on her face at all. "That was a pretty tight move. What the heck did you do in the Army, anyway?"

"My last gig? Rangers."

She stopped looking at Henry and stared at me, gap mouthed. "You were an Army Ranger?"

"No, I trained Rangers. Gaither worked for me."

A brief silence ensued. "And before that?"

"Classified."

"Hmm. So, you used to be a badass."

"Still am."

She said nothing for fifteen seconds. Then, "I am so turned on right now. Are you turned on? I'm really turned on."

"Babe, focus."

"Henry, right."

I turned to Henry.

"Sex later though, okay?" she asked. Her nostrils were flaring.

Just then Henry groaned and rolled over onto his back. A huge knot was forming on his forehead. I knelt over him and he jumped, looking fearful. "Henry, honest to God, if you had nothing to do with this, I don't want to hurt you. Just tell me the truth."

"Okay. Just ask your damned questions and go." His voice was caught midway between angry defiance and a whimper.

I helped him sit up. "One, who was Fadil's boyfriend? I need a name. The Georgetown house came up empty."

"How'd you know about that? Chas? I told him to stop talking to you."

"Uh uh, Cindi," I answered.

Henry looked surprised. He didn't know we'd spoken to Cindi. That led me to believe he couldn't have been behind the attack in D.C. unless he was a pretty good actor. Then again, he'd fooled Kari for over a year.

"Henry was seeing David … David Hinton."

"David Hinton. Where have I heard that name before? Mina asked.

Henry was rubbing his face and scowling at her. "Do you mind getting me some ice? My jaw is starting to swell."

"Big baby. You broke two of my nails with your hard head. You don't see me bitching." She returned to the kitchen for some ice.

"Who is this David?" I asked.

"He's a former colleague of Kari's and Fadil's from when we were at Columbia. I believe David introduced them, in fact."

"That's where I've heard the name," Mina called from the kitchen. "Kari likes him."

"Of course, David wouldn't have known Fadil was gay then," I suggested.

"No, Fadil was most insistent that no one ever reveal his … indiscretions, he called them. But after a time, his attraction to David became apparent. They started seeing each other shortly after Fadil married, from what I understand."

I sat down opposite him again. "Is that why you didn't come out for so long? To protect Fadil's secret?"

He looked away. "Love can make one do foolish things." He looked back. "Or it can make you brave. It depends entirely on what type of love it is."

I caught his drift. "Chas seems genuinely happy."

Henry gave a weak smile.

Mina handed him a towel with ice in it. "Sorry for slugging you. I think I had some misplaced anger there." She gave me a pointed look.

"Henry, we believe Fadil was murdered. I'm guessing you think so too. Whoever is behind it has already killed an innocent woman and they could come after anyone who helps us. We need to know who would want Fadil dead."

"Other than his wife?" Mina's face turned angry. Henry raised a hand in front of his face. "She's earned the right to hate him, don't you think?"

"Yeah, she has. But she's not capable of that," Mina said.

"So have you," I told Henry.

"I suppose I have. But Chas has helped with that. Well, being able to admit I'm gay has helped. I don't know why I let Fadil convince me I should hide myself in the first place."

"That was Fadil's idea?" I asked. That never occurred to me.

"Yes. We had a brief…fling, when we were roommates. He said if I ever came out, people would know he'd slept with me."

"He was a pretty self-serving asshole," Mina said. Henry agreed.

"Who do you think killed Fadil?" I asked Henry.

"Try his uncle, Emir Sunay."

"We've heard of him. But what's his angle?" I thought I knew, but wanted confirmation.

"He's not ostentatious about it, but Emir adheres to a very strict form of Islam. He believes adultery is a sin, drinking is bad, etc. He wasn't initially happy that Fadil married a non-believer, but she seemed like a good, conservative wife, so he gave Fadil his blessing. But homosexuality? He'd never okay that."

"Enough to kill over?" I asked.

"Enough that Fadil spent his entire adult life pretending to be something he wasn't just to keep his uncle from finding out. Now, I'm guessing it's Emir who's trying to keep anyone from finding out."

"And I'm stirring the pot," I said.

"It's apparently what you're best at."

Mina and I let that be the last word and headed out to Queens, where Henry told us we would find David. Henry revealed David had retreated to his parent's home to recover from what he referred to as his "period of mourning." Eighteen months later, he was still there. Mina made such a face when Henry told us that I made her give me the gun. She made for an awesome Bad Cop." The problem was that she wasn't faking it.

"Mina, there's nothing wrong with mourning someone you love," I said, just after boarding the bus at 125th Street heading to Astoria, Queens.

"There is when that someone is married." She cut her eyes at me. "I guess some people don't believe in the sanctity of marriage."

That pissed me off. "If you and I were married I would never cheat on you, ever. But I still might have left if you spent the evening at an ex-boyfriend's without telling me first."

She got quiet. "I screwed up, huh?"

"Little bit. Why'd you do it?"

"I don't know, babe. I guess because I know you're happier with her than you are with me." I opened my mouth to protest but she just plugged in her ear buds, drowning me out. "Like the man said, love makes you do stupid things," she added.

I turned forward, listening to the dieseling of the bus's engine and wishing I could choke to death on its fetid exhaust.

We finished our long ride with the questions I had for David running through my head. I wasn't even sure how I should feel about him. On one hand he'd cheated with Kari's husband, but in a way, he was doing her a service. What if this had happened when she was fifty and most of her life was behind her? Mina, by contrast, saw things in black and white. He was a cheater, and in her book cheaters should never prosper. I wondered if that applied to me as well.

We approached the nondescript little single-family house that David's parents owned and spotted him right away, mowing the small front yard with an ancient-looking hand-powered mower. Mina stopped where we were, fifty yards away and across the street, and watched him. After a short while, she said, "He doesn't look like a monster."

"No, he looks pretty normal."

"By the way, I felt stupid riding to do big-time detective work on the M60 bus. We should have taken a cab. You'd never see Sam Spade or Nick Charles on the bus."

"The last time I got in a cab, somebody tried to kill me."

"Well then, you should have rented a car."

"This is my first trip to New York. I don't want to spend my time being lost."

"It's my twentieth trip. I could have driven us."

"I didn't think of it."

"You would have if Kari had suggested it."

"Kari would have suggested it. You didn't. You waited until after and then yelled at me about it."

"I'm not yelling."

"Feels like yelling."

All the while we never took our eyes off David, who was working hard, pausing only to wipe his brow on the sleeve of his white shirt. The house was small, covered in white siding and barely shaded by a green-covered stick that was fooling itself into believing it was a tree. I'd used bigger sticks to pick my teeth. The air was filled with the peppery scent of freshly cut grass mixed with garbage from a bin left too long at the curb. It was an older neighborhood, lacking the sounds of children, but painted by some fervent dog's barking. "This city kind of blows," I said.

"Oh please. You love it here.'"

I looked at her. "Why on earth would you think that?"

"Because you want to marry my sister, and this is where she lives." She started across the street towards the house. I started after. "Wait here," she said.

"Mina…"

"She stopped, her hands on her hips. "Do you trust me or not?"

"Completely. I was going to say good luck."

She smiled and turned, heading back across the street. When she reached David, he stopped and clasped both hands to his mouth. He took a few tentative steps closer to her. A look of surprise crossed his face and he extended his hand to her. To my surprise, she used it to pull him into a hug. He stood there, shuddering, crying in her arms. I couldn't see her face, but I imagined she must have shown him the side of her she normally hid from me or he wouldn't have opened up so readily.

Mina led him to the front steps and sat with him. She waved me over. "This is my partner and Kari's boyfriend, Eddie Daley." The label made me frown at her. She started frowning at my frown. That, of course, made me frown harder. Fortunately, David was busy pulling himself together and didn't notice. He took my hand and shook it. "David Hinton," he said, sitting back down.

He was a decent-enough looking guy in his mid-thirties, blond, with a trim, rectangular build. He looked like the type who'd cut the grass by hand for the exercise.

"I was telling Mina how sorry I am for what happened. I felt so bad that Fadil…before he was able to give Kari her divorce. It must have made things that much more complicated for her."

I gave Mina a look. She returned one I interpreted to mean I should allow David to lead the talk. I did. "Did Fadil tell you when he expected the divorce to be final?" I asked.

"Oh, he wasn't sure. The one-year period for the Separation Agreement had passed, but he said he and Kari were still working through custody arrangements and the like." He sniffled and flicked hair from his forehead. "It was so much more complicated with the distance. People always assume you can just take the kids for the summer, but summers can be more complicated than the rest of the year."

"Tell me about it," Mina said. "Mom seems to think I've turned over custody of Nona to her."

David laughed. "Fadil said Kari would have the same worry."

I looked at Mina and she gave me a wink. She was a clever girl, that Mina.

"Have you been staying here long, David?" I knew the answer, but again, often one answer can get them talking enough to give you information you didn't know to ask.

"Oh, since Fadil…" I noted that was the second time he couldn't say the word "died." He flicked hair from his forehead again, which I recognized was what I call a grief gesture. He was unconsciously signaling emotional distress: quite an important tell. "I used to teach at Columbia in the International Development department, then Georgetown offered me a tenured position and I jumped at the chance. Luckily, they've been very understanding." He looked me directly in the eyes and I was surprised to find not weakness, but strength in his gaze. "It's not the city or the job I'm avoiding. It's not even Fadil's…death. It's the fact that we were so close to finally having it all. He came to New York to finalize the separation agreement so that the divorce could be finalized, but he died on the way back home. We were going to be married right away, in Maryland." He blinked back tears, better than I would have managed under the circumstances. "I just can't bear to live in that house again." He inhaled and stood. "So I'm here. But I've been here too long." He turned and looked at us. "It's time to go back home, to D.C. Maybe Kari will want the house in Georgetown."

"So Fadil did own it?" I asked.

He nodded. "I wanted to rent a smaller place, but you know Fadil, always needed status symbols."

Mina nodded. "He was kind of traditional," she said.

"He was an anachronism," David said. His lip curled just slightly and briefly. It was a contempt tell. I pounced on it.

"Must have frustrated you at times. The world is changing quickly."

"Yes! Ohmigod, yes." He thrust his hands forward, his fingers extended, and sat on a lower step facing us. He was subconsciously placing us in a position of authority. We were counseling him now, not interviewing. I liked the guy. He looked at Mina. "You look so much like Kari." He laughed. "That was a pretty dumb statement. You're twins. I meant, you're both so lovely." She beamed a smile back at him. "Did she tell you I introduced them?" Mina nodded. "Know why?"

"No, I was wondering," she said, quietly.

"I've been *out* since I was out of the womb. Yet Fadil was so far in the closet I had zero idea he was gay when we met. He just seemed like this handsome, dark-haired guy who needed a good woman. I thought Kari would be perfect."

"So you ended up introducing the man of your dreams to her," she said.

"Yes, and almost ruined Kari's life in the process."

Mina's face flashed anger and she looked at me. I mouthed "Go for it."

She did. "Then dammit David, how could you sleep with Fadil if you cared about her so much?"

"I'm an ass. I was stupid." He sniffled. "We met up again when I did some consulting for the Turkish government. I was so surprised when he started flirting. Then the flirting got serious. We began to meet, but only in secret. He told me he was being...*discrete*—his word—because of his position and to keep his uncle appeased. He even told me Kari knew he was gay but went along because all she really wanted was comfort." He touched Mina's arm and her face softened. "I should have known better. Heck, I'm sure I did. But I was so in love, Mina. I'm sorry. By the time I figured out for certain she didn't know about him we'd already been together for a year. And...and this is terrible, but I knew she'd be better off without him. I mean, can you imagine being married to a man who's secretly in love with someone else?"

Mina looked right into my eyes. "Yes. That would suck."

This was a great time to change the subject. "You mentioned his uncle. Did Fadil ever indicate he was afraid of his uncle finding out about the two of you?"

"Afraid? No. Fadil had told Emir, finally, he was gay. It was at my insistence, of course. I told him I'd never lived in a closet and I wasn't about to start living in one now."

"Good for you," Mina said, and touched his shoulder.

David smiled at her and blushed. She was charming his pants off. Rather, she was charming his mouth open. "Well, he finally worked up his nerve and told his uncle. He claimed that Emir told him he'd always known and had appreciated his discretion."

"That word again," she said, shaking her head.

"I wanted to throttle him every time he used it."

"Kind of like when you use the f-word, Mina," I added.

"Shut it. Go on, David."

"Emir fully supported our relationship, even though we were doomed to burn in whatever Islam says is the fiery pit of hell. Good thing I'm agnostic or I'd never be able to sleep at night." That made me snicker and Mina offer a gesture of support. "Anyway, according to Fadil, it was Emir's advice to 'wean' Kari of the idea of being married. He said she deserved to be told and to have time to make a dignified transition, instead of just being abandoned."

"So Emir knew Fadil was gay and understood he'd not told his wife," I said.

"Exactly. That's why he followed me to D.C. and told her not to come."

"Told her not to come?" I asked.

"Right. That's when he finally told her about us. After a few months he said she'd agreed they would eventually divorce and had even found a boyfriend. But *eventually* turned into months and then a year had passed. All that fighting over assets. You know the rest."

Mina and I never corrected any of David's false impressions. If he was going to find out the truth, it wouldn't be from me. We thanked him for his cooperation and headed toward the subway, figuring it would be easier to find a cab there. We could have called from David's parent's place, but I wanted some walking time to put the pieces together.

David fully believed that not only was Fadil finally out in the open, but that even Kari knew about it. That part was obviously a lie. However, Fadil told him that Uncle Emir knew he was gay too. I still needed to understand if that was true. In any case, from David's demeanor and speech patterns, I received no signals that he thought Emir was a threat at all. In fact, it was clear that it had never occurred to David that Fadil suffered anything other than a tragic accident.

I was beginning to wonder again if he had.

"You know, I never played you," I told Mina, as we rode in the taxi to lower Manhattan.

"I never said you did. I sort of played myself. But still ..." She punched me in my bad shoulder. I almost passed out, it hurt so much. "Oh my god, Eddie, I'm sorry. I forgot." She was fawning over me, not that it helped the pain.

"Yeah, I bet."

"How come you never trust me?" she asked.

"I do trust you."

"When I called myself your partner, you frowned at me. Deb gets to be your partner, but not Mina, no. Never crazy old Mina."

"I was frowning because you called me Kari's boyfriend."

"You are her boyfriend. You picked her."

"You and I haven't talked about it. She and I haven't talked about it."

"You can be such a girl," she said. She gave me an intense frown that I returned. "Tall, handsome, hard-bodied, and sexy with gun-metal gray eyes, but a girl."

"I'm not so tall." I was trying to be clever. She didn't get my jokes any more than Apache did.

"You're like, six feet. That's tall."

I gave up on the joke. "No, my brother's tall. He's six four and a half. I'm…normal."

She stared at me. "You have a brother?"

"Yeah." Her surprise surprised me.

"Wow. You are full of revelations today." She leaned toward me, allowing her lips to brush mine. She dragged them along my cheek to my ear, lingering there, breathing warm air into my ear canal. Then she whispered, "Fucker."

"You are such a jerk."

"You love it."

I wanted a subject change. "Haleh is the last one I want to see before we talk to Emir. We can't even nail down motive, much less means and timing. If it's neither of those two, we're in trouble."

"Eddie, how long can you really afford to spend on this case? It's not like we're paying you."

"I'm okay for now, thanks to Deb. But much longer and I'll have to go back to work." In truth I could give another week, week and a half tops.

"You can't marry both of us, Eddie."

Shit. "I know that."

"So you're also running out of time to figure out who you're in love with."

"What do you want me to do, Mina?"

"Love us both. Figure it out." She gave me a peck on the cheek. "Stop expecting one of us to freak out if you act on your feelings. We both still love each other way more than we do you." She leaned back and looked me in the eyes. "Your happiness depends on making one of us love you as much as we love each other. That's the best advice I can give you, as your friend."

"So if I kissed Kari, you wouldn't be mad?"

"I wouldn't be happy, but no. I created this mess by throwing you two together and sending you both mixed signals. I just want it straightened out." She poked a finger in my chest. "You've helped Kari heal."

I was dubious. It smelled of girl trap to me. "And if I kissed you, Kari wouldn't push me out of her life before I got my head on straight?"

"Don't know. One way to find out."

I took her up on it. I kissed the hell out of her. It was the first time she'd shut up since she got back to New York.

We reached Lower Manhattan in record time: four kisses and one opened button later. I tipped the driver and we climbed out, right in front of the first genuine New York City skyscraper I'd ever been to. We'd called Haleh's office and learned it was her day off, which was the opportunity I'd been waiting for. Given the new info we'd found I wanted to talk to her in a setting wherein she'd be less inclined to keep a professional demeanor.

The building had a doorman and a security desk that was filled to the brim with exactly one guard. I could outrun him on my knees, but not before he'd hit the alarm that would lock the elevators. There were stairs, but Haleh was on the thirty-second floor and the staircase locked from the outside, where we were. There would be no way of getting by the desk short of pulling the gun out of my pocket. I didn't want to give Haleh notice we were coming, so I had no choice but to unleash Mina. I stayed outside, chatting up the doorman while she went inside. Ten minutes later she opened the door and gestured for me to come inside. The guard was there, still looking stern, but no longer watching us. Mina led me to the elevator and we stepped inside.

"What's the damage?" I asked, assuming she'd resorted to bribery.

"I have a date."

I looked at her. "You gotta be kidding me."

"Nope."

Up ten floors.

"He didn't seem very happy."

"I told him he needed to keep a professional demeanor so no one would think anything improper was happening."

"And he bought that?"

"I can be very persuasive."

"I've noticed."

I received a broad smile. Eleven more floors.

"He'll be calling for me tonight."

I laughed. "I can't wait to see that."

"Well then you better get to Tanya's place. That's the address I gave him."

Ten more floors and then the elevator door opened. "She's going to kill you."

"Nope. I told him my name is Eddy. It's short for Edwina."

"I'm sorry, what?"

"He's gonna knock on her door at ten o'clock and ask for Eddie. She'll probably bring him to you. Tanya's very romantic."

"Now I'm going to kill you."

"Knock on the door, baby."

Baby knocked.

We could hear movement on the other side of the door, but no one answered. The light through the door's pinhole disappeared, then reappeared. I knocked again, this time, louder. "Ms. Asker, I need to speak with you. It's an FBI matter," I added. Gaither owed me a favor; I figured he'd back me up. Otherwise I'd just committed a federal offense.

After another thirty seconds the door opened a crack. All I could see was her dark eyes and hair, which she quickly tucked under her scarf. "How can I help you, Mr. Daley?"

"I have a few follow-up questions I need to ask, Ms. Asker. It will only take a few minutes."

"Can we do this tomorrow at the office? I'm...I'm babysitting for a neighbor today."

"I'm sorry, but it can't wait." She made no movement toward letting me in. "If you'd prefer I can have my colleague, Special Agent Gaither, speak with you." I handed her his card through the door. "He'll be happy to see you in his office at your earliest convenience."

"I can't afford to take off more time from work," she said. She stepped back from the door. "Come in, but please make it fast." I entered and she added, "Please remove your shoes. And do speak quietly. I just got the neighbor's kid to sleep."

I removed my oxfords and Mina slipped in the door behind me. She said not a word. I watched Haleh's face turn from shock to what could only be described as hatred. She caught my gaze and affixed a blank mask over her emotions.

"Come in," she said. "We can speak in the living room."

The place was huge, as Manhattan spaces go. I was no expert on NYC cost of living standards, but I estimated she could just about afford the kitchen on her salary. "This is a very nice place," I said.

"Yes, my fiancé is an investment banker. I'm living here while we finalize the wedding plans. It became too much of a hassle to commute back and forth from Long Island." We sat. "How can I help you?" she asked. Niceties over.

"Ms. Asker, when I spoke to you before you told me that Fadil wanted you to go with him to his new job in Washington. Is that correct?" She flashed Mina with wide eyes as if she'd taken a photo, and then looked back at me. It was a fear tell. Good, she completely bought the idea that I'd brought Kari with me. "Haleh? Is that right?" I reiterated.

Finally, after narrowing her eyes to slits, she answered, "Yes, that's correct."

"That's odd, because I spoke to Ken Satterhorn, Fadil's boss, and he said even though he specifically asked Fadil if he wanted to bring someone on, Fadil said no."

For a split second she looked away from me and then back. I knew the next thing she was about to say would be a lie. "Well, sure. That's because I told him I wasn't interested."

I pulled out my fake notepad and pretended to read. I really needed to start taking actual notes. "Let's see: according to Mr. Satterhorn, *Haleh was basically just a secretary*. That was coming from Fadil." I closed the notepad and looked at her. "As far as anyone knew, you were no more important to Fadil than his desk phone. Isn't that so?"

Haleh stood erect. "That is not so! Many times Fadil—Mr. Sunay told me that my work was invaluable. He was quite distressed that I couldn't go, but I had other involvements." She flashed me that damned gaudy diamond again.

Right on cue Mina muttered, "Oh brother," and rolled her eyes.

Haleh's mouth turned to a sneer and she took a step toward her.

"Bitch, I wish you would," Mina said. Her voice was as calm as the sea, as if she'd just said "Yes, I'd like a cup of tea."

Haleh stopped in her tracks and sat back down.

"Let me read you some other comments we've accumulated from Fadil's friends, those who knew him well." I pulled out the notepad again. This time, in Deb's handwriting, there were actual notes. "*Fadil never would have taken that crazy bitch, because she was a pain in his ass.* Oh, here's a good one. *Fadil said the woman couldn't even type a letter correctly.* And, oh, this is priceless. *She was constantly trying to get him in bed. He said she wasn't his type. In fact, he doubted she was anyone's type.*"

"Those are fucking lies!" she shouted. Haleh stood and this time charged me. I didn't move and let Mina push her back onto her chair. I wasn't about to touch a Muslim woman without permission. "Get your damned hands off me," she said, jerking away. "Maybe if you had been a better wife, he wouldn't have constantly been hounding me."

"Whatever, bitch," Mina said, calmly sitting back down.

"In fact, that's the real reason I didn't go. He was obsessed with me, constantly asking me out. I couldn't wait for him to leave so I could have a little peace of mind."

"Is that why you sent him this lovely internet card?" I asked. It was a fake I had Deb create. "My darling Fadil," I began reading.

She charged me again and began a stream of invectives that would have made a sailor blush. I let her grab the paper and she ripped it to shreds with the venom of an oversized Chihuahua. Apparently, we'd guessed right about the cards.

"This is your fault," she said, pointing at Mina. "If you'd been a better wife, maybe he wouldn't have been a fucking queer. If he'd had a real woman—"

"Like you?" To her credit, Mina was smiling. "I think we both know between us who is more likely to have turned him gay." Mina crossed her shapely legs.

"Get out!" Haleh shouted. In the next room I could hear the neighbor's kid start to cry.

"You woke up the baby," Mina said. Knife. Twisted.

"Get out!" she shouted again. "Or Allah help you if you don't."

"Can I use your restroom first?" Mina asked. "I think you made me wet myself with fear."

I stood and started guiding Mina toward our shoes. "Okay, that's enough. We're leaving. I think we've gotten what we need." We slipped on our shoes; I could hear Mina humming to herself.

She stopped just as I opened the door. "You may want to get the kid a bottle. I'm not sure you're equipped to breastfeed." Bigger. Knife.

Haleh picked up what looked to be a very expensive piece of pottery and hurled it at her. Mina ducked and the pot went crashing into the hallway. I gave Haleh my best two-fingered salute and closed the door. At the elevator I said to Mina, "I knew your ability to be completely annoying would come in handy one day."

"That was so much fun. Can we go back and do it again?"

"Nah. I think we can officially pencil her in as a suspect. We still need to rule out Emir though."

"Can we go out to celebrate first?" she asked.

"As long as celebration doesn't require walking. My feet are killing me."

"Too bad. Kari and I are Lakota. We celebrate with dancing."

"Oh, good. For a minute, I was afraid the evening would end well."

Ten floors down.

"What are we celebrating, exactly?"

"The way I see it, that's the bitch who would've been sleeping with Fadil if he were straight."

"Maybe he would have been faithful," I said.

"You obviously never met Fadil. He would have slept with somebody either way. Cheaters always cheat. You're like the first good guy Kari ever fell for."

"Okay, now I feel guilty for making out in the cab."

"Wow, you just give yourself permission to hurt my feelings whenever you want, don't you?" I reached for her shoulder, but she shrugged me off. She turned her back to me, holding her face. We rode down twenty floors in silence.

Mina, I...I didn't mean to make you cry."

"Psyche." She grinned in my face.

"You are a real pain in the ass, you know that?"

"Shut up and kiss me again." I did, but I wasn't sure if I'd reconciled with my girlfriend or if I was cheating on my girlfriend.

The three of us went to a late dinner at a pretty upscale Italian place in Bensonhurst. I knew right away it was swank because they were playing classical music instead of Sinatra like all the Italian places I ate in at home. Kari told me that in New York, Sinatra only went with red sauce places like pizza joints, but I think she may have been pulling my leg. It was a nice crowd, with enough people to make you feel like you're being trendy but not enough to actually be trendy. Mina being Mina had made reservations sometime between when we'd left Queens and reached Manhattan. The place was elegantly appointed, lit by chandeliers and draped in the white tablecloths that always made me afraid to spill my food. I was staring at a mural that covered an entire wall when a round man with smiling eyes and a receding line of white hair approached the table. He'd been working the room when he spotted the girls and made a beeline. They were decked out—Mina in a figure-hugging green dress that stopped just below her scar line and Kari in a short red number with a belt that Tanya had made out of faux diamonds to match her jewelry.

"*Buona sera*, thanks for coming," the man said, taking Kari's hand. "I'm Alphonse and I own the place, unless you don't like the food, in which case my wife owns it. Who might you beautiful ladies be?" He turned, looked at Mina, and said, "Whoa. How the heck did you get over there so fast?"

Kari grinned at his twin joke and Mina did her best to avoid rolling her eyes.

"I'm Kari Good Crow. This is Mina Good Crow. No relation."

Alphonse looked startled for a split second and then laughed in a deep bellow that made me want to loosen my tie and order wine for the room. "Ah, you're pulling the old man's leg." He leaned in to Mina. "Which is as close to sex as I'll get tonight." He pointed to a chubby grey-haired lady instructing two of the wait staff. She did not look happy. "See what I mean?"

To my surprise, instead of her usual muted response Mina broke out in a huge smile.

He looked at me. "So, are you Mr. Stop or Mr. Go tonight?" It took me a moment to figure out what he meant, until he pointed to each of the girls. That was long enough for them to decide I was wavering. Kari shot me a look that indicated she was more worried that his question stressed me than she was at the fact that I didn't know whom I was dating.

Mina didn't hesitate. "That's Eddie," she said. "He's our boyfriend."

I looked at her.

Kari looked at her and grinned. "Right, although it's not looking good for him in the sex department tonight either."

"I dunno," said Mina. "Jury's still out."

Alphonse made a point to stare at me with an exaggerated gaping mouth. Then he stood erect, walked around to my side of the table, and pulled me to my feet. I was laughing at this point, but didn't know what he'd do next. He wrapped me in a huge embrace and gave me a kiss on the cheek. "Paisan! You are my hero." I swear to God he wiped a tear from his eye.

"Uh, Eddie's not Italian," Kari said.

"He is tonight!" replied Alphonse. "Tony!" he called, gesturing to a busboy standing nearby. "Get my friend Eduardo two bottles of our best champagne."

"What's that for?" I asked. My real question was "What's that cost?" but I wasn't going to ask it with the girls both looking so happy.

"My friend," said Alphonse, placing his meaty hand on my shoulder. "You're gonna need it. It's on me." He blew kisses to the girls and walked to the kitchen.

That was followed by the most amazing meal I'd ever had. It made Henry's food taste like peanut butter sandwiches. I nearly ruptured myself on the baked ziti while Kari nibbled around the veal and Mina made the baked oysters look like foreplay as she slid them out of their beds with her tongue. Midway through she caught me staring and really turned on the show. My arousal was heightened by the wine, the music, and Kari's pretty toes, which had taken residence in my chair. She was feeling no pain, but I increasingly was as she continued her teasing.

From there, after thanking Alphonse and his wife, we rolled on to a local club where Mina proved once again she was capable of dancing seemingly without touching the floor. She and Kari were stop-and-go mirror images of each other on the floor, and I was the temporary King of Brooklyn Nightlife despite being a terrible dancer. I had the fortune of being quite certain not a single soul was watching me dance.

The first downer of the night came when a bag of steroids in a cheap suit kept insisting Kari dance with him. "The lady said no," I told him. "Just move along and nobody has to ruin their nice clothes."

"Hey man, I wasn't talking to you. You can focus your ass on Twin Number Two over there. The lady here is with me." He grabbed Kari's shoulder and pulled her to him.

I saw Mina open Kari's purse and signaled for her to stop. She did, but left her hand on it. "Okay, you win," I said, taking a step toward him.

He stood straight, pushed Kari behind him, and stepped toward me, placing his face close enough to mine that I could smell the cheap brandy on his breath. He stopped, opened his jacket, and showed me his twenty two-caliber pea shooter. I'd been shot by bigger. I smiled and snatched it from his belt before he could move a finger, the dumbass. I should have just pulled the trigger and blown his steroid-atrophied balls off. Instead, I stuck the tip in his mouth. I figured he got the metaphor. He stood still, wide eyed, saying nothing. I released the gun's clip, pocketed it, and handed him his empty gun. "Next time," I said, "I let my girlfriend shoot you."

"Let's get out of here," Kari said, taking me by the arm. Mina joined us and we headed out into the warm night air.

"Where'd we park?" Mina asked. She was wobbling despite being so graceful while dancing.

"Up the block," I said. By this time, between the dancing and the surge of adrenaline from our little conflict, I was as sober as a deacon. I wasn't about to take chances with the NYPD in a rental car, especially for a potential DUI charge. "There's one problem," I confessed. "I don't remember what kind of car we rented."

"It was a blue piece-of-shit import," Mina said. "I remember because I hate imports."

"That's not really that helpful, babe," I said.

"How come she gets to be *babe*? I should be *babe*," Kari said.

"No, you're *sweetie*. I'm *babe* because I'm more of a babe than you."

"That's diriculous. We're identical." The two girls were leaning on each other, their foreheads almost touching—not due to conflict, but to Kari's being a total lightweight when it came to liquor. She was drunk from the enormous sum of almost two glasses of champagne.

I smiled and was about to reassure Kari she was every bit as much a babe as her sister when I felt the unmistakable sensation of a stub-nosed pistol at my back.

"Don't say shit," he said, and gave me a quick pat-down. When he came up empty, he said, "Start walking." He indicated the dark street ahead. "That way." Mina and Kari hesitated. "Naw, Christmas tree, you two go first."

"That does it," Mina said, "no more red and green."

"Shut the hell up and move." His head was swiveling from side to side like a lawn sprinkler. I was surprised to see it wasn't the guy from the club. He was alert, though I didn't think him nervous. If I had to guess, and I did at that point, I'd peg him to be a pro. That was not good, especially with my backup Marine in the pretty green dress, drunk. After a block and a half, he jabbed my back with his gun and indicated for us to turn into a dark alley. This was a problem. If you are accosted by a stranger, and he wants to take you from someplace crowded to somewhere quiet, it is invariably to kill you.

"What is it you want?" I asked. I knew the answer.

He said nothing. Instead he pulled me away from the girls and pointed his gun at me. It was a thirty eight-special, snub nose. This wasn't some pissant twenty-two. At this range I was a dead man. "Which one of you is Kari?" he asked. Neither girl moved. Smart. "I asked you a question. If I have to ask again, I shoot this asshole in the head." He raised his gun, pointing just above my nose. I estimated the end of the barrel to be eighteen inches away. He was around four inches shorter than me.

"It's cool, babe," I said. "He's gonna shoot me anyway."

"Shut the fuck up." He cocked the weapon like they do in the movies, although the gun didn't require it. That was good; it was meant to scare me.

He didn't know me at all.

Kari looked at him with hazy-looking eyes. Mina was to her left with her arm around her, holding her up. "I'm Kari. Whashoowant?" she asked.

"I have a message for you. Next time, keep your fucking mouth shut."

That was it: my cue. As he turned his eyes to me, a second before he squeezed the trigger, I ducked, being sure to clear the angle he was aiming at. The pistol fired, the blast loud enough to make my ears hurt. I felt the bullet whiz over my head. My ears buzzed. At the same instant I slammed one fist into the underside of his extended upper arm, which caused it to jerk upward. I continued the motion, stepping forward and grasped his rising forearm, twisted it, and turned the gun toward his startled face. He fired again, the bullet sailing wide of both of us. I leaned my full weight into his arm and squeezed the trigger. At that instant I heard another shot, muffled to my ringing ears.

My bullet took off the top of his head. Mina reached around her sister into Kari's purse, which Kari had opened while pretending to be incoherent. At the moment I took my shot, Mina fired my gun without removing it from the purse, shooting our attacker in the chest. It would have been a kill shot had he not been wearing a Kevlar vest.

Kari looked at me, her face blank, but I suspected from shock, not alcohol. "Are you okay?" I asked her. She nodded, and Mina turned her sister's face away from the dead man.

"You don't need to see this, baby," she said and led her sister out of the alley.

In an instant I had wiped down his gun and reinserted it in his hand. I took his vest, picked up three spent shells and the bullet from the gun Mina fired, and left him in the alley.

"The cops will find nothing but a suicide in the morning," I said. "Let's get the hell out of here."

I took the girls back to Kari's townhouse and we grabbed a few days' worth of clothes, then dropped Apache off at Lauria and Tanya's place. In route I'd called Gaither, who told me to get the twins to a safe place until he could get NYPD to assign someone to watch the house, which could take up to a couple of days. I told him where to find the body.

"I'll get someone to fast-track an investigation and see who we can tie this asshole to," he said. "Plus, I'll need to clean this up with the DA's office."

"Sorry for tampering with the scene," I said, "but I wanted to make sure I got the girls outta there in a hurry. For all I know, he wasn't alone. I didn't want a hundred police cars looking for a shooter in the area."

"No, that's fine, good in fact. Suicides don't get much press in a city this size, so it'll be like it didn't happen for a few days as far as the press is concerned. Let whoever sent him wonder if the deed was done. We'll be watching your suspects to see if anyone gets nervous." He paused. "Who do you like for this, Eddie?"

"With the timing, the obvious choice is the Asker woman. Mina got into her head pretty good pretending to be Kari, and the shooter specifically said his message was for her. That was almost like a confession as far as I'm concerned. Still, I have a feeling there's more to it."

"I'm liking her for this too. The simple answers are usually the right ones," he said. "You just get those women to a hotel somewhere. Make it out in the country."

"I still want to check out Emir," I said.

"Okay, but wait a day or so until we see if he starts acting jittery. I'll be in touch." He paused, then added, "Oh, and Eddie, keep your head down. From what you told me, this was a professional hit. Somebody's been tailing you. This might not be the last attempt."

"We'll be safe," I said. We had to be.

Chapter 11

We took Gaither's advice and found a nice hotel in Jersey about midway between I-95 and the Jersey shore. It was summer and the place was packed, which was what I wanted. If anyone was tailing us, as I'd come to realize they must be, we would get lost in the crowd of tourists and golf enthusiasts. I tried to get a suite, but pragmatic Mina decided it was too pricey. I didn't argue much, as this case was already costing me more than a normal vacation. We ended up in a nice room that had a king size bed and a foldaway sofa bed.

It was after three in the morning when we got settled in. I was tired enough that I would have happily crashed on the sofa bed without even changing my clothes. Unfortunately a quick lights out was out of the question, as night owl Kari was wide awake from the excitement of checking in and fastidious Mina wasn't about to go to bed with a layer of travel funk on her. I lay on the bed, watching them, trying to figure out the dynamic of the room. Sure, the idea of being in a hotel with two gorgeous women was fun, but any guy who'd ever shared a hotel room with even one woman could tell you the reality could be very different. Women were a lesson in logistics, and these two were no exceptions. Forget ideas of a passionate *ménage à trois*; I just wondered if I'd ever get a turn in the bathroom so I could brush my teeth.

Just when I spotted an opening, Kari went into the bathroom, still dressed in the jeans and top she'd traveled in, and shut the door.

With my luck I figured she was pooping and I'd have to brush my teeth while holding my breath. I heard water running in the sink and the usual commotion. Thankfully, there was no flush. Five minutes later the door opened and out she walked, completely naked. I was already standing, ready to make my dash; her nakedness caught me off guard, however, and I froze. I stood gawking, wondering how she'd gotten even sexier, while she fumbled around with her suitcase looking for the God-knows-what that women put on at night.

Mina barely glanced at her, saw my toothbrush in hand, said "My turn," and ran in the bathroom. Just as I blinked myself to alertness, she slammed the bathroom door shut. The sound of the tub filling roared into the room.

"Damn," I said. I now had to pee too.

"What's wrong?" Kari asked. She was squatting by her bag, casually looking over her shoulder.

I wanted to answer *I want to screw you while your sister's bathing*.

I actually answered, "I need to brush my teeth and I have to pee."

Kari stood up and yelled. "Mina! Eddie needs to pee."

Mina opened the door and leaned out, also naked and with a mouthful of toothpaste. "Pee then. Who's stopping you?" she said, not even pausing her brushstrokes.

"I'm waiting for you to leave so I can go."

"I can't believe you're shy around Mina when you guys have already had sex."

"I know, right?" Mina said, spitting in the sink. "He must have forgotten about it."

I ignored her, let her rinse out her brush, and pushed her out so I could do my stuff. Before I'd finished brushing Mina invited herself back into the bathroom. She walked by me, turned off the water in the tub, and stepped in. She'd ringed the tub with candles from her bag. "Perfect," she said. "You coming?"

I could see Kari sitting on the bed, putting up her hair. Even if I was officially Mina's boyfriend, Kari and I had feelings for each other. I wasn't comfortable taking a romantic bath with one woman when I'd recently confessed love for the other. Okay, I'd done that before, more than once, but this time I meant it. Hell, I loved both of them like crazy.

This new warm, fuzzy Eddie was starting to get on my nerves.

"Mina, I don't think bathing together is a good idea."

She was stretched out. Her eyelids were already beginning to droop. "Why? That's why we got the Jacuzzi room. There's plenty of space in the tub."

"What about Kari, Mina? Do you really think it's cool to bathe with Kari here?"

"I'm not invited?" Kari asked. She'd just walked through the bathroom door with her personal soap in hand. "Why am I not invited?" She was pouting at me so hard I felt like kicking my own ass for hurting her feelings.

Mina said, "Of course you are, sweetie. Eddie's just being weird." She held open her arms as if she could hug her from across the room.

Kari closed the door and flipped off the bathroom light, washing the room in candlelight. She walked over to the tub, still frowning, and climbed in. "If you don't want to bathe with us, then poo on you," she said.

They both sat there scowling at me. I never undressed faster in my life. Once they both understood I wanted to be with them, they relaxed. Kari relaxed by bathing me, purportedly as a thank you for saving all of our lives. Mina, the early bird, relaxed by falling dead asleep in the tub next to me. Kari and I enjoyed the bath while taking turns preventing her sister from drowning. When we'd had enough I lifted Mina from the tub, wrapped her in a terrycloth robe, and set her in the big bed. Kari finished drying her off and slipped her under the covers while I pulled on my sleeping shorts and climbed in the sofa bed. No more than a minute later Kari turned off the light and padded over to me.

"That was really romantic," she said, and climbed onto my bed.

"You mean the bath or Mina's snoring?"

"No, silly, I mean this." She patted the sofa bed and pulled back the covers. I felt her skin on mine, still hot from the bath. She was deliciously soft, like warm butter. I felt like playing toast. She said, "It's sweet you want to make love the first time in private."

I looked at her, trying to ensure I really heard what I thought I heard. "You don't feel like we're sneaking behind Mina's back?" I asked. I'd not bothered about conscience too much with women before I met the twins, but now I couldn't turn the fucker off. Damned useless thing, a conscience.

"Nope. Why do you think she nixed separate rooms?"

"Because she's even cheaper than I am."

Kari laughed, sliding herself on top of me. "Because you need to choose."

I kissed her, and a wave began to take me. I surfaced, breaking the kiss, certain that if I didn't I'd soon drown. "Why are you okay with this, baby? After all the shit you've endured, you deserve more than half a relationship."

"Two reasons. First of all, this isn't half a relationship. You're healing me, and you're healing Mina. And we're both healing you."

"What makes you think I need healing?"

"Because you're a single, beautiful, thirty-one-year old man with your own business. You've got no kids, no steady relationship, and your puppy is the first long-term commitment you've made since you left the Army. You've been living with two pretty women for weeks, both of whom have made it obvious that we're in love and would sleep with you anytime. All you had to say is, 'I pick you.' We even stopped saying 'Pick me' and you still couldn't choose." She kissed me again. This time it was more urgent than the first. I wrapped her inside an embrace and held on, waiting to breathe again. She released her kiss. I came up for air.

"How ... how does not sleeping with you two mean I'm broken?"

"Because, baby, you can't pick because you haven't figured out what you want. That's why you've been a player all your life." I started to object, but she shushed me. "You think you're in love with both of us because you don't know if you want excitement or compatibility. Settle down with me or have wild adventures with my impulsive sister? Are you Mr. Stop or Mr. Go? My guess is that you never once thought about marriage until you met us. Before you showed up in Mina's motel, you'd probably decided to die a bachelor. But all that's changing, isn't it?"

"It already has changed. But you're right, I still don't know what I want."

"Sure you do," she said. "You want both of us. The calm life plus bursts of adventure. You want us to stop making you choose." I said nothing. Her words resonated truth. I wanted it all. "So for now, at least until Mina has to leave again, you're married to both of us." She kissed me on the cheek, my ear, my neck. I heard myself groan. "I'm betting you'll figure out that's not really what you wanted."

"It's feeling pretty good so far," I admitted. "What's the second reason you're okay with this? You said there were two."

She started nibbling on my ear. "Oh, that. I haven't had sex in close to two years. I am very, very, very horny." She bent down and, in a single stroke, removed my shorts. "But you're about to fix that too."

Lovemaking with Kari was very different than with her sister…or any woman I'd ever known. There was no lightning, no booms of crashing thunder, no startling storms of passion. It was a breeze blowing over a lonely ocean, gaining strength. I was a ship against the sea unfurling my sails, searching for my way and trying not get dashed upon her rocks. Gradually, however, as the tide turned, as ripples became waves and waves became tsunamis, I found the rhythm of Kari's roiling seas. I was lost there, lost in her riptides, pulled under, joyous to drown. And when I was spent and her tide still churning, with a gasp she met my eye and my startled cry, and her waters finally calmed. We were marooned there together, waiting for the waves to build so we could begin again. I feared I would never find my way to shore again.

Mina woke first, before the first morning light breached our windows and before either Kari or I had awakened. In my arms Kari still slept, her naked body pressed against me. When I opened my eyes Mina was sitting on the king-sized bed, wearing one of my shirts. She couldn't have slept more than a few hours. She was watching us, and when I stirred, she waved. In her hand was a cup of coffee.

Kari felt my movements and turned, groaning in a sleepy, slushy voice, "Mina's not drinking coffee is she?"

"Yes," I said.

Kari blinked at the clock and squinted toward Mina. She rolled over and reached to the floor. "Put these on," she said, handing me my shorts.

She climbed over me, went into the bathroom to relieve herself, and reemerged wearing my shirt from the night before. Her eyes were more closed than open. To my surprise, she climbed on the bed with Mina. Her sister didn't react until Kari took the coffee cup and set it on the night table. Kari kissed her sister's cheek and pulled back the covers. Mina climbed inside without a word. Kari joined her. That felt like my cue. I left the sofa bed and joined the girls in the king bed. Almost without looking they rolled apart and made room for me between them. Kari slid her back against me and began breathing deeply, instantly nearing sleep. Mina rolled herself to face me, placing her leg over mine.

"You two are good together," she whispered. I wondered how long she'd been watching us. She lay there, her eyes closed, lower jaw clenched and body stiff, saying nothing.

"So are we," I said. After a time, when I didn't feel the tension in her body ease, I asked her, "Are you upset?"

"Horny," she said. We lay there another thirty seconds before she asked, "Is it my turn yet?"

From my right side, Kari began laughing. I took that as a yes.

Two days after our little *honeymoon à trois* began we were back on the road to see Emir Sunay. By then I was both exhausted and invigorated. The day began with someone atop me as I slept, with a different someone curled under my arm, asleep. I didn't even open my eyes once the gentle rocking awoke me. I figured this was about her, so I let it be so. We'd hit an odd rhythm, we three. I don't think any of us realized the amount of strain we'd been under until we'd given ourselves a physical release. Once the sexual genie was out of the bottle, it proved impossible to put back in. In two short days the girls had tried to love me to death. I was willing to die for the cause.

The only interruption to our romantic interlude was a phone interview I conducted with the funeral home that handled Fadil's cremation. I had to take the call wandering around the lobby, as I didn't want Kari to hear me. It was interesting, for two major reasons.

First, the funeral home director was very nervous. Now, I could foresee his being stressed before the actual event, given how important interments are to the surviving families. But Fadil had been cremated eighteen months earlier. What the hell did a glorified crypt keeper have to be stressed over? In my experience, people get nervous when they are afraid they might fail or afraid they might get caught. This had to be the latter.

Second, when I did my usual dance—which was to lie my ass off—he broke. The police records that Gaither had shared with me told me Fadil's and Jeremy's bodies had been burned beyond recognition and the coroner's office mistakenly turned them over to the funeral home. This gross error was exacerbated by Sanford and Sons Funeral Home's mistake—and I swear to God it was the place's actual name. They almost immediately cremated the corpses. It was a coincidence. Coincidences piss me off.

I pressed the elder Mr. Sanford for answers. He sadly was not named Fred, but Jim. "Mr. Sanford, my colleagues have already contacted the New York District Attorney's office. We've been informed that, in addition to the hearty civil damages my clients are likely to seek, the DA will be looking at you for conspiracy and accessory after the fact charges. Given these are in conjunction with two first-degree murders, you could be looking at ten to twenty at Rikers." It was all a bluff.

Sanford, as I guessed, folded right away. "I-I wasn't a party to any crime. In fact, I was assured the coroner had already cleared the bodies."

I couldn't see his face, but nothing in his voice led me to believe he was lying. Still, it wasn't enough. "That's all well and good, but Mr. Sunay and his son were cremated without Mrs. Sunay's approval, or even the ability of anyone to verify the identity of the bodies."

"I … we understood the police found Mr. Sunay's finger. It was on that verification that we were able to take possession of the bodies."

"Well, yes, we can officially say you did in fact cremate Fadil Sunay's finger." I let that sit for a moment. "Who authorized the cremation, Mr. Sanford?"

He was quiet at first, and then tried to lie his way out of it. I knew it was a lie, because they take longer to think of than the truth. I wasn't listening to any of it; I was looking at my watch. Right on cue, Sanford got a call on the other line. I encouraged him to take it and told him I'd hold. I already knew who it was. It was Deb, calling under the auspices of the DA's office, asking Mr. Sanford about his availability for an interview. She did give him an alternative, however. He could consent to a phone interview with her consultant, me, and it would obviate his having to come downtown for questioning.

Good old Deb.

When the call was over Sanford came back on line and was very forthcoming. He told me it was a woman claiming to be a family member who signed off on and paid for the cremation. She said it was imperative that the bodies be cremated and their ashes interred as soon as possible after death. After being paid twice his normal fee, he complied. By the time Kari had found the bodies had been transferred to Sanford and Sons, it was too late. I asked him to describe the family member, and he gave me the description of an accented woman in her twenties, dark hair, very skinny. Sounded a lot like Haleh Asker.

I thanked Sanford and broke off the call. Like I said, very interesting.

As we neared the coast Mina sat in the front seat on full alert, with Kari in back working on sketches she'd done of us during our hotel stay. Less than thirty minutes from our objective I got a call from Gaither. I put him on speaker.

"Daley, Gaither. Got some news for you."

"I'm listening," I said. "Mina and Kari are with me."

"Good. This concerns all of you. You remember our friend, Gus Sandersen?"

"The Staff Augmentation Specialist, yeah. Were you able to make a case against him?"

"Is that the guy who hired the two idiots back at mom's house?" Mina asked.

"Yeah," Gaither said. "Anyway, I don't have a case, but I've got something better."

"Okay, I'm intrigued," I said.

"Sandersen came to us. He wants in Witness Protection. Seems the bosses have heard rumors he'd been freelancing and talking to the feds."

"Lovely," I said.

"Yeah, funny things, those rumors. They can start anywhere."

I laughed. "You son of a bitch."

"We do what we can. So, anyway, I made a deal with him. We get the DA to drop all outstanding charges, get him in the Federal Witness Protection Program and, in turn, he gives me the names of local guys who could have brokered the guy who…" He caught himself, probably realizing the girls were listening. "The guy who assaulted you in the alley."

"You mean the guy who tried to execute us," Kari said.

"Uh, yeah," Gaither said. "Anyway, it'll take some time but I'm confident he'll eventually lead us to whoever's behind this."

"Not sure that *eventually* is a timetable I can live with."

"We're working it, Eddie." He cleared his throat, which he only ever did when he was nervous. His being nervous made me nervous. "Well, the DA is happy, because he'll have a ton of names of hired muscle, which puts him one step closer to the bosses." He paused. "Which is lucky, because it got him to drop pending murder charges against you."

Kari and Mina immediately began arguing until I got them calmed.

Gaither continued. "I think he was mainly posturing anyway. He was major league pissed that you tampered with the crime scene. He knew it was a righteous kill, but I do think he'd have hit you with tampering if this hadn't come up."

"Well, thanks for cleaning up my mess," I said. "Now you wanna tell me what's got you so nervous?"

Gaither laughed. "We've been friends too long. It's just Sandersen's early info is leading me to believe somebody's being paid to know where you all are. I think that's how these attempts keep happening. Somebody's gone through a lot of trouble to cover their tracks."

"You mean there's a killer following us around?" Kari asked. The stress in her voice was beginning to return. She set down her tablet.

"No, not a killer, more like a private eye. We theorize either Emir or Asker hired an investigator to watch you. Then, when you were in vulnerable situations, they called in the hit."

"Betrayed by another shamus," I said.

Gaither was quiet for a moment. Then, "What the hell is a shamus?"

"Don't ask him that," Mina said, frowning. "We'll be talking about Bogart again for the next thirty minutes."

"In that case, I'm gonna hang up. You guys just watch your back. If you see anyone suspicious tailing you, don't be heroes. Call me and I'll get the cops on it ASAP."

"Rod," Kari asked, "should we be worried about going in Emir's house?"

"I don't think so. To be honest, I'm liking the Asker woman for this more every day. She's disappeared since your visit. We've even started watching the international airports in case she tries to slip out of the country. Think of this trip just as a nice ride to the coast."

"Your mouth to God's ear," I said, and hung up. Five minutes later I started noticing a tan sedan with New York plates around a quarter mile back. I was almost certain I'd seen that car parked at our hotel. Gaither and I often think alike. After all, I was his teacher once upon a time.

I didn't have much trouble ditching the sedan. I pretty much only needed to drive the way I normally drive back home in the wide open spaces. Once he realized he'd been made he had to decide whether to make it a full-on chase or back off and pick things up later. I was disappointed he chose the latter. Likely he knew where Kari lived, so I was certain we could re-convene there.

We arrived at Emir Sunay's house, which could accurately be called an estate, shortly after noon. My initial reaction was that both Deb's and Gaither's estimates of Emir's wealth were low, by a lot. Deb was extraordinary at her work, so I had little doubt she'd ballparked his official wealth closely. That meant either he had an under-the-table source of income—meaning illegal—or somebody was fronting him some prime real estate. The damage in this part of the state from Hurricane Sandy was devastating. Much of the state was still in recovery mode almost a full year later. However, there were no signs of damage on Emir's property. Either he had outstanding insurance or he had an inside track to God his neighbors didn't have. I suppose that beats insurance any day.

The property was gated and, after I gave my name, we were buzzed in with the twelve-foot iron gate swinging open noiselessly. The house sat on a grassy hill, which was bifurcated by a manmade stream that flowed into small pond, filling the air with the sound of miniature rapids. We followed the multicolored stone driveway up the hill to the house. It was a large custom home, shaped like an elongated U with a two-story central entrance made almost completely of glass. It was mirrored on each side by smaller rooms, each comprising more window than stonework.

"The room on the right is the dining area," Kari said. "The one on the left is mostly open space that Emir uses for prayer. The house faces Mecca, to the extent the landscaping allows."

"How many rooms is this place?" I asked.

"I've never been past the dining room," she said. "I know it's more than six bedrooms, I just don't know how many more. Fadil once told me the master bedroom is bigger than our first floor."

Mina responded, "It's not like your place is for paupers. I couldn't pay one month's mortgage in six months."

"Fadil's insurance paid off the mortgage," she responded. "If it were up to me I'd be in a box somewhere in Prospect Park. I don't know what this place costs, but Fadil once told me our entire mortgage would've made a nice down payment on it."

We were greeted at the door by a large man dressed in a dark business suit. He was in his mid-twenties, around six foot two with close-cropped dark hair and a couple of day's worth of stubble. My eyes were drawn to his large nose, probably to avoid the blank stare in his eyes. Though he was looking directly at us, I got the impression we hadn't registered with his brain. He was flanked by an even larger man with an even bigger nose and a fuller beard. If you had inflated the first guy's head with air, you'd have gotten the second one. He was joined on the other side by a woman who shared his handsome face, minus the beard. She'd probably shaved earlier.

The first guy was packing: I spotted a Sig Sauer P226 on his hip belt, and a familiar bulge at the back of his suit coat I determined to be a sizeable piece of armament. I guessed his wide pants leg hid a little pea shooter, maybe a Sig P290. It was neat and compact, but still could kill you quick. Either we'd been greeted by Security or this was one paranoid motherfucker.

A bit of a surprise, considering I was escorting a former family member.

Mr. Friendly caught me sizing him up. "Mr. Sunay will be with you in a minute," he said. His rapier wit was punctuated by his making actual eye contact for the first time. His mouth said nothing more, but his eyes accused me of raping his grandmother. I didn't even know his grandma. "I'll pat you down now," he said, as if I'd been waiting for that.

I bristled, but raised my hands nonetheless, all polite guest like.

"What's this about?" Kari asked. She was a cool kid. I could see her surprise, but I doubted Friendly could. Her voice was steady, as if she'd spent a lifetime ordering the servants around. "I've been here several times, and no one's ever frisked—" Her words were cut off by the female security buffarilla's beginning her pat-down. I caught the clench of her fists, but she quickly let them go.

Ms. Security reached for Mina, who said in a supremely calm voice, "Touch me and I'm gonna shoot you with his guns." She was pointing to both of Mr. Friendly's supposedly hidden weapons.

Mr. Friendly had finished with me and took a step toward Mina.

"Don't." It was all the warning I was going to give him. He touched the butt of his side arm and gave me a look. I didn't like it. Mina folded her arms. Mr. Friendly was just about to die; he'd likely reach hell as surprised as fuck.

"That is enough, Ozan!" came a voice at the base of a large staircase. The speaker was a wizened gentleman with tired, dark eyes, a salt and pepper beard that had turned mostly to salt, and thick black eyebrows that seemed to punctuate his face. He wore a white cotton garb that draped him from head to foot, covered by a black suit coat. At his words Mr. Friendly, apparently a Turk named Ozan, retreated.

Mina unfolded her arms and I exhaled.

"Emir," Kari said. She managed to squeeze a smile out of her voice and she and the old man embraced.

"Please, come in," he said, gesturing to lead us to the adjacent room.

It was a small room and empty except for Turkish rugs and pillows that covered the floor. On the walls were typical art from the Muslim world, geometric and floral patterns. There was one piece, however, that caught my eye. On the far wall was a painting of what appeared to be a camel trader haggling with two Arabic men. I looked at Kari and could tell she noticed it too. Given our encounter with Ozan, I'd already decided this would be an asymmetrical interview. In short I planned to piss Emir off. I understood security. I lived in that world myself. However, Kari was known to Emir and we were treated as a threat. That made me wonder why.

I caught Kari's eye and nodded toward the painting. She picked up my cue exactly. Our host had seated himself amid a stack of pillows like Jabba the Turk. I expected him to drag out Carrie Fisher any minute and start puffing on a hookah.

"Uncle Emir," Kari said, "is that an original Gérôme?"

Emir turned and considered his painting. He turned back, a look of pride swelling his sagging jowls. "Yes, and I had to pay a pretty penny to get it. Doesn't exactly fit the décor of the room, but I'm planning to make the décor fit the painting. One must start with one's prize possession." He looked at me. "That is the reason for Ozan's exuberance. I neglected to tell him I expected guests, so he went through the normal protocols."

"Must be worth millions," I said.

Emir laughed, although his eyes didn't. I got the feeling he was trying to decide whether to be flattered or insulted. "The price was in the four hundred thousand dollar range I believe. Something in that order."

"It is lovely," I agreed. "Do any of your guests object to the piece?"

His already narrow eyes narrowed further. "No. Why do you ask?"

"Well, when I was in Afghanistan more than a few people told me that the Qur'an expressly forbids depicting the human form as being idolatrous, and not of God."

"Yes, well, it is not a uniformly held viewpoint." I could tell he wanted to move on from the discussion. Behind him, Ozan glared me a warning.

It made me smile.

"Well, that is true," I said. "And again, it is a lovely work and certainly worth the investment."

Emir answered without humor. "Many investments disappoint in the end, but art rarely diminishes." He turned to Kari, attempting to brighten the atmosphere in the room. "That is why I was delighted that Fadil had chosen a talented artist."

She gave a polite smile.

"And her religion wasn't an issue?" I asked.

"Of course at first I had some reservations. After all, some of my clients will only do business with those who are true believers. However, after meeting her, I was certain he had chosen well. Her willingness to raise her children as Muslims sealed my approval."

When I'd planned this interview I had intended to things polite and airy. That was based on my belief that Haleh was behind this case for no other motivation than feminine jealousy. However, I couldn't get my questioning of Jim Sanford out of my head. All my instincts told me the information he provided pointed the way to solving this case. Ozan's belligerence let me know the polite route would lead nowhere. I was running out of time.

"Am I correct in assuming, Mr. Sunay, that your company's business depends on keeping your client base intact?"

He gave me a patronizing laugh. "All businesses depend on that, Mr. Daley."

"In your case, however, it should be easier, since you share similar beliefs."

He gave me a squinty-eyed stare. "Which beliefs are you referring to, exactly?"'

Whoa, there was a plum worth picking. I hadn't intended that to be a provocative statement, yet he'd prickled. "I was referring to Islam, of course. Are there other beliefs you share?"

His smile faded completely and was replaced by an upcurled lip. "Islam is a faith to which I have dedicated my life. Any fortuities I've encountered in business are blessings from Allah." I nodded my understanding, and he continued. "Of course, some clients have other views of...politics...that do not gel with Western sensibilities. However, as you can see, I have embraced the West as well." The broad swipe of his hairy arm indicated the plush surroundings.

"Indeed," I said. "And in any society, commonality of faith is enough to secure ties."

He squinted at me the squintiest of possible squints. I doubted he could even make out my face. "What, precisely, are you getting at, Mr. Daley?"

"Only that what God hath joined together, man can still put asunder."

My misquoting the Bible had the intended effect. Emir didn't blink, but Ozan touched his sidearm. That made me smile too.

"Are we still discussing my firm's private business or my nephew now?" Emir asked.

"As I see it, one thing leads to the next."

"How so?"

"If Fadil's marriage was threatened, and in a way that reflected poorly on the firm, being a family-owned concern it might have made some of your more...conservative, shall we say, clients nervous." Emir frowned, but said nothing. "For instance, if he were found to being having an adulterous affair, all the while using contacts he'd garnered due to being related to you, it could put some of your clients in embarrassing positions."

"And what makes you think he was using my clients as contacts?"

"His boss told me that Fadil had developed high-level contacts that his firm didn't have. I put two and two together. Of course, I can send him a list of some of your clients and ask him if they are the same people."

He stood erect. "My client list is confidential information! You should not—"

"And yet I do have it," I said.

Ozan took a swift step in my direction. It was time to stir the pot to boiling. "Mr. Sunay, I'll have to ask you to leash your bulldog or else my security will have no choice but to shoot him in his ugly face." Mina, whose arms were again folded, unfolded them. When she did, she unsheathed two palm-sized thirty-twos from holsters on her upper arms. The woman was a concealed-carry genius.

Ozan grabbed his holster, but Emir reached back and stopped him. "We'll have no gunplay in my house." He nodded to the female security guard, who pulled out a two-way radio. "Perhaps now it is time to ask you to leave, or perhaps to call the police."

I didn't stand. "As much as I hate cops, I'd welcome their company. Maybe they would be as interested in your client list as I was."

Emir's face went through a litany of expressions before settling on resignation. He sat back down. Ozan returned to his place, never taking his eyes off me. Mina holstered one of her pistols, leaving the other sitting in her lap.

"As I was saying," I began, "I think your clients would be uncomfortable were they linked to business dealings with Fadil and his employer, especially given that the penalty for homosexual relations in some of your clients' homelands is death."

The elder Turk's nostrils flared and he nearly spit out his next words. "My nephew was not a ..." He pursed his lips and turned away.

"Fag? Bunghole jockey? Dick licker? Damned to Hell and spurned by God?"

"That is enough!" shouted Emir.

Ozan charged me and I broke his damned nose with my elbow. He looked stunned for a second before recovering and reaching for his gun. Mina was on him with her gun to his head before he could unholster his.

"Bitch please," she said. "I come from South Da-damn-kota." She took his sidearm and the pistol from his back holster. "Now sit the fuck down. And if you reach anywhere near your ankle, I'll shoot you in your tiny little dick."

I got a slight erection. That was my girl.

Ozan sat on a large pillow pinching his bleeding nose.

I continued after Emir. "No, Mr. Sunay, you are right; he was none of those things, and he deserved none of those labels any more than you do. He was just a normal guy, wanting to please his uncle by fitting into the fucked up little hate-filled world you squeezed him into." I pointed to Kari. "And then he married that sweet woman and broke her heart, all so you wouldn't risk embarrassing your clients."

I looked at him for quite some time, but he wouldn't meet my gaze. David told us Emir accepted their relationship and wanted Fadil to "wean" his wife. Emir's reaction now told me that the old man had done no such thing. It was likely that little Fadil told David was true. A liar always lies, as Mina would have said.

"I'm guessing, Mr. Sunay, that you initially had no idea that Fadil was gay. In fact you probably believed what others did: that he was sleeping with Cindi Roark, with whom he'd been negotiating in Turkey. You had given him the contacts he needed to secure an executive position, and Fadil repaid you by having an affair right under the noses of your clients."

Emir remained silent.

"It wasn't until his accident that you discovered the truth. How'd that happen, exactly? A dying confession?" I looked right at Ozan. "Maybe a little game of waterboarding."

Ozan practically snarled. Mina shook her head and he stayed tame.

Emir exhaled and stood. I stood too. "And now, I really must insist you leave, Mr. Daley. This has become tiresome."

I allowed Emir and his security to escort us to the front door before playing my last card, courtesy of Jim Sanford. "The funeral home that handled Fadil's and Jeremy's cremations told me a family member authorized the work."

"So they said," Emir stated. "However, there is no evidence that is the case. Kari generously discouraged my filing a civil suit on her behalf."

"Yes, that was generous," I said. "It was especially generous since cremation was your idea and Islam expressly forbids it. I find it really difficult to believe a faithful Muslim like Haleh Asker would convince the funeral home to cremate the bodies. Unless, of course, she was being directed to do so by someone who has already shown a willingness to break some of his faith's directives." I turned away and then turned back. "But it really was a lovely painting, wasn't it? Some rules you just have to break."

I saw Ozan tense and Emir hold his arm, shaking his head. No explosion today, Ozzie. Mina handed Emir the guns she'd taken from his security chief. To her credit, she didn't crack a smile. The girls and I left before the old man changed his mind and shot us in the back.

What the hell was that?" Kari asked, as soon as we were in the clear. "I thought you and Gaither decided Haleh was behind this."

"Gaither decided that on his own. I don't think Haleh is smart enough to pull this off alone. My guess is her part in this drama consisted of giving the funeral home director a few thousand dollars to dispose of the bodies before they could be examined. It was probably just as a favor to Emir. I'm thinking that's why she was so uncooperative, to hide her role in this."

"So what exactly do you think Emir did?" Kari asked.

"What if Fadil didn't die right away in the crash? What if someone were following him the way they are us? What if that someone caused the accident and then took him to Emir?"

"I don't believe he would have tried to kill his own nephew, and he surely wouldn't have risked hurting Jeremy. He adored him."

"I don't think he meant for the accident to happen. Besides, you told me Fadil snatched Jeremy on impulse. Emir wouldn't have known he was with his father. Look, all of this isn't clear in my head yet."

Kari got quiet while she digested the information. I heard her sniffle, and she spoke. "Fadil took Jeremy out of spite when I demanded a divorce. Maybe he was finally going to run away with David."

"Emir never would have allowed that," I said.

"Eddie," Mina asked, "if you think Fadil didn't die in the crash, is he alive somewhere?"

"I don't think so." I didn't elaborate. However, I figured if Fadil were alive, Cindi Roark wouldn't have been killed. I looked in the rearview mirror and saw Mina's confusion, so I continued. "Look, if he were alive, the only reason to cover it up is if they were hiding him somewhere, trying to deprogram him from being gay or something. But no one in their right mind is going to commit multiple murders to cover up kidnapping a family member."

Mina said, "So at the end, Fadil really was killed because he was gay. See? That's why I hate religions."

"Look, I've been to the Middle East and to Turkey. People there are just like anywhere else. It's not like homosexuality is a crime in all those places or there's a Taliban on every corner. This was Emir's personal hatred, not Islam's. As faithful as he supposedly is, he has an idolatrous painting in his prayer room. He lets unbelievers sit in there on the prayer rugs. I knew families who weren't religious but still wouldn't have dreamed of doing either of those things. He's a hypocrite who's just pretending to be religious for money."

"Then why did Fadil die? What did they do to my son?" Kari's questions came out as long wails. I was glad Mina sat with her in the back seat.

Even so, I pulled over onto the shoulder. This wasn't the kind of conversation you have with your back turned. I turned in my seat and answered. "Because Emir thought your husband might cost him money. It's always about the money in the end. The way he bragged about the painting instead of hiding it convinced me. I can't prove it, but I think Emir confronted Fadil, and when he found out the truth he flipped out."

"And Jeremy?" Mina asked. She was speaking softly. "Why wasn't his body found?"

"I'm guessing they took him to cover up Fadil's death. They probably shot Fadil and faked the vehicle fire to cover their tracks. But they were smart enough to know forensics would still have found a gunshot wound even in a burnt body."

"Which means they would need another body that could pass for Fadil," Mina said.

"Right. There had to be a cover-up with someone in the Coroner's Office and with the funeral home as accomplices."

Kari chimed in, sniffling. "So, they use some other body as Fadil's and then make sure it's cremated before anyone can test it."

"That's my guess," I said.

"Oh lord," Kari gasped. "That means they burned poor Jeremy's body for nothing."

I interjected before she went too far down that path. "Jeremy is alive."

"How do you know?" the girls asked, almost in tandem.

"They took pains to leave Fadil's finger in order to ensure he was identified. If Jeremy had died, they'd have done the same thing with him." I looked at the twins and they both looked skeptical. I have to admit, it was a pretty thin theory at this point. "Look, everyone thinks both Jeremy and Fadil really died in a car crash. We know that's not true because Haleh paid the funeral home to cremate the bodies. Emir's reaction tells me he knew she did, which means she wasn't acting alone out of spite."

"Okay, I buy that," Kari said. "She's crazy enough to do that, but Emir loved Jeremy enough that he would have flipped if he'd only now found out she'd had him cremated on purpose."

"Exactly," I said. "Emir had her dispose of the bodies. He would only have arranged for a cover up if somebody died and if he had a hand in that person's death."

"He wouldn't have hurt Jeremy on purpose," Kari said.

"So that leads to the only real possibility, Fadil died after the crash."

"Agreed," Kari said. "But how does that relate to my son?"

"Okay, we know Fadil survived the crash, right?"

She hesitated, but answered, "Yes. Then he was somehow killed later. Maybe even by accident."

"Let's say it was an accident. That's still enough of a reason to cover it up in order to avoid a scandal. But see, Jeremy had to have been alive." I started smiling at this point because I was beginning to believe it myself.

Mina jumped in, more excited than I was. "If Jeremy had died in the crash and Fadil survived, there's no way Emir would've covered up a fatal traffic accident and then killed Fadil anyway."

Kari was the somber voice of reason. "He might have if he'd been the one who caused the accident."

I thought about that for a time, sitting by the side of the highway listening to tractor trailers roar by. Just as we were about to slip into a three-way depression, it hit me. "No! Because if that were true, he could have just left Jeremy's body in the car. Sure, he still sets it on fire, but he also leaves DNA for both victims, not just Fadil."

"That's right," Kari said in a hush. "They never found a trace of Jeremy's DNA. The policeman who investigated thought that was suspicious right away. He couldn't prove anything, though."

"No way you open yourself up to suspicion if you have the real body. Muslims don't cremate, but I don't see Emir as the type to swap out bodies just so Jeremy's real body isn't cremated."

"Not with infidel women sitting on his prayer rug," Mina said.

Kari began to smile. "No Jeremy DNA because he wasn't in the car they found."

"And he's not wherever they buried Fadil's real body …"

"Because my baby's still alive."

It sounded like a prayer. I almost answered, "*Amen.*" Instead I said, "Yes. I think that's what Emir has been fighting so hard to keep us from finding out."

She burst into tears, as did Mina, and they held each other there in the back seat.

I didn't want to feel it, not yet, because the job wasn't finished. These were all theories and could be wrong. I started the car and re-entered the highway.

"Eddie, where is he?" Mina's voice was anxious. She sounded less certain than her sister.

"I have no clue. But I bet Uncle Emir does."

"So, what do we do next?" Kari asked.

"Time to bring in the Feds," I answered. The words almost burned my tongue.

Chapter 12

We'd been holed up in Kari's townhouse for almost three days before I got antsy. Kari was working and Mina was on video chat with Nona and her mom. Gaither had promised to keep a tail on Ozan and his security crew. We'd still heard nothing regarding Haleh. A search for her fiancé came up empty as well. According to Gaither, Emir rarely left the house. Given his tight resources, he pulled the watch on Emir and focused on his dangerous employee and on finding Haleh, who he still believed to be the prime suspect. Gaither was a good man, but as hardheaded as they come.

While Mina was busy crying over the webcam and lamenting how her daughter seemed to be growing up without her—she looked exactly the same to me—I snuck out. It was nearing eleven p.m. and I'd been inside all day. No sooner did I hit the street, meaning to take a short jog around the block, than I spotted the tan sedan we'd seen on the way to Emir's place. It was parked down the block on Kari's street, which enabled him to see the front door. With her limited view he was invisible from inside the house. I ran around the block the other way, which would allow me to loop behind the car. If he were sitting facing the Kari's house, hopefully he wouldn't see me.

I came around the corner bent low, which put me fifteen feet behind the sedan. It was a Volvo. Who the hell tails someone in a Volvo? It was like being shot up in a drive-by from a dude in a minivan. As I crept up to the car I could see the driver's window open and a shirt-sleeved arm poking out. At five feet away I made a leap for it, lunging to the window and grabbing the guy's arm. I meant to twist it under, bending the elbow joint in a direction it didn't want to go. The theory was that would make him yield and I could take him from the car with ease. The reality was that I grabbed his Popeye-size forearm, twisted, and, though he was caught off-guard, he was strong enough that with one tug he pulled me through the car's window.

So now I was half in the car with my legs dangling out over the street while King Kong in the front seat and I wrestled for position. He pounded me in the face a couple of times and I saw stars, but didn't go out. I managed to lock onto one arm and drive my other elbow into his throat. He slammed into my sides two or three more times with enough force that I thought he'd broken a rib. By now my mind was racing, zooming between hoping I'd not just assaulted an innocent man and wondering if I was about to be beaten to death by the most muscular human ape I'd ever seen.

Though I hate cops on a bad day, this turned out to be a good one. Just as Kong finally pulled my arm off his throat—with one hand—and reversed my arm lock on him into a submission hold against me, the NYPD came racing down the street. For the briefest of moments the big ape stopped, his eyes checking the side mirror to see if the cop was coming our way. It turned out to be just another midnight donut run, but the distraction was long enough that I was able to rear back and head butt the hairy monster.

The theory was that I would stun him and give myself a chance to gain some leverage. The reality was that I knocked us both the hell out. The head does not make a good weapon unless your target is a hat.

I didn't die, it turned out, because I managed to wake up first. I had the worst headache of my life and probably at least a mild concussion. When Kong woke, grunting and cursing, he was handcuffed to his steering wheel and had one of my footprints in his groin. That was pure spite. I texted Mina and got her to bring out one of my friends. If Kong broke loose there wasn't a chance in hell I'd have survived another bout with him. She tried to stick around but I shooed her back into the house.

"Give me two minutes and then call Gaither," I told her.

"What are you going to do?"

"Shoot this guy's dick off and then come inside. I need to lie down."

She shrugged and left. I love that girl. Now, I was bluffing, but with Kong's balls still ringing from my drop kick, I guessed he didn't know that. Once I aimed my empty pistol and pulled the trigger, he became quite talkative.

"Once again," I said, "who's paying you?"

"Some guy, calls himself Oz. I call him, tell him where you are. That's all I know."

"And it doesn't bother you that people turn up dead afterward?"

His jaw clenched and he pursed his lips. "I don't read the obituaries. I just follow you and tell my client who you've been talking to. Maybe you need to learn when to shut up."

I decided to teach him to shut up instead by popping him in the head with the butt of my gun.

By the next morning Gaither had the guy in protective custody. Once the FBI made it clear he was facing possible accessory to capital murder charges in Virginia he became a lot more cooperative. More importantly, his arrest gave the Feds the first concrete link that tied Emir to Cindi Roark's murder and our attempted murder. Even Gaither had to agree it was likely that Ozan had been the killer in Maryland and D.C. or had hired whoever was.

It was enough for Gaither to start filing arrest warrants, though custody battles with Maryland, D.C. and New York were likely. He advised all of us to "lay low for a couple days" until they could pick Emir and Ozan up for questioning. Given I was now nursing a bad shoulder, bruised ribs, and a concussion, it was advice I was happy to take. Hell, I wanted my mommy. Less than an hour later, we got a call back from Gaither informing us that David had been shot a block from his house. He was alive, however, and in good condition at the hospital. There were no witnesses.

It made no sense that someone would try to take out David to hide the crime at this late stage. We knew Fadil was gay. We knew he'd been killed, whether purposely or accidentally. We suspected Jeremy had been taken. The only reasons for shooting David were either revenge or because Emir and his stooge had decided to kill anyone who knew the real reason for Fadil's death. That list included David, Henry, possibly Haleh, the twins, and me, plus absolutely everyone any of us had told. Doing so would be the work of an irrational mind. Certainly Emir must know that it was too late for a cover up.

To make matters worse, both Emir and Ozan managed to elude

Gaither's crack crew of agents.

"You're killing me," I said to Gaither.

"Quit whining. You're not dead yet, and we'll find the Turks. I've got NYPD watching Kari's house." He paused, then continued. "Do me a favor. Don't leave home with those guns again. I can't help you if you get slapped with a weapons charge."

I hung up, not even bothering to remind him that he was the one who gave me my gun in the first place. I wasn't about to tell Mina what to do with hers.

Kari was delighted to have us housebound for a few more days. She took up most of the time by having Mina and me pose for a sculpture she wouldn't let either of us see. I'd never been naked for so long in my entire life. Finally, after three days of suffering, Mina and I were allowed clothes. I was pretzeled around Mina wearing just a pair of jeans. She wore a flowing white dress that accented her curves. We'd been there a half hour and she was losing focus.

"Kari, did you know Eddie has a brother?"

"Yeah, Stevie. He's a sweetie pie."

"You met him? How'd you get to meet him?"

"Eddie and I FaceTimed with him a couple of times." She frowned. "Stand still. I'm trying to get your calves right."

"Face what?" she asked.

"Video chat, babe," I said.

"Nerds," she answered, rolling her eyes. "How come I haven't met him? You didn't even want me to know you had a brother."

"I wasn't hiding him from you. You never ask me any questions about myself."

Mina's scowl grew deeper.

Kari spoke up. "You'd like him. He's even cuter than Eddie."

I gave her a dirty look. She was right, of course, he was better looking. That didn't prevent it from being a major sore spot between us. Little brothers should be taller, smarter, or better looking, not all three. My angst was exacerbated by Mina's glassy-eyed response.

"Can I meet him?"

Kari must have noticed her interest too. "Have you told Stevie about us?" she asked.

I hesitated. "You mean about you-and-me us, or the three-of-us us?"

"The three of us, of course."

Mina's frown returned and she straightened, causing Kari to throw up her hands and walk over. "Why, are you ashamed of us?" Mina asked.

"Yeah," Kari chimed in.

"No, of course not. It's just that I wasn't sure if you'd be okay with my telling people I'm dating both of you. Sounds kinda like bragging."

"Oh brother," Kari said.

Mina hit me on my good shoulder. "See? That shows how arrogant male-centered society is. If I were sleeping with you and your brother people would say you were exploiting me and I'd be a slut. But since Kari and I are screwing you—"

"Nuh uh, making love," Kari interjected. She was pouting.

"Making love," Mina corrected, gesturing toward her sister. "Even though we're both willingly with you, people will still say you're the one doing the exploiting and we're a couple of saps. Sounds like you agree with them. Well, maybe we're both exploiting you. Did you ever think of that?"

Kari began giggling.

I admitted that I didn't. To be honest, her way of thinking made me feel less of a creep.

"You need to accept we're with you because we enjoy sharing you. I'm finally learning how to give myself to someone without worrying about where it's going, and Kari's getting her bad girl on. Plus, the sex is amazing." Emphasis: hers. She frowned at her laughing sister. "What the hell are you laughing about?"

"You. You called us 'a couple of saps.' Eddie has you talking like his detective movies."

Mina starting smiling too. "Yeah. I'm gonna buy myself a fedora and stiletto heels and go into business with him."

"You'd be awesome together! Eddie and Crow Detective Agency," Kari said. "You could finish getting your helicopter license and—"

To my great relief that's when the phone rang and I removed myself from the conversation. I'd never admit to the girls that a good shamus can never have too many stilettos on the ground. When I returned they were yammering away about copter adventures and "living the film noir life" as if they were completely unaware that most of the characters in those films lived shitty lives. Me, I was busy trying to live the romantic comedy life; the pay was just as good and the benefits were worlds better.

My happy thoughts were interrupted by Kari saying, "I like being a bad girl." This I wanted to listen to. "I've always had to be the Goody-Goody," she said. "Well, if you don't count the time I ran away with my teacher."

Mina cut her eyes.

"But even then...and don't laugh, I barely let him touch me. I just wanted a ticket out of South Dakota. He went along because he wanted so badly to get in my pants he was willing to *be patient*. So even when I was bad, I was being good." She covered her face in her hands. I could see her smiling underneath. "But earlier today I spent an hour lying on the floor, watching a movie while my sister had sex with my boyfriend on the sofa. You guys are still really loud, by the way. And before that he and I were doing it in the kitchen with her in the next room, playing with the stupid dog."

"Hey!" Mina said. "Don't call Apache stupid."

Apache yawned his indifference.

Kari raised her voice. "Do you know how liberating this is for me? Sweet Kari Goody-Goody is sharing her boyfriend with her sister!" She thrust her fists in the air.

Mina rolled her eyes and pulled out her e-cigarette. She puffed while Kari tried to frown her out of existence. "I'm thrilled for you," Mina finally said, blowing minty smoke rings at her twin. "We should all move to Utah and get married. Meanwhile, I'm going to go scrub the kitchen table because that shit is nasty."

"You can be such a bitch," Kari growled.

To my great relief, that's when we heard a knock on the door.

After we finished jumping out of our socks, we peeked out the window and saw Gaither and a suited guy in his early fifties that couldn't have been anything but a cop. Everything about the guy was gray, including his crew cut. Kari let them in and Apache starting growling at the cop. That is one smart dog.

"Daley, girls, this is Detective Conroy from NYPD's Homicide Unit. He's here investigating the death—"

"If you don't mind, Agent Gaither," Conroy said. "Mr. Daley, where were you three nights ago between the hours of nine p.m. and three a.m.?"

I gave Kari and Mina a look and hesitated. "What's this about?" I asked.

"Please, Mr. Daley, just answer the question."

I looked at Gaither. His shrug told me this was out of his hands. It wasn't out of mine. "I asked you a question," I said. "Answer it, lock me up, or get the fuck out." Apache began growling louder.

"Shush, Apache," Mina said. She looked at Conroy. "Excuse him. Eddie hates cops and Apache's picking that up." She smiled sweetly. "We, however, very much appreciate the protection you guys have been providing us."

Conroy gave his best cop almost-smile. Mina made a good point. I'd forgotten NYPD was currently outside saving my life. I managed to mumble an apology myself.

"Look Eddie," Gaither said, one of the few times he'd called me by my first name, "Emir Sunay has turned up dead. We went to serve him with a search warrant and found his body in an upstairs closet of his home."

"And you think I killed him?" I asked. "What about his security staff, especially that clown Ozan?"

"We found a male security officer in a first floor pantry, dead of a gunshot wound," Conroy said.

"I don't understand," Kari said. "I thought you said Emir and Ozan had disappeared."

Gaither answered. "We saw Ozan take off in his car and he managed to lose the agent I had tailing him. Emir left in the middle of the night and we traced his car to a lot at Newark Airport. We assumed he'd skipped town, but he showed up at home the next morning. He didn't leave after that."

"Didn't you have someone watching the house?" I asked.

"Yes, but you've been there. There are thick woods down the hill in the back. Anyone could have parked a couple of blocks away and snuck up through the trees in the dark."

"Why would I kill him?" I asked. "I'm on the case trying to find Kari's son. Emir was my number one hope. Hell, I had him pegged as Fadil's killer."

"I thought we liked the Asker woman for that," Conroy said.

"Gaither liked her. I liked Emir. Looks like he was right. I figured Emir confronted Fadil about his supposed fling with Cindi Roark. Fadil panics, figuring it was only a matter of time before his real secret was found out. He thinks *What the hell* and decides to run away with his boyfriend. But Ozan or whoever runs him off the road and grabs him up."

"And discovers Jeremy is in the car," Kari said.

"Right." I said. "So now they have to take Jeremy and Fadil. Emir confronts Fadil again, and this time he's got his back up a little, so he tells his uncle he's gay and finally, maybe, proud to be gay."

"And gets shot for it." Gaither said.

"Yeah. Love is bad for business. Emir stages an accident to avoid a scandal."

Kari looked sad. "All because he loved his money more than he loved his nephew."

Conroy looked at Gaither. "You know, I like that scenario. Makes more sense than the Asker woman killing him in a jealous rage, given the Roark shooting."

Kari gave a little squeak and looked at me. I'd managed to hide Roark's death from her until then. To her credit, she held it together enough that I don't think anyone but me noticed her reaction.

"Yeah, well, we still need to find Asker," Gaither said. He pointed at me. "And you need to produce an alibi so we can get the DA off your ass and after the killer."

I wasn't going to be able to stall them any longer. Conroy had that look cops get when they are through taking your shit. If you've ever seen it, you won't forget it. I said, "I have a damned good alibi, but it's a little embarrassing."

Gaither said, "It's gonna have to be air tight. The DA already wants you for leaving the scene of the Joyner shooting."

"Remind me again who Joyner is," I said.

"Jesus, Daley, the guy you killed in the alley last week. The DA hasn't forgotten it, even if you have."

"That's why I hate DAs," I said. "So nitpicky."

"You hate everybody," Gaither responded. "And I'm serious. Conroy can tell you, the DA wants to chew your ass."

Mina interrupted. "We're Eddie's alibi. The three of us were having sex all night."

Gaither said nothing. Neither did Conroy, though he did begin to look a little flushed around the collar. After around forty-five seconds of silence I started to think maybe they hadn't heard her.

"Is that airtight enough?" I asked.

I wasn't bragging. I'd never needed an alibi before. I was worried they'd want sex tapes or something. The way Conroy was looking from Mina to Kari, I was certain he would, at least. He didn't answer directly. Instead, he asked, "She's kidding, right?"

"I never kid about sex," Mina said.

"I can vouch for that," I said.

Mina gave me a kiss.

Conroy grew silent again. After a time he cleared his throat. "Um, together?" he choked out.

"Together what?" Mina asked.

"The three of you were having sex together?"

"No, Kari and I take turns. Don't be weird." She was frowning at him, completely serious.

Gaither finally spoke up. He'd been staring in my face since Mina spoke. "I really hate you," he said. The lack of humor in his voice made my heart sing.

"Aw, don't be mad, Rodrigo," Kari said, touching his chest. Her voice was saccharine. "I hear Deb wants to come back to New York for a visit. Maybe we can hook you up."

"I'll hold my breath," he grumbled.

"Now, if you don't mind," Kari said, "Eddie and Mina have to finish posing for my piece, and then we're going to have celebration sex." She kissed me. "If you're not too tired, that is."

"No, I'm good," I said.

She looked at Conroy. "Maybe Mina and I *will* do him together. That was a good idea."

Mina made a face.

Neither man said another word. Conroy just flipped his little pad closed and walked somberly to the door. Gaither followed him out, turned, and opened his mouth. Kari slammed the door in his face. I threw both hands in the air and did a little touchdown dance. "That may have been the highlight of my life," I said.

"Wow, you were a total bitch," Mina said, laughing. She gave her twin a fist bump.

Kari glowered. "He deserved it. The nerve of him, calling you a player before."

Mina gave me an "*Is she kidding?*" look.

I just shrugged. Kari's mind was an interesting and lovely place.

Without warning she started sobbing, to the point where she was gasping for breath. I picked her up and carried her to bed to lie down with Mina right behind us. Neither of us needed to ask what was wrong. Emir, the only person we believed could lead us to Jeremy, was dead. Kari, finally, was running out of hope.

My guess was Ozan was already on his way back to Turkey. It

wouldn't have surprised me to find out he'd killed his boss in order to cover his tracks. I was almost out of suspects. Now there was Haleh or no one, and we'd lost sight of her for days. I hoped her disappearance wasn't linked to Emir's mystery trip to the airport.

Around noon the next day events began to get strange in a hurry. It started with a surprise visit by a Mr. Adnan Fatayri, a handsome, dark-haired man with a haircut that probably cost more than my suit. He introduced himself as Haleh's fiancé. I took him to the back room to talk, out of Kari's earshot. She'd been on enough of a rollercoaster as it was.

"How may I help you, Mr. Fatayri?" I said, gesturing for him to take a seat.

"Adnan, please." I returned the pleasantries. He sat across from me, hunched over his knees and with his hands running over that expensive cut. "I'm hoping you can help me. It's about my fiancée, Haleh."

I resisted the urge to refer him to a shrink. "I'm afraid I haven't seen her since our interview in your apartment."

"Yes, she told me about that."

"So you know we didn't exactly part on the best of terms."

"This is true. She was nearly climbing the walls when I got home. I'd never seen her so upset."

"Then I'm not sure what I can do to help," I said.

"I don't know where else to turn. I'd go to the police, but Haleh becomes deathly afraid whenever I bring up the subject."

I considered telling him that the cops were looking for her. However, she'd obviously not told him and I didn't want to scare him off. Instead I said, "I'd be glad to help, but won't she be even less open to talk to me?"

His brow furrowed and he rifled his hair again. "I'm more concerned about getting her help than whether she's open to it," he said. "I don't know all the details of your conversation, but I do know that whatever it was she was surprised by how much you had learned about her." I didn't say anything. He sat straight in the chair. "Eddie, ever since your visit she's been acting odd, and it's getting worse. It's like you opened some door that she'd been leaning against, and now a bunch of bad stuff is pouring out."

"Is that why no one's seen her?"

"Yes. Even I couldn't find her for most of a week. I finally tracked her down at her parent's old place in Long Island. There wasn't even power there. She'd been living in the closed up house." Then he added something that made my ears perked up. "I was worried about her son, living there in that heat."

"Her son?"

"Yes, she has a son, almost three years old. I couldn't even get her to let me in at first to check on him."

I was beginning to get an anxious feeling in my stomach, one that said I was about to make someone very happy or permanently break their heart. "Did she finally let you in?" I asked.

"That's why I'm here. She did let me in and she was a wreck. It turns out it's because her son is missing."

My heart sank. I tried to keep a professional demeanor, but all I could think of was Kari's tears.

"I know you're a private investigator and money is no object here. Haleh…Haleh has fallen apart. I can't get her out of the apartment and she won't even let me call the police." He was fighting back tears and I let him gather himself.

"I'll be glad to help," I said. "Do you have a photo of her son?"

"Sure," he said. He reached in his coat and pulled out a photo of the most beautiful little boy I'd ever seen. He looked just like Kari. Mina and I had been in the same apartment as Jeremy and neither of us suspected a thing. I was closer to tears than Adnan was.

As if some unseen radar were working, Kari and her sister both came bursting through the door, with Kari's eyes wide, searching mine. "Where is he?" she asked.

I handed her the photo. "We don't know just yet," I said. Those were the hardest words I'd ever had to speak. I hoped I wouldn't have to top them soon.

She gasped and sank to the ground, crying silently. Mina, her hands shaking, took the photo from her sister, and stared at it. She said nothing, only stared, tears streaming down her cheeks. After almost a minute and Adnan's gaze going from confused to worried, she spoke. "This is my nephew, Jeremy Alexander Sunay. Is…is he alive?"

"How can this be?" Adnan asked. He was standing, although I don't remember his moving.

I stood, took him by the shoulders, and gently sat him down. "You better brace yourself," I said. "You're not going to like this story." Then, as Kari and Mina held each other, I relayed to Adnan the story of Jeremy's supposed death. I'd never seen a man apologize so vigorously for something of which he was completely innocent. Of all the people wrapped up in this case, I felt for him the most, next to Kari. He'd been duped just as much as she, and for the same reason: an irrational willingness to trust a person just because they were supposed to love you.

Thirty minutes later I was en route to Long Island, madder than a hornet with a headache. I ignored Gaither's request that I leave my gun at home. The crazy bitch Haleh was going to tell me where Jeremy was or I was going to do her right there in that old house.

Twilight's shadows claimed the city as I wound my way through the ebbing traffic toward Long Island. It was enough time that I could formulate my view of events. Haleh's role was obviously more than just helping Emir cover up Fadil's death and making it appear that Jeremy had died with him. As a reward she'd been given the man's son to raise as her own. She'd shown her hatred toward Kari, whom she considered her rival, when Mina showed up pretending to be her. We knew right then she was unstable, but not enough to raise a kidnapped child in the city where the mother lived. I guessed that once she'd learned Fadil's true sexuality she must have been all too willing to help Emir cover up his murder. Maybe she'd even done the killing. That made her dangerous; perhaps David had recently discovered just how dangerous.

I only hoped Jeremy's disappearance was the result of Emir's attempts to cover his tracks and not something more sinister. Just in case, I made Kari stay behind. It took all of Mina's strength to restrain the woman so I could slip out of there. As I drove away I could see Kari screaming and trying to tear herself out of her sister's grasp.

"This better end well," I kept muttering as I neared the address Adnan gave me. I wasn't sure how I could face the girls if it didn't. I'd been ten feet away from the boy and let him slip out of my grasp. Any shamus worth his salt would have barged into that kid's bedroom, just in case. The truth was slapping me in the face. I hadn't done so because deep inside I never believed Jeremy was still alive. Now maybe he wasn't because of me.

The Long Island house was perfectly normal. I'd had in mind

some palatial retreat straight out of The Great Gatsby. What I found was a two-story A-frame house with pristine white siding and no lights. Given what Adnan had warned me was her state of mind I didn't bother to knock. Instead I crept along to the rear of the house. There was an old-fashioned kitchen door with glass panels and no discernible security system. I pulled out my pouch of locksmith tools and within thirty seconds had the door open. I crept in, being careful to make no noise.

"I wondered when you'd show up," Haleh said. She was sitting in a kitchen chair holding a gun. She gestured for me to sit.

"I spoke with your fiancé," I said.

"Ex-fiancé," she said, and inhaled deeply on a cigarette. "I had to break it off. He was terribly upset. Started making up wild stories. Then, when he threatened to get you involved—"

"Save it, lady. None of that stuff is true, and I didn't come here for your delusions. I came to get Jeremy."

She took another drag on the cigarette. "Jeremy who?"

Before she could react I rolled out of the chair and swept my legs across her chair's legs, sending her spilling backward. She didn't have time to brace herself, and her head smacked the linoleum floor hard enough to stun her. I grabbed her gun and stepped back. She sat up wide eyed, her messy hair haloing her in the dim moonlight. She was no angel, however.

"Now, here's what's going to happen," I said. "I'm going ask you again where Jeremy is, and you aren't going to lie. If you do, tomorrow they'll find you've committed suicide here in the kitchen. Not a soul will doubt it."

She looked into my eyes for signs of bluffing and found none. "He's gone. If you've talked to Adnan, you already know that."

"Gone where?"

"I suppose that answer depends on whether you are a believer or not."

I knelt beside her and placed her pistol to her head. My hand was shaking because I wanted to shoot her so very badly. After a few tense moments I leaned back and pulled the gun away. "The next time you piss me off, you are one dead bitch. I'll just take my chances Ozan knows." That must have registered as credible with her because I saw a change in her expression. It also gave me the answer: Emir had taken the boy. "What did Emir do with him?"

"How…?" She stopped herself and a look of fear crossed her

eyes. "I will tell you, but it will anger you. Will…will I die for it?"

I meant to shake my head no but found myself nodding. Catching myself, I said, "If you're honest, I won't harm you. I'll let God deal with you."

"Then His will be done." She closed her eyes, inhaled, and said, "Emir killed him. He sent the jackal Ozan, and he and a cohort took my son."

The wind gushed out of me as if she'd kicked me. I wished she had so I could have killed her with a clear conscience. After an eternity of trying to still my raging heart, I managed to grind out words. "Why…why…why would he kill him?"

"Because," she spat through gritted teeth, "you were closing in on him and he refused to allow him to be raised by his mother."

"Why?" was the only word I could form. I was glad to be sitting in the dark so that she could not see my pain.

"Emir blamed Fadil's…wife for his homosexuality. He swore that Jeremy would never be returned to her."

"How in fuck's name is Kari to blame?"

"Were she a good wife, he would have stayed at home instead of lying with the faggot." Even in the dimness I could still see fury in her eyes.

"You missed, by the way," I said, "David is still alive."

"No matter," she said. "God will sort him in time."

"God already has," I said, "that's why he's alive and you're about to die." I lifted the gun, aimed at her temple, and, my hands shaking, pulled the trigger. Then again. Nothing happened. Her gun wasn't loaded. Mine was, but by then I'd regained control.

She began to cry, though her face was awash in rage, not grief. Her tears helped to still my own anger. I'd almost done her a favor: suicide by angry Eddie. I called Gaither. Maybe a cop would be mad enough to accommodate her death wish.

"I did as he asked," she moaned. "I did everything he asked. I negotiated with the coroner and the damnable funeral director."

"You mean bribed." I knew this story, but it kept my mind pointed away from revenge.

"Yes." She wiped her eyes with the back of one hand. "We procured the bodies of some unclaimed homeless souls the coroner couldn't identify. The child wasn't even a male. Then the funeral home cremated them."

"What happened with Fadil?"

"Emir's clients heard rumors that he was sleeping with the Roark woman. He came to Fadil's home and told him it must stop as he was jeopardizing important contracts. I suppose Fadil decided it was time to..." She made a face that I won't even attempt to characterize, other than she would have looked happier had I been force-feeding her excrement.

"Fadil decided it was time to finally admit he was gay," I said.

She nodded. "I am surprised Emir didn't kill him then. Instead he tried to talk sense to him. Fadil claimed to repent and promised Emir he would immediately go into counseling."

"But instead he came to Brooklyn to see his son because he was about to run away with David."

"Yes. And he and that...woman argued. Ozan was following him and called Emir to say Fadil had already broken their agreement. Emir later told me Ozan was only to capture him and bring him back to Emir's. But he attempted to flee and the jackal ran them off the road, nearly killing him."

"Why did he kill Fadil?"

She looked at me as if I'd asked the dumbest question in history. "Because he would not renounce his perversions. He certainly couldn't let Jeremy be exposed to such."

Jesus Fucking Robinson. She was even crazier when she was being sane. "How'd you end up with Jeremy?" I was no longer hiding my contempt.

"I knew Emir from his visits to the office. He was of great comfort to me when Fadil left for Washington."

"Meaning you slept with him."

She cut her eyes at me. "I was in pain and I had yet to meet Adnan. Emir was kind. When he asked me to raise Jeremy as my own, I could not refuse. I should have taken him and fled home." She began to cry again.

"You killed Emir."

"Of course I did. He took my son. When I confronted him he admitting killing him. He even went so far as to promise me another child, as if one can simply replace a son."

"You have no fucking sense of irony at all, do you?" I asked.

Making a stupid, puzzled look at my question was the last thing she ever did. The back door slammed open and gunshots rang out. I dived under the kitchen table, but Haleh slumped over backward, eyes open. I fired, giving myself cover from the hulking figure in the doorway. He returned fire, diving to his left. That gave me enough time to race through the kitchen doorway to the next room with bullets whizzing over my head and buffeting the walls. I bolted through the empty room, kneeling down in a dark hallway.

From the kitchen I could hear Ozan's gravelly voice. "You cannot escape. This—"

I clicked off six shots in the direction of his voice. It immediately shut the hell up. I wasn't in the mood for bad-guy speeches. I heard the satisfying thump of his body's crumbling to the floor. He lay there groaning until the sound of police cars filled the air. It was sour music, but the perfect tune for my mood.

I let Gaither deal with the New Jersey State Police. I had no stomach for it. They impounded my vehicle, asked me questions I ignored, booked me, and later released me into Rod's custody. I pretty much said nothing to anyone except him. He called Ozan a "good collar," but I called him irrelevant. Around four a.m. he dropped me back off at Kari's wherein I proceeded to break what was left of her precious, fragile heart. The sound of her wailing will haunt me until the very second I die. It is a reminder to never fail again, to always be vigilant, to never trust, and to always check. It was an important lesson to learn, and one I wished I'd learned earlier.

She and Mina held each other for hours until they both passed out sometime before noon. I spent most of the time sitting on the front step, holding my puppy. Or maybe he was holding me. I suppose I'll never be certain. I was sure of one thing, however; whatever the twins felt for me changed in the moment that I'd had to utter the words, "I was too late." Remorse didn't matter. Tears didn't matter. The solitary thing that did was that I'd gone from being their last hope to just another guy who'd let them down.

I couldn't wait for the next flight home.

Chapter 13

After a bad day, rough evening, and a worse night, I awoke alone on the sofa. Even my dog didn't want anything to do with me. He'd spent the night before curled up next to Kari. I'd made the mistake of announcing I'd be leaving soon with him. She jabbed a middle finger at me, called me the f-word, and then took him in the bedroom with her and locked the door. Mina called me "a coward like every other man" and vowed to never sleep with me again. She sagged off to bed thereafter with her soft footfalls almost disappearing into the hardwood floors. It was odd considering that, despite her small stature, she usually stomped around with the impact of a bull. Only when she danced or loved did Mina choose to show her elegance. But with my final failure, my brash, blustery girl had seemingly swapped emotional places with her twin.

At around ten o'clock in the morning I still hadn't heard a peep from either of the sisters, so I got up and made myself some coffee: midnight black and bitter, to match the mood in the house. That's when I heard a rap on the door. I opened it, more to keep whoever was there from waking the girls than any desire to see another human. It was Adnan, looking even worse than I felt. He was bleary-eyed, wearing purple running shorts, an orange polo shirt, and Adidas with no socks. His expensive coiffure looked like crap. I liked him even more than the first time.

"Here," I said, handing him coffee. "You look like you need this more than I do."

He nodded a thank you and took a sip. I led him to the kitchen and grabbed myself a cup. We sat there in silence sipping acid-strong coffee while we both tried to broach the subject of his fiancée's death. I wasn't directly responsible but, given I'd tried to kill her myself, I didn't exactly feel innocent either.

Adnan broke the impasse. "I'm still trying to get my head around all of this," he said. "I spent much of yesterday speaking to the police and Haleh's family. It's like most of what I thought I knew about her was untrue."

I didn't have good words for him, but I thought he could use some nonetheless. "She did love you, at least. She was talking about you right before…before Ozan showed up."

Adnan looked at me and gave a weak smile. "You are a terrible liar, my friend."

I returned the smile. "Yeah, I've been told that. Kind of sad, considering I've been trained to detect deception."

"Ah, then you will know the truth of this statement. Much of what I feel is not sadness, but guilt."

"Guilt?" I bristled. The last thing I needed was more bad news.

"Yes. I should be heartbroken, she deserved that much. Instead, I feel relief." He looked to me for an understanding look. He got it. "She had me completely fooled. I can only imagine what my life would have been."

"She fooled me too, and I'm a professional. But yeah, you did sort of dodge a bullet."

"An ironic turn of phrase," he said.

"Oh, god. I'm sorry, Adnan."

He waved a hand. "No, it's alright. Can I tell you a secret?" he asked. I nodded, and he leaned forward in his chair. "She really was one crazy bitch."

I tried not to laugh, but it came spilling out. Soon we were both laughing, in tears and not all of them from joy. It had been a trying month for both of us.

"Oh, what is wrong with me?" he suddenly said. He reached in his pocket and pulled out a cell phone. "I completely forgot the reason I came. Here." He handed me the phone.

"What's this for?"

"I found it in my apartment. I wanted you to see it before I turn it over to the police." He gestured with his head. "Check out the text messages."

He sat grinning at me while I pulled up Haleh's recent texts. A long string was whiny gibberish to her mother. Another, shorter one was to some wedding planner on mundane details of Adnan's almost-imprisonment ceremony, and the last…

"Holy fucking shit!" I yelled and went running upstairs. Adnan followed me to the foot of the stairs, grinning.

Kari's door was still locked, but it didn't matter. I hit it in full stride, almost knocking it off its hinges. She shrieked and Apache bolted from atop the covers, then stopped and looked at both of us as if we were insane.

"What is wrong with you?" she asked, her eyes struggling to focus. Her little fists were balled.

By way of answer I handed her the phone and pushed the side button, turning on the display. She read the messages from Haleh and Emir:

Haleh: Bring back my son!

Emir: Haleh, for the last time, gather yourself. The boy is safe in Turkey. I got him on a private jet two nights ago.

Haleh: Where is he!!!!???

Emir (two minutes later): He is safe.

That was followed by a string of epithets that no godly woman should ever put in writing. Emir did not answer, and I imagine that bit of silence sealed his death warrant. The time stamp of the texts corresponded to the hours before Emir and his bodyguard were found dead. They probably never thought Haleh a threat and weren't on alert. She'd shot them and fled straight to punish David before returning to Long Island.

"Does that…?" was all Kari asked.

"It does," I answered. I knew the question. Her son was still alive. It never felt so good to smile. "Adnan found her phone and brought it to us."

"Where is Adnan?" she asked, her voice rising.

"He's downstairs."

Kari jumped from the bed and raced downstairs, blowing past Mina who'd emerged in a sleepy fog from her bedroom.

"What's going on?" she asked, rubbing her eyes while her sister raced down the stairs. "And why's she running naked to see that guy?" Mina stood at the top of the steps pointing at her sister and looking utterly confused and adorable. I needed to kiss someone, so I strode over and kissed her while Kari, completely nude, hugged the pleasantly surprised Adnan. If he wasn't missing Haleh before, he really wasn't missing her now.

After kissing, stroking, and crying her thank-yous all over Adnan's face, Kari suddenly remembered she'd gone to bed naked. She screamed and ran back upstairs and into the bedroom. Mina followed her inside—to laugh at her, most likely.

I rejoined our guest downstairs, and gave him back the phone.

"I don't know where in Turkey Jeremy might be," he said.

"That's okay. I suspect Kari knows."

"Yes," he said, smoothing his hair, "she did seem to." He looked back up the empty stairs to where she'd escaped. "Does she…um, is she…seeing anyone?"

"Me," I said.

"Oh. Oh! I thought you were dating her sister."

"I am." He raised both eyebrows. "It's a long story," I said.

He blinked and a fog crossed his face. "I see," he said.

"No, it's not like that. She's really a good, sweet, spiritual woman, the kind you introduce to mom."

His expression eased. "That was my feeling as well."

"Yeah, right up until the time she tackled you butt naked."

He inhaled and exhaled deeply. "No, I was hoping that meant she liked me. My disappointment was only in finding she's not unattached."

I was going to explain the situation, but realized I understood it no more than he. Fortunately I didn't have to. Mina came tramping downstairs, her bare feet slapping hard on the wooden steps. It was good to hear the physical power had returned to her stride. She walked up to Adnan and hugged him. "Thank you," she said.

He shrugged. "I did nothing but find the phone."

She shook her head. "You found us all." Adnan smiled and turned to leave. "By the way," Mina said, "That was how it feels to hug one of us with clothes on."

He broke out in a wide grin. "Most pleasant either way," he said.

We shared a smile and I escorted him out. When the door closed I asked Mina, "Am I forgiven yet?"

"You mean will I have sex with you again?"

I looked at her. "No, that's not what I mean at all."

"We're good." She smiled at me and took my hand. "Come on, we all need to pack. You're taking Kari to Turkey and I have to go see my baby before I lose my mind."

I followed her upstairs, wondering if I'd thought to pack my passport. I hadn't been to Turkey in ages.

Mina and I said our goodbyes at the airport. She held onto me as though I were flying off to my execution. "Aren't you coming back?" I asked.

She shook her head. "It's over, baby. She kissed me on the cheek. "It's been..." her mouth twisted. She turned and began running toward her gate. Just like that, she flew out of my life.

Kari and I touched down in Ankara and checked into adjoining rooms at our hotel. To avoid any legal wrangling we would have to go through the U.S. Embassy and proper channels. Fortunately, between Gaither's contacts and favors I called in from former Army buddies who were now in the foreign service, we'd made good progress. It would be a few days, we were assured, but Kari had all the proper documentation to secure her son. The fact that he looked exactly like her didn't hurt either. To ensure there were no claims of impropriety I introduced myself as her investigator, a role we fell into easily.

Kari was at home in densely packed Ankara, occupying her frantic mind with shopping for art objects and taking in tourist sights and restaurants while we waited. Finally on day four we were called to the Embassy for good news. They'd worked through channels and found Jeremy living with his elderly great grandmother.

"I know her," Kari said. "She came to our wedding. Fadil adored her."

"Good," said Mr. Treadworthy, the Embassy staffer. "That will make things easier."

"Do we know what the grandmother was told?" I asked.

"Her son, Emir, told her only that both of Jeremy's parents had been killed in a car accident, and he wanted him safe with her. She believed that Jeremy had no other family in America except her grandsons and their families. She doesn't know of Emir's death. Due to her advanced age, her siblings' children have asked we not tell her."

"We understand," Kari said. "When can we see Jeremy?"

Mr. Treadworthy handed us the address. "First thing in the morning. He'll be prepped and ready to go."

"What ... what did they tell him about me?"

"I'm afraid I don't know," he said.

We thanked the staff and I took Kari by the arm and led her out. She was shaking like a leaf.

"What if he doesn't remember me?" she asked as we climbed into the little Celica we'd rented. "He's only three. Kids don't even develop long-term memories until they're four or so."

"The human brain is flexible. Besides, you're his mom. He'll remember you."

"But how can you be sure?" Her face was a roadmap of worry lines.

"Because I know you. Nobody who's ever met you will forget you." I started up the car. "I bet Adnan is still thinking about you."

She grinned, blushed, and hit me. "Stop it. Why'd you let me run downstairs like that naked?"

"I figured the guy deserved a reward. Besides, you told me nudity didn't bother you."

"I just said that so you'd shower with me." She frowned and shook her head. "You don't know women nearly as well as you think."

"So I'm learning."

We spent a final night in Ankara sitting on the hotel balcony of my room, sipping wine. It was a warm night, and the city was beautiful. Kari was a wreck. Finally, around eleven, she excused herself and went to hit the sheets. I turned in as well since the Embassy told us Jeremy would be available promptly at eight a.m. Kari and I planned on taking him on a plane to New York as soon as possible, just in case any remaining family members changed their minds and tried to tie us up in Turkish court.

Shortly after two a.m. there came a soft rapping at the interior door that separated our rooms. I opened it to Kari standing in a sheer gown, shaking like a leaf. She'd not slept a moment. I lifted her, kissed her, and set her in my bed. We spent our last night together like that. She fit in my arms as though she were born to be there. Still the mood was unmistakable: our nights together had come to an end. It was hard to describe the emotions that passed through that night. We held each other, loved each other, wanted each other. But she summed it up in a single sentence. "Sometimes, sweets, it's all about timing, and this isn't our time."

I'd arrived in New York with one love, found a second, and lost them both.

We woke before sunrise and headed out over winding modern highways some thirty two miles towards Çubuk. The region beyond Ankara reminded me of driving through the Southwestern U.S., with its sprawling highways and open spaces. Kari was silent the whole way, but her mood began to brighten like the sunrise. By the time we'd gone the sixty minutes over hilly terrain to our destination she was positively radiant. We parked on an ordinary-looking street, which Kari was disappointed to find looked as if it had been transplanted from suburban America.

Fadil's grandmother lived in a square apartment building on a side street atop a sandwich shop. Except for the TR on the cars' license plates it could have passed for Anywhere, USA. I was pleased, to be honest, since I figured that would make the transition back to the States easier on Jeremy.

I knocked on the door to the apartment since Kari was shaking too much. To our surprise the old lady herself opened the door. She squinted, her short frame bent even lower with age, and grinned a half-toothed smile that made angels dance. Without even a word, she swept Kari into her arms and flooded her face with tears and kisses. In Turkish, she kept repeating a single refrain that I didn't need translated. "You're here," she was saying, still in disbelief her beloved great-grandson's mother was still alive.

In short order a dark-haired boy with Kari's face stood in the doorway. The world inhaled and Kari dropped to her knees. "Do you know who I am?" she asked. Her arms hung at her sides like timid serpents, not daring to awaken.

Jeremy blinked, wiped his eyes, and nodded. "Mommy," he whispered. Then, on wings borne of hopeless but requited love, he flew into his mother's arms.

I turned away—not due to my own tears, but to allow this moment to be theirs and theirs alone. The old lady took me by her shaky hand and slipped a piece of paper in mine. It was a note, dictated by her and translated into English by some unseen stranger.

They think because I am old, that I am a fool.

*I am, sadly, the first, but most assuredly not other.
Never, never, never have I believed that boy's
mother to be dead as Emir claimed. Jeremy never
took the Asker woman as his mother. And entire
time he was here, he would ask me when he was
going home. I knew which home he meant as he
loved to talk about how he remembered his two
mothers who looked just alike. Dear, sweet Kari,
hold him, and never let him go. His heart is one
with yours.*

It was signed in her old hand, a shaky scribbled name that I could not make out. With another exchange of silent hugs and kisses, we departed the small Turkish apartment and jetted for home. Not once did Kari stop touching her son until we were safely in Brooklyn's arms. I am certain the tear-stained note penned for Jeremy's great-grandmother is still framed on her wall.

We had one last errand before I left New York for home. Jeremy and Kari were bonding quite well, and I'd spent a couple of days becoming reacquainted with my puppy. He missed Mina, but I was okay as a distant second to him. Gaither contacted us the first day back to inform us that cadaver-sniffing dogs had found a grave on the Sunay property they were certain belonged to Fadil. Ozan had signed a plea agreement in the hope that he might one day be eligible for parole. Fat chance of that. One of his first acts was to confirm Fadil's burial place, which was precisely where the dogs said it was. Emir's two sons erected a grave marker there, avoiding having to disinter Fadil, which violated his religion's tenets.

We held a brief memorial at the site, with Kari, Jeremy, Fadil's two cousins, and David. At the end of the ceremony Kari walked to an easel we'd set up by Fadil's grave and pulled off the small cloth covering. It revealed a painting she'd done of Fadil, which she'd entitled *Fadil Sunay, as God Made Him*. It was a startlingly beautiful portrait of a young man with piercing brown eyes, dark hair and brow, and a two-day-old growth of beard. Instead of the business suits that he had donned for all his adult life, trying to be what his uncle wished, Fadil wore a simple black and white rolled-up shirt and a black headscarf embroidered with a pattern that looked like butterflies peeling out of a dandelion patch. A shock of dark brown hair jutted from behind and below the scarf. He wore a white bandana tied to his right wrist along with a half-dozen beaded and leather wrist bands. He stared blankly out of the frame, his eyes following viewers wherever they walked, daring them not to see him as he was. On the ring finger of his left hand he wore a jeweled band.

David stood in the center of the group, mouth agape and both hands to it. After endless moments, he turned to Kari with misty eyes. "He is beautiful," he said.

Kari smiled. "He always was, but you were the only one to notice."

David walked closer to the painting and leaned in. "That's…" His voice fell to a whisper. "That's the ring I gave him," he said. His expression and voice were apologetic.

"I know," Kari said. "I figured it out when I saw yours." David looked at his own hand, which sported a matching ring, and slipped it behind his back. He averted his eyes. Kari walked to him, lifted his face, and smiled. "It really is okay, sweets," she said. She lifted up the painting and gave it to David.

"I, I can't take that," he said, although his shaking hands were already reaching out for it.

She whispered to him, but I was standing close enough to her to hear. "You were the love of his life," she said.

David shut his eyes and clutched the painting to his chest. After a moment he opened them and said, "But what about you? Don't you want this to remember him?"

Kari laughed and lifted Jeremy into her arms. "I have something better," she said.

Later, as we were driving back to Brooklyn for the final time, she said to me, "I hope that was true. I hope Fadil had a love of his life."

"What about you?" I asked once we were in the car. "Don't you want a love of your life?"

She didn't look at me, but shut her eyes and leaned her head against the window. "I'll give you the same answer I gave David. I have something better."

I looked at Jeremy asleep in the back seat and understood. It was all about timing, in the end.

I only spent an hour at Kari's once we returned from New Jersey. I grabbed Apache from the neighbors, thanked them for their kindness, and my pup and I headed to LaGuardia for the trip home. I didn't let Kari take me to the airport. We never even said goodbye. Instead, I kissed her on the cheek and she said, "I'll pray for good timing for you from now on." I left having no idea what she was talking about.

I figured goodbyes would just make things harder on both of us. We knew whatever we had was over. At the end I realized that maybe a lot of what she and I shared had been temporary. She needed someone to rely on and she fell for me because I was her last remaining hope for bringing home her son. In truth, it wasn't even me who did it. If Adnan hadn't found that phone there was no telling if the cops would have ever found out what happened to Jeremy.

On the plane home I wondered how long it would be before Adnan came calling. If it were me I'd already be on my way over, like that Amish dude at the end of *Witness*. After all, he already had a relationship with her son.

Chapter 14

Apache turned out to be something of a gentle giant. At nine months old he was already tall enough that, when he sat in my convertible, his ears practically stuck through the roof. Of course, since he was still a puppy, most of the time he tried to sit in my lap. That was fine at home, but we were on the road and he was close to causing me to wreck the car. After reuniting with the Camaro after such a long stretch, I was in no mood to wrap her around a tree. I finally pulled off the side of the road just outside of Trinidad, Colorado, to strap him in with a seat belt. Patchy—as I'd come to call him—and I were returning from one of the most satisfying moments of our partnership. It ranked right behind helping Kari reunite with her son.

Four months after we'd hit Arizona I got a call from Gaither. He was on scene in Colorado.

"Daley," he said. "I forgot to tell you. We got a hit on that face you gave me." For a minute I couldn't remember what he meant. Then I recalled the phantom from the Eastern Plains Bed and Breakfast and all the memories came flooding back. "His name is Adam Lovejoy. He was released from the federal penitentiary in Florence, Colorado in March. He'd been serving fourteen years for rape."

"Florence. Isn't that the supermax prison?" I asked.

"The supermax is in the same facility, but Lovejoy was in the ordinary high security segment. Supermax is reserved for the real hard cases. You'd fit right in; it's full of Al Qaeda operatives now."

"No, thanks. You and I met enough of those bozos already. What's Lovejoy's story?"

"Serial rapist. He got charged with murdering a prostitute as well, but the local DA couldn't make the charges stick. He had a knack for cleaning physical evidence. He'd commit a rape and make a video of the victim with her own phone. Shrinks think he got sexual satisfaction playing back their torment."

I tried to choke back the bile that was filling my throat. "I'm guessing that was the screaming we heard back at the bed and breakfast. How'd they catch him?"

"Guy is not only a sociopath, he'd got some kind of OCD. Dude would go back to the scene of a rape, not to do the woman again but to clean the place and make sure he didn't miss any spots. One victim had security cameras installed and they caught him breaking in to scrub her bedroom while she was at work."

"Jesus, I don't know if that's insane or stupid."

"Both. It seems he's particular about the kind of cleanser he uses. Has it special made."

"Don't tell me: it goes on red but dries clear."

"Yeah. How the heck did you know that?"

"It explains all the blood I thought I saw that night. Does that mean you could trace him to the other murders via the cleaner?"

"Yep. Not as good as DNA, but a close second. Anyway, thanks to your lead we're looking at him for a string of unsolved murders across Colorado, Nebraska, and Kansas. I've got a crew up at that old bed and breakfast you told me about right now. I still don't know how you found the place."

"Call it the luck of the stupid. Tell me, did the name Kennedy come up with this guy at all?"

Gaither whistled into the phone. "That's one of the vics we're looking at. How the hell'd you know that? You finally getting good at this detective business?"

"Talent is overrated. I prefer to rely on luck. And since I'm on a roll, let me try another one. Mrs. Kennedy has an identical twin."

"Ah, now I know what's going on," Gaither said. "All that time you spent with those two spooky twins made you some kind of shaman."

"I'm pretty sure that comment is racist," I said.

He wasn't listening. "Kennedy seems like the last one. It was right after her death that he got arrested for the B and E. We got circumstantial evidence for the murders, but still no DNA. The pros are interviewing him something fierce, but this guy's a hard case for sure. I'm not certain we're gonna get anything from him."

"Do me a favor," I said. "Have the boys tell him Frances Kennedy said to tell him hello and she'll be around to see him soon. See what he does."

"The dead woman? I don't know, Ed, Lovejoy doesn't seem the superstitious type."

"Maybe not, but I'm guessing he doesn't know Kennedy had a twin."

Gaither got quiet for at least fifteen seconds while he played that scenario in his head. When he spoke I heard the old excitement he used to get in Afghanistan right after we'd identified a hostile's hideout. "So, Lovejoy gets out of prison and his old compulsions are fully intact," he said, laying out my theory perfectly. "He goes back to the scene of his last murder and is scrubbing to beat the band, even though the place is closed. He hears someone rustling around in the next cabin."

"The one his victim's twin sister stuck us in," I added.

"Yeah. She must have had a good feeling about you. Anyway, he sees you poke around outside and decides he better do you too. Must have gotten real excited when he saw you were with Mina."

That made my stomach lurch, but I kept quiet.

"You do your shootout at the OK Corral bit, but he always wears a vest."

"Plus he has the advantage of being crazy as fuck," I said.

"That does seem to help. So once you're out of bullets, he chases you around the front." Gaither was huffing as he talked. I could tell he was acting out the scenario as he laid it out. "And who does he see but his last victim? He nearly shits himself and takes off through the field."

"Except he doesn't know it's the victim's sister," I said. Then I asked the question I knew we both must be thinking. "Why in fuck's name would she be living in that abandoned motel?"

"I met her briefly," he said, his voice low. "I think losing her sister made her snap. Wouldn't surprise me if we have a female Norman Bates going on."

That took my wind. "Holy fuck," I said. "You mean…"

"Yeah, she might have been planning to kill you two herself. But she saw her sister's killer and that snapped her out of it."

I sank to my sofa with that bit of news. "Do me a favor," I said. "Don't ever tell Mina about this. She thinks that *sweet little old lady* saved my life. And if you can, see about getting Mrs. Kennedy's sister some professional help. I'm kind of partial to twins these days."

"You got it, buddy. Besides, she kind of did save you, even if she might have been planning to off you herself." Gaither started laughing, although I couldn't find a bit of joke in what he'd just said. "Hey, Eddie, for real," he said, once the laughing stopped, "I owe you one, big time. Between wrapping up the Sunay case and this guy, I'm looking at a major promotion. If we can get a conviction, I'm probably looking at a post in D.C."

"That's great, dude. We'd never have found Jeremy without you."

"Yeah, well, I'm kind of getting used to covering your rear. Oh, and there's something in the Lovejoy bust for you too. Seems the locals put up a fifty thousand dollar reward for information leading to the arrest of a suspect."

I whistled. "Seems like my trip might have paid for itself after all."

"Yeah, too bad I work for the good guys. I could use that kind of money myself."

"Sucker," I replied, and hung up.

That phone call was barely two months earlier. Within days of planting Mrs. Kennedy's name in Lovejoy's head he was confessing up a storm. It seemed he firmly believed in ghosts and had no desire for another visit. He even confessed to be cleaning cabin ten of the Eastern Plains B&B when he found some "vagrants" sleeping in the next cabin. He claimed to have tried to chase them—meaning Mina and me—off, but he ran into some "interference." It was still mostly a lie, but enough to tie him definitively to the crime scene. He was indicted on capital murder charges less than a month later.

Gaither, in order to publicize the case enough to secure his promotion, arranged to have me travel to Holyoke for the reward ceremony. I'd texted Mina hoping she'd join me, but as usual got no answer. So me and my now-famous pup did the trip alone and picked up the check. I put ten grand in the bank to cover expenses from the New York trip, gave Deb a five thousand dollar bonus, and wired the rest to Mina's bank account. That was one day prior to our stop in Trinidad.

I have to admit, the money felt empty without my partner to share it with. I don't mean Deb, who I made a full partner as I promised; she'd have gladly taken the trip to Colorado. That little taste of New York had energized the road dog in her. She'd spent much of the previous six months on the road drumming up clients, including quite a few in the D.C. area. We'd been considering opening a branch of Daley and Tuohy, LLP there. It was no wonder Rod Gaither was working hard for an assignment in the capital city. Like I said before: whither Deb goeth, men follow.

In truth I was hoping the trip to Colorado would finally put me in touch with Mina. We kept in contact awhile, sharing webcams and the like. I'd even bonded with Nona, of all people. It was she who renamed Apache, since her take on the name always came out sounding like "Patchy." It sort of stuck. Then, abruptly, Mina stopped taking my calls. I think the distance became too much of a strain. After Brooklyn we never discussed romance or the future. As with Kari, that part of our relationship seemed to have run its course for her. Then again, she was a beautiful girl. I figured she probably just found another guy.

So six months after our Brooklyn trace it was just us two guys, panting on the side of the road in another western postcard of a town. I stopped at a little diner that advertised take-out and grabbed us both a couple of burgers. I like mine medium well and Apache likes them bunless. He's a low-carb man. I pulled out the bag, waited for him to settle and, before I could react, somebody pulled what felt like a pillowcase over my head. I tried to swing, but a powerful hand grabbed my arm and I felt a stick. Just before I went out, I could hear not barking, but the sound of a ferocious German Shepherd chowing down on my share of the burgers. That damned dog eats too much.

We'd been going through an unseasonably warm spell for January, but I woke warmer than I remembered being in Colorado. It had been nearing sunset when I went out but, as I blinked away the fog in my eyes, I could see within the crystalized mist the golden rays of sunrise. I looked around. I was in the middle of a field, lying in an open tent. It could have been anywhere. Just inside the tent flaps I could see the silhouette of two large men. It was still too dark to make them out, but I could see they were holding rifles. That made them in charge. Seeing I was awake, the larger of the two brusquely pulled me to my feet with a jerk of one arm. I considered moving on his gun, but the other was pointing his squarely at my chest. I squinted, having trouble making out the features of his face. My eyes still hadn't readjusted from whatever drug they gave me, however, and I mostly saw a monochromatic blur.

"Walk," growled one of them, pushing me through the tent. As I emerged into the sunlight the world flashed into a blinding white light. I walked, my hands in front of my face, blinking from the brilliance of the normally subdued dawn's radiance. One of my captors poked me in the back with a rifle and I stumbled forward. Within a minute I was able to see, squeezing the water from my eyes. I could hear drumming in my head and soft chanting. There was an enormous bird with brilliant feathers of turquoise, green, red, and black ahead of me. She was spinning, lightly tapping the ground to the rhythm I thought only I could hear.

"Birds don't dance to music," I heard myself say aloud. I squinted harder at it, and it stopped being a bird. It became…Kari. Her smile was radiant and she turned, dancing, with a small flock assembled beyond her. She looked at me and, with barely a motion, nodded a hello in my direction. I found myself standing still, stupidly waving back at her. Regaining my senses I spun around to confront my captors. There I saw the two large men: Anthony and Mika, dressed in some formal ceremonial attire. Anthony's grin made my stomach begin to churn.

They shouldered their rifles and gestured for me to proceed. "Don't worry," Mika said. "They weren't loaded."

Anthony stopped and looked at him. "Mine was. You didn't tell me we weren't loading them."

I decided there were too many witnesses for me to kill him. Mika shrugged and motioned for me to continue. The guys led me through a group of dancers in the midst of celebrating God knows what. There were singers praising something but, since I don't speak Lakota, it was all a mystery to me. We walked and the dancers thinned into a long procession. At the head was Katherine, smiling beatifically. She was standing next to a man in a dark suit I'd never seen before. Spotting me, she grinned and waved. Then she pointed to a huge rock on her ring finger I could spot from twenty feet away.

"Holy crap, it's Katherine's wedding." I was still woozy enough from whatever Mika had drugged me with to be speaking aloud. It would have fit Mika and Anthony's perverse sense of humor precisely to find out from their sister where I'd be and abduct me to her wedding rather than just inviting me. I'd seen Anthony drive. I hoped at least it was Mika who brought my Camaro here. "Where is here, anyway?" I asked Mika.

"We're in Oklahoma," he said. "It's too cold back home for an outdoor wedding unless you want to freeze to death."

We stood there for a time in an Oklahoma field I was only now recognizing as bordering Mina's brother Randy's house, watching Kari dance. Her movements displayed the same grace she showed during our many nights together but, watching her here, it seemed a million years earlier. She'd done well in six months, with the sculptures she made of Mina and me getting her much acclaim back home. From what I understood, she had a backlog of commissioned work that was likely to keep her from ever needing to teach again.

After her solo, for which I was the only idiot who clapped, Kari came and stood next to me. Next came Mina, finally, dressed in a long native dress covered with a lovely white cloth that draped like a cloak. Her entire face was covered except her eyes. She was dancing a simple, graceful step that reminded me of the movements of a hunting bird. She made eye contact with no one, merely proceeded with her dance, which by now I'd theorized was meant to honor her mother. Mina's dance proceeded slowly, as if she were winter's snow gracing the plains. Winter was a gift, once you understood her, as she made it easier to track prey and survive until the spring. I thought it beautiful, if odd, given her dance made her outshine the bride in the way a galaxy outshines the sun.

I blinked, realizing I was waxing poetic in my head because my heart was jackhammering as soon as I saw her. Only then did I realize what I'd really done in New York. Kari and I needed to love each other—and we did—in order for me to risk my life to find her son. I would gladly do it again, but I'd lost Mina in the process. Maybe she'd agreed to share me in the hopes that I'd realize what I was doing, but I never had, not until Jeremy was returned to us and the bond was severed. That reminded me: I'd not seen the little guy, or my little Vulcan princess, Nona.

Even as the thought crossed my mind Nona came walking past

her mother, scattering flowers. She was focused on what she was doing and barely looking up. As she neared me she suddenly lit up into a smile and yelled, "Hi, Eddie! Where's Patchy?" The entire congregation began laughing. In the distance, behind the crowd, I heard her buddy bark an answer. The smiling Kari walked over, took her niece by the hand, and stood her next to me.

To my surprise Mina stopped dancing, slipped off her shoes, and walked, barefoot, on the petals Nona had spread toward us.

I turned to Mika and whispered. "Is this a Lakota ceremony?"

He shook his head no. "This is all Mina."

Mina reached us the next moment, stopping six feet away. She looked me in the face for the first time and lifted her white cape over her head and onto the ground behind her. She was six-months pregnant. I nearly fainted.

"See what I meant by timing?" Kari said, smiling. "It was her time, not mine." Kari stepped back.

"Who gives this woman away?" asked the preacher, to whom Katherine happened to be engaged.

"I do," said Mika, frowning and waving his shotgun. He gave me his fiercest grimace. It would have made his enemies tremble and his ancestors cheer. I was honored to be about to call him brother.

Still, I started to laugh. "A shotgun wedding? Seriously?" I said, speaking to Mina. "Why didn't you just tell me you were pregnant?"

"You're the detective, you should have detected it yourself. Besides, last time I asked you to marry me, you said no."

"I never said no. I just didn't answer."

"Well, look here, dude, this time I need an answer." She quieted and the entire congregation seemed to hold its breath at once. "Do you want to marry me or not?"

I stepped toward her. "Even more than I want the sun to rise," I answered. I sucked in a breath and added, "*Lila waste chi lake*," which is pronounced *lee la wash tay chee la kay*, and was as close as to saying "I love you" in the Lakota language as I could learn via the interwebs. So yeah, I'd been working up my courage to ask her. The congregation exploded in cheers. Anthony, Mika, and Randy all waved their rifles and began firing them in the air. Somewhere above, an entire flock of winter birds found their lives in peril. I gave Mika a dirty look, since he hadn't loaded his gun after he told me it was empty. He grinned.

When the ruckus died down I said, "Um, I don't exactly have a ring with me."

Just then, Jeremy seemed to magically appear like some Turkish-Lakota Leprechaun, his shoulder-length hair in braids. He held rings on a pillow.

"Tanya said to tell you you're welcome," Kari said, and handed me a ring.

"So, am I the only person who didn't know I was getting married?" I asked.

"Hi, Mr. D," Deb called from behind me, waving. She was sitting next to Gaither. He owed me big time for that promotion…to Deb's boyfriend. Maybe he could get her to stop calling me "Mr. D."

"I take that as a yes," I said.

"Pretty much," Mina answered. "Now shut up and marry me already."

We exchanged our vows right there, under the rising Oklahoma sun, with Mina being quite probably the most beautiful mother on the planet. It was a lovely, romantic ceremony, accompanied by soft Lakota songs and punctuated by Mina's grinning acceptance of my hand in marriage by saying, "I do. Fucker."

Katherine clasped her forehead and the reverend winced. I was overjoyed.

We spent the evening of our wedding night driving toward lovely Santa Fe, New Mexico. My bride insisted on wearing her wedding dress the entire day and was looking forward to checking into the hotel in her gown and bare feet. She'd even found one that took pets.

"So what's next?" I asked, once we were across the New Mexico border. "We haven't talked about where we'll live or what we'll do."

"First things first," she said, and kissed me. "I just kissed my husband." She grinned.

"Not that I care in the least, but did you get pregnant on purpose?"

"I agreed to share you. That didn't mean I was willing to be stupid about it." She gave me a devilish grin, followed by a look so earnest I kissed her again for being cute. "I didn't mean to get pregnant. I just got careless. Are you mad at me?"

"I should be, but I'm not."

"You're fun," she said, smiling at me. "So, did you, like, sow all the wild oats you needed sowing with Kari?"

"All I'll ever need. It's just you and me, kid."

"Good. I was sick of sharing you." She leaned on my shoulder as we rumbled along in her truck with Nona humming in the back seat. Apache sat next to her, blocking my view of the rear window.

"This isn't going to be exactly the honeymoon you've always dreamed of," I said.

"Oh this isn't the honeymoon. I figure that can wait until the baby's born. Plus, by then I'll have my CFI license from flight school. The reward money will more than cover it." She was speaking in a matter-of-fact tone of voice, her head not lifting from my shoulder. "Then we'll be ready to go."

"I'll bite. Ready to go where?" I asked.

"Oh, I don't know, maybe South America, maybe an island somewhere. It depends on which client makes the best offer."

"Mina, what in the hell are you talking about?"

"Don't curse in front of Nona. She repeats everything she hears now."

On cue, from the back Nona said, "Mommy, the hell you talkin' 'bout?" Then she giggled.

Mina frowned at me. "See? You need to be more careful, Daddy." She kept talking, but I didn't hear any of it because my brain was busy grinning inside at the word "Daddy."

That stopped when I heard Nona parrot from the back seat, "They pay bunch money!"

"Um. Who will pay us a bunch of money?"

Mina sat up straight and frowned. "You've only been married eight hours and already you've started tuning me out." She folded her arms across her ample chest and sulked.

I apologized because I was the husband and it was now my job. "Sorry. I was too busy being in love with the two of you to listen."

"In that case, I'll let you live. I figure if we're going to honeymoon on a beach somewhere we may as well make some cash. I mean, I am a partner in Eddie Daley, Inc. now, right?"

I started to correct her on the name of the company but, knowing her, she'd already filed the incorporation papers. I looked at my little round firebrand, the same girl who'd had my back in New York on multiple occasions. She risked losing our relationship just to ensure her sister got her own life back. It was an easy call. I just had to ask myself WWBD – What would Bogie do?

We grew silent and I watched Mina's expression slowly change to serious, then to what looked to me like guilt. Finally, she spoke. "I have a confession to make."

"I'm afraid to ask."

"We aren't exactly legally married."

"Say what?" To my surprise, I felt my heart sink to my lap.

"Mom's boyfriend isn't officially licensed. Still, the ceremony looked legit, we committed ourselves to each other in front of the world, and now Mom and everybody are happy." Mina turned to me. "Except … now you don't look happy."

"Well, I'm not sure how to take this news."

"You have the best of both worlds. You have Nona, me, and the baby, and you get to convince yourself you have your freedom."

"Convince myself?"

"Yeah, 'cause if you ever try to leave us, I'll kill you."

I waited three minutes for her to smile. She did not. Finally, I said, "Raymond Chandler said *A really good detective never gets married.*"

"Raymond Chandler never met me, Eddie Daley. Now shut up and start planning our real wedding. Think mountains. Beautiful view. Big honking diamond." She leaned back and closed her eyes. "Unless you're still wavering, in which case Kari wants to marry you on the beach. She said to tell you you're wearing a white tux." She rolled down the window and stuck out her swollen feet. "If you pick her, can I be your best man slash wife?" she asked.

My headache was back, along with my doubts. Mina was a storm that shook my life from its stable, dreary foundations. Kari was a strange ocean to me, opening a side of life I'd read about but never lived. The storm or the sea? Mr. Stop or Mr. Go?

Raymond Chandler was a very wise man.

About the Author

Bill Jones, Jr. is committed to delivering fast-paced adventures laced with romance and full of characters you fall in love with. Before focusing on writing, Bill spent years working as an analyst and business development professional for some of the world's largest technology companies. Having acquired his tech parole, he now spends his time predicting the future, writing, reading, playing with the cat, and doing street photography with his smarter and more talented wife.